WIFE
BY THE HOUR

WIFE
BY THE HOUR

WIFE
BY THE HOUR

*For Megan,
Thanks for your interest in my book! Enjoy :)
Gail Treasure*

GAIL TREASURE

TORONTO, 2024

RE:BOOKS

Copyright © Gail Treasure

All rights reserved.

www.rebooks.ca

Published in Canada by RE:BOOKS

RE:BOOKS
Brookfield Place
181 Bay Street
Suite 1800
Toronto, Ontario
M5J 2T9
Canada
www.rebooks.ca

No portion of this publication may be reproduced or transmitted, in any form, or by any means, without express written permission of the copyright holder.

First RE:BOOKS Edition: March 2024
ISBN: 978-1-998206-06-3
eBook ISBN: 978-1-998206-07-0

RE:BOOKS and all associated logos are trademarks and/or registered marks of RE:BOOKS.

Printed and bound in Canada.
1 3 5 7 9 10 8 6 4 2

Cover Design By: Chloe Faith Robinson and Jordan Lunn
Typeset By: Karl Hunt

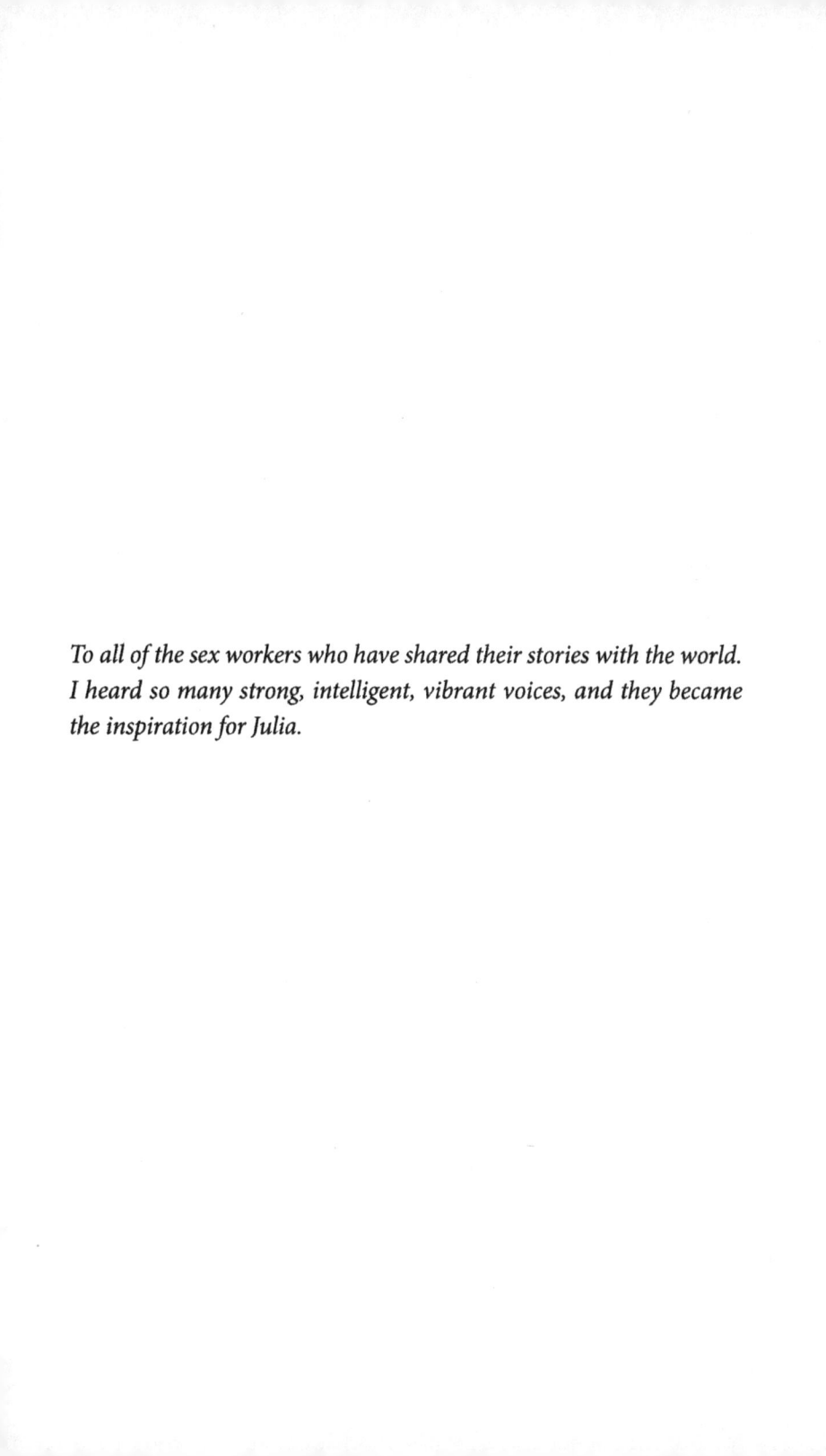

To all of the sex workers who have shared their stories with the world. I heard so many strong, intelligent, vibrant voices, and they became the inspiration for Julia.

CHAPTER ONE

I'M APPLYING THE finishing touch, a coat of shimmering clear lip gloss, when my work phone rings.

"You're halfway through your last day! I'm crying here. How can you leave this long list of clients with no one to cater to their needs?"

It was Kate. Kate's enthusiasm always lifts me up. Her steadfast friendship and shrewd business savvy got me through ten years of escorting with a smile on my face, and a sweet pile of money in the bank. But I swore to myself this would be my very last day.

"When the guy walked in this morning, he kept looking around as if there must be a younger woman stashed in the closet. I'm almost as old as these Percys now and my push-up bras are losing the battle."

"Impossible! You're the most sought-after mistress to married men in Toronto. There could only ever be one *Just Julia*."

Kate heaves an exaggerated sigh, continuing, "Well, this last guy is all checked out. His name is Alex, and he looks like a lot of fun. I think he's some kind of bigwig scientist and he could be into experimentation . . . if you know what I mean."

"No problem. You know me, always the professional."

"Is there nothing I can say to keep you working?" Kate asks.

"I appreciate you, Kate. You're one in a million. But Belle is everything to me. She's almost twelve years old and I've never been able to explain this to her. Full-time teaching is my future. And who knows what else is in store for me?"

"Tell me the truth," Kate says. "Are you going out on your own, or worse, with another agent?"

"Absolutely not. I'm ready to trade in my thong for something with a little more coverage. This was always going to be temporary."

Temporary, but "temporary" had lasted for ten years.

"Oh, please don't say it! Did some guy finally turn the head of my most sensible girl?"

Kate's babbling, so I clear my throat.

"Time to go greet the Percy. Wish me luck!" I say, interrupting.

I switch the phone to silent mode and begin my deep breathing. I've got five minutes to get into the zone. To become the woman who Kate baptized: *Just Julia*, an homage to the actress who portrayed everyone's favourite onscreen escort in *Pretty Woman*.

Kate is a big fan of the descriptive adjective for escorts. She was pushing for something like Sultry Julia or Refined Julia. Then she suggested Juicy Julia. I choked and said, "No way. It's *just Julia*." Well, Kate got the last laugh. She always says I named myself. I like to imagine that *Just Julia*, spoken in a seductive tone, answers the question, "Which of these ladies can fulfill all of your desires?"

I know that my last ever client is called Alex, but the first one was Percy, and if I think of them all as Percy, it's easy to forget them as soon as they go back to where they belong. I plan on making the most of my time with this last one.

The usual session includes: the offer of a beverage, some well-practiced banter layered with teasing sexual innuendo, a section of slow over the clothes touching and even slower kisses, a short check-in to assess the situation, to verify consent and to jump back a step or two if I need to kill more time, and then the meat and potatoes activity culminating in a joyful explosion. This is followed by a delightful denouement. I relish in the sense of accomplishment as we lay together afterwards, breathing the air of satisfaction, going nowhere in particular, lying naked and languorous on silky sheets

CHAPTER ONE

with a man who thinks I am the most appealing woman in the world, regardless of the fact that he has paid highly for my rapt attention.

Of course, a few of them just wanted to talk, cuddle, or dance. I've also had clients whose request was to watch me read a book, watch me eat a sandwich, watch me have a bubble bath, even watch me peel oranges. People fascinate me.

Kate knows that I am open to exploring a range of desires and that I fancy myself to be a bit of an untrained therapist. Today, no matter what experiments he has in mind, I hope that this last of all Percys smells nice and has a good sense of humor. A small dose of laughter can go a long way in the bedroom.

I rise and close the window in my quiet guest room. Between clients, I crack it open to let the musky odours of sex float away on the breeze and, like the most efficient of hotel housekeepers, I take a fresh set of sheets from the closet, and expertly remake the bed.

My home is always meticulously clean and tidy. No detail escapes my sharp eye. There is so much more to being sexy than dirty talk and lingerie. My clients appreciate the calm and order of my sensual space, which is decorated with dark oak furniture, elegant crown molding, and a huge gilt framed mirror that leans against the wall opposite the bed. When they enter this sanctuary, it's always spotless and polished, crisp and unsullied—the illusion is of a room that has remained empty since their last adventure, a secret hideaway known only to each man, an oasis in their ordinary lives where they are free to explore their fantasies.

It's showtime.

I blow a farewell kiss to my reflection in the mirror and run my fingers along the pearl-coloured Egyptian cotton sateen on the king-sized mattress. I intend to go out in the exact same manner as I came into this business—with my bare butt on a brand-new set of sheets.

In the living room, I get into position standing ten feet from the front door, which I have left slightly ajar, wearing an ivory-coloured satin corset framed by a floor length translucent negligee. I pull my wavy chestnut-coloured curls forward, so they tease the tops of my small, but significant, breasts. I don't wear heels because I'm already a little too tall, but my legs are shapely, and my butt is round, and I've learned how to move like a cat and talk with a breathy voice which is usually enough to make a neglected husband's penis jump to attention when he walks through the door. I'm neither too outlandish nor too comfortable.

During a decade of sexual encounters with rich, married men, I have honed the ability to hit the sweet spot where they throw open the doors on their classic Mercedes and invite me in for an orgasmic joy ride.

He knocks twice. "Julia?"

Alex made my name sound deep and Shakespearian. I like it.

"Please, come in," I say.

This seems like an interesting man walking through my front door, along with a pleasant dose of midday sunshine. He's taller than me and he's got curly salt and pepper hair, sharp grey eyes, and full red lips curved into a shy smile. "Uh. I parked in front of your neighbour's house?"

"I'm so sorry. Kate was supposed to tell you to park at the MiniMart," I respond.

"Right. I knew I was forgetting something." Alex taps his head and backs out of the room. "I shall return."

I know that man, I think. I grab my work phone and text Kate.

What is Alex's last name?

Confidential, she replies immediately. *Is everything okay?*

Great. Just curious.

I replay our brief encounter in my mind several times and I realize it's his voice, not his face, that I recognize. And then I know for sure. He's Alex Green. Zoe's husband.

CHAPTER ONE

Zoe Green. The once upon a time friend I was positive I would never meet again, for the rest of my life.

Alex Green is my last Percy. And he's already back and he's closing the door behind him. I like his black leather jacket and shiny low-cut boots.

He's staring at me.

"Oh, I apologize," I say. "What just happened to my manners? Welcome to my home, Alex. Please make yourself comfortable." I motion to the cozy couch, in front of which sits a table set with iced tea, water, and a few nibbles. If it was winter, I'd have the fireplace on, but today there are pots of red tulips in front of it.

"You look like you've seen a ghost," he says, his brow wrinkling with concern. I find myself laughing.

"Not at all. But I have to be honest. You're the most handsome Percy I have ever met."

Alex's puzzled expression and nervous laughter cause my heart to start beating hard inside my chest. I can feel a surge of heat through my body and I'm grateful for my scanty clothing and the cool breeze wafting into this room from the open kitchen window.

As usual, I let my client sit down first. I like to decide how close I should position myself next to my clients. I don't want to rush this last Percy of my career, so I leave a twelve-inch gap between us.

"It's a gorgeous day," I say, pouring two glasses of iced tea. "Spring is my favourite season."

"There's a pair of robins making a nest on top of your front light," Alex says, accepting a glass from my hand.

"I know. I can see inside the nest from the hall window upstairs. They're there every year." He looks interested, so I keep talking. "When I was a kid, a robin made its nest in my bike basket, so I couldn't ride it for a month. I was annoyed at first, but I put my bike in the same spot the next spring on purpose and they did it again."

Alex nods. "That's called nest-site fidelity. If they are able to successfully raise their young once, robins keep using the same spot to nest. But they don't like to build a new nest on top of an old one. It's too messy."

This man is definitely a lot more interesting than the guy this morning who wanted me to listen to him recite a list of all the ways his neighbours make his life miserable. Also, Alex has good cheekbones, a straight nose, kind eyes, and maybe the best lips I've ever seen on any man. I would be happy to kiss those lips right now, but I have a feeling he's taking a moment to size me up as well.

"Right," I continue on the topic of robins. "When the baby birds fly away for good, I knock the nest off the light with a broom and the parents often raise another clutch of eggs in the same season. Or they come back the next year."

"Although, robins don't mate for life, unlike barn owls, swans, and even Canadian geese," Alex laughs for the second time, but now it's conspiratorial laughter. "Your robins are probably getting a lot more action than you know."

"Well, I'm glad for them, then. They seem to be happy birds. I love hearing their cheery song. It makes me feel like everything is right with the world."

Alex puts down his glass and places his hand in the space between us. "Your profile didn't say you were a bird lover."

I put my hand on top of his and begin to explore the surface with my fingertips. Alex's hand is big and his fingers are long, but I sense that they are capable of performing intricate work. "I love birds as much as the next person. I also love mystery novels, Thai food, rollercoasters, and thunderstorms. Are you familiar with this quote by Walt Whitman? 'I am large. I contain multitudes.'"

Louder laughter. It's working. He's relaxed now.

"I am. So you are also a lover of nineteenth century poetry," he says.

CHAPTER ONE

"Yes, but sadly, that quote is the only thing that stuck with me from my compulsory Humanities class in university. My professor said that Whitman's expanded sense of self led him to believe that he was at once himself, and every other person he met. I get that. I've met a lot of people in this business and each one has taught me something."

Alex is staring at me.

"I want to kiss you, Julia," he says abruptly, but he doesn't lean in.

"Me too," I assure him. "I want that, too." So I get to work.

I try to tell myself that it just feels sweeter because he's my last Percy ever, but the hour flies by in a rosy haze of blissful discovery.

I forget to say all the regular comments I usually make like, "Oh, honey, your dick is so big and hard" and "You're so good at this."

Instead, as if I was new to this act, I am astonished by the way our skin seems to be joined by a thin film of pulsating sweat and I wonder if it's possible to become drunk on sex. Coiled together like human spaghetti, we share deep, languid kisses, and I realize that I have lost all sense of where my body starts or ends.

The creature that is us undulates until I gasp and feel surprised at the sound of my own voice. Our eyes lock onto each other and I know that he is watching the flush of pleasure on my face as I experience two orgasms in a row.

As I emerge from the cloud of passion, the room comes back into focus and I catch the reflection of our bodies in a precarious position. Alex slides off the bed and drags me along with him at the height of his orgasm. Blushing, he declares, "I'd like to try this again next week."

I say, "I couldn't be happier about that," and I pop back up on the bed.

Feeling like I've just had a person-sized Band-Aid ripped off my flesh, I reach out my arms toward him. "We can cuddle for an extra half hour. No charge," I offer.

He smiles, stands up, and arranges the sheet over my lower half. "Thank you. But I've got to go."

I watch him get dressed and I think his legs look muscular for a scientist. His butt is tight and I like the way his back is shaped like a long V.

Looking like an important man with places to go, he strides over and lifts my chin with one finger. I hope he will speak, but instead, he meets my eyes with an expression of amused curiosity. Then he kisses the tip of my nose with his sex-swollen lips, and I have to brace myself as he exits the room.

I hear the front door close with the softest "click" and I'm staring at the ceiling, trying not to cry, because I just had sex with Zoe's husband, and I think I might be in love.

CHAPTER TWO

25 YEARS AGO...

September 6, 1999, St. Paul de Vence, Cote d'Azur, France

Chère Diary,

THIS TRIP JUST got fun! I mean, Monsieur and Madame Dubois, Alain and Pascale, are great, the twins, Émilie and Georges are so sweet, and St. Paul de Vence is everything I could hope for in a Medieval-walled village perched on a hill on the French Riviera: picturesque, seeped with history, soaking in sunshine, and bursting with more flowers than a florist's wedding. But today, I went to my first *leçon de français* with the other au pairs and I met the best friend of my dreams!

Her name is Zoe and she's got everything I wish I had been born with, rich parents, big boobs, and an impressive knowledge of French art and culture.

The professor, Madame Gaudet, who was showing off fishnet stockings and a garter belt under her black leather mini skirt with a deep slit up the side, was annoyed that we had to wait fifteen minutes for the tenth and final student.

When Zoe breezed through the door like she owned the place and apologized by saying, "Je suis très désolée de vous faire attendre," the teacher couldn't be upset anymore. Even I knew her pronunciation was flawless. Zoe slid into the seat beside mine, winked at me with her sparkly blue left eye, and whispered, "I bought some French cigarettes on the way here. You can smoke with me after class."

Which I did. Zoe was impressed that I could inhale the strong French Gitanes without coughing. I said I love them because they taste like the air in a dark forest at midnight and they made my head feel dizzy like I'd been twirling in circles.

After that we went to the Distillerie Bar to drink local white wine that is cheap and a bit sour and to also eat little individual quiche Lorraines. These are delicious pastries filled with eggs, cream, and ham, and you can buy them everywhere.

Zoe and I sat on fancy metal chairs at a tiny table on the narrow stone road and she told me about all the boys she has met so far. There were so many names and she made each guy sound sexy and brooding like Brad Pitt or Justin Timberlake, but French. So, therefore, better.

I asked her when she has time to go looking for boys, since we are expected to mind the family's children and help with the housework before and after school, as well as attend French lessons during the day.

Zoe shook her head at me like I knew nothing, and I guess she's probably correct. She spread her arms wide and said, "Open your eyes, mon amie! We're in the land of Cézanne, Van Goth, Chagall and Picasso. Try looking at the whole picture and understand what it's trying to tell you."

I was getting more confused. She leaned in until our noses were nearly touching and I felt almost assaulted by the strength of her cigarette and wine breath. With her eyes, she led me to a group of three men who were washing the shop windows on the street.

Zoe fixed her gaze on them until the one with the longest squeegee gave her a sneaky smile and a low, sexy chuckle.

CHAPTER TWO

Zoe looked at me again, leaned back in her chair, and said, "This place is literally crawling with men who want nothing more than to make love to you like you are a precious rosebud ready to unfurl its petals. Don't be afraid to be that flower, because you'll be old and withered before you know it."

CHAPTER THREE

"CAN I ASK you a question?" the gloriously naked Alex says while teasing my hard nipple with the feather light touch of the back of his hand. I think he's proud of his performance on our second date. He looks satisfied, like he just got great results from his experiment and proved his hypothesis.

"Shoot," I answer coolly. Inside, I'm freaking out. Is he going to ask me if I love him? Is he going to ask me if I think he should redecorate his mansion before Belle and I move in to live there in unimaginable bliss for the rest of our lives? Is he going to ask me how I survived the last week without his kisses? Because I almost didn't.

On three occasions, I got a pain of longing inside my belly, so strong that I doubled over and sobbed for five minutes before I could continue with my mundane activities. The pangs happened in the shower, in the teacher's washroom at lunchtime, and in my car on the way to the grocery store. I had to pull over and suffer through the mini nervous breakdown in a gas station parking lot. I've never experienced so much intestinal discomfort.

Love is a harrowing physical experience.

"Do many of your clients like to tie you to these bedposts?" Alex asks, as he indicates the tall ornate corners of my bed.

"Hmmm..." I look at his quizzical raised eyebrow expression and give him one right back. "It's not usually me who's tied up."

CHAPTER THREE

He nods.
"Would you like to give it a go?" I ask.
He nods again.

CHAPTER FOUR

September 9, 1999, St. Paul de Vence, Cote d'Azur, France

Chère Diary,

BOYS ARE DRAWN to Zoe like swarms of orange butterflies coating the lush-scented lavender that borders the winding roads in the Alpes-Maritimes. What is Zoe's magic? I have been pondering this question for three days since she made her first spectacular appearance in my life.

It's the weekend, so the Dubois family and I had a "family" outing. We drove to the nearby town of Grasse, which is considered the perfume capital of the world and, in my opinion, should also be known as "the most wonderful smelling place in the world." There is literally lavender everywhere, growing in gardens and pots, hanging in bunches from ceilings and filling fancy glass bowls on counters and shelves. We visited three perfume factories and an eleventh century cathedral. That means that I walked through a building that is nearly one thousand years old. Wow!

The Dubois, Alain and Pascale, call me their grande fille and treat me like their long-lost daughter. How is it that they have no fear of opening their home, showing kindness to a total stranger, and leaving me in charge of their belongings, not to mention their children? I am constantly overwhelmed by the generosity

CHAPTER FOUR

of the Dubois and by their appreciation for the simpler things in life.

They seem to stretch out every sensory moment. Like at breakfast, when they rip off hunks of baguette, load them up with fresh butter and jam, then chew in slow motion, moaning out loud with pleasure so everyone knows how much they're enjoying their food, even though it's the exact same thing they ate the day before.

But I digress. I need to write about Zoe. I need to analyze what she's got, so I can get that sort of magic too. She told me that she has made out with five French boys so far and that they kiss you like they're trying to stuff a whole tomato into their mouth at once.

So far, I have only kissed Monsieur Dubois on the cheeks too many times to count because that is what people do here instead of saying "Hello." And Georges and Émilie, who run into my bedroom in the morning, jump on me while I'm still trying to sleep and repeatedly peck the air on either side of my face, much like chickens who keep missing the target. It's funny. I'm getting used to it.

Zoe is a boy magnet. I think it has to do with her confidence. She says you get confidence from experience. So therefore, what I need is . . .

I'm ashamed to admit to Zoe that the sum of my experience is one awkward fumble in my next door neighbour's garden shed during a pool party to celebrate the end of high school. It was over so fast I wasn't entirely sure if it happened the way it was supposed to. I'm still not sure, really. And the worst part was that Joel stumbled out of the party shortly afterwards with his team of friends, leaving a bunch of disappointed wet girls. On his way out, he slobbered on my neck and said, "Call me next time you wanna fuck."

Yeah. That happened. And since I just jotted that down, I now feel ready to move on.

In St. Paul de Vence, the local boys hang out at art shops, or cafés, or art shops with cafés. They drink pastis or even absinthe, which I

15

gather is some kind of alcohol that can actually make you go crazy. It's illegal in many countries. French boys prefer leisurely sex with girls who wear pretty lingerie and high heels, unlike rough Canadian boys who drink frothy beer and only want to have quick sex between periods of the hockey game. Well, that's what Zoe says anyway.

Tonight, I'm going to the soirée Zoe's host family, the Martin's, has organized for the Au Pair group. The Martins own the *La Cave Bar* and they know everybody in St. Paul de Vence, which isn't that difficult, really.

There are only just over three thousand people, including those who live outside of the walls. If you only count the residents who live inside the walls, it's just over three hundred people. I think it's possible to know three thousand people. Some day, when I'm back in Canada, and I'm bored of watching reruns and on snowy days, I'll write down all the people I know and see if I can make three thousand.

For this soirée, a bunch of local youths have been invited to eat pizza, drink wine, and converse with us. Madame Gaudet said it's to help improve our *technique d'expression orale*. This made Zoe and I convulse into laughter and the whole class was glaring at us like we were idiots. I'm sure that the rest of them think about sex just as much as we do, but they're letting their North American conventionality hold them back.

They'll probably loosen up before the six months is over. Honestly, who could resist the intoxicating effects of the French Riviera?

Zoe found out that it's an annual tradition among the local boys to see who can kiss the most Au Pair girls. So, for fun, she's keeping her own tally of Frenchmen kissed, hence the five conquests so far. Can I ever hope to rival Zoe's success?

I've got to stop thinking and start dreaming. Of course, Zoe also said that.

Pascale and I are going to walk the short distance to La Cave. The entire walled area of St. Paul de Vence is less than three square miles.

CHAPTER FOUR

Everywhere is within a short walking distance, and the streets are all narrow, winding stone alleys that were designed for horses and carts. So cars, even the tiny French cars, can't fit, and they're only allowed outside the walls.

None of the streets in St. Paul are perpendicular and it seems that around every corner, there is another corner. But there is also shop after shop, with baking, sweets, lovely smelling toiletries, and art, every kind of art and then some more art. I am reserving one hundred francs of my spending money to buy the perfect picture to take back to Canada with me as a souvenir. *Souvenir* is a French word that means "to remember." I'm certain I'll know it's the picture I'm meant to have, as soon as I lay eyes on it.

What will I remember when I'm an old lady and I look back on this trip?

CHAPTER FIVE

MY MIND IS in a complete swirl this morning. After Alex requested the second date, Kate texted me asking if I would agree to doing just one more. I've got to let her know that I will continue seeing Alex for as long as he's interested, or until I begin teaching full-time in September, whichever comes first.

What I really want to do is to stop charging him and become lovers. I want to give away my affections for free and hope that a genuine spark of connection will ignite between us.

That hasn't happened since my brief fling with my daughter Belle's father. For the last ten years, I wasn't interested in pursuing any men, outside of escorting, because I had all the emotional attachment I needed with my sweet little Belle. My needs were compartmentalized, sex in this box and love in that one. I honestly never believed I would ever be gifted a box that contained them both.

I'm lying like a starfish on my bed, irrigating my nostrils with the scent of sex that lingers in this room like a mysterious olfactory message only I can decode. I won't wash these sheets until the night before I see Alex again, because a foolish part of me is afraid he might not be real.

The salty, sweaty aroma recounts the story of two strangers, connected by the thread of another woman, who came together in an extraordinary surge of passion and who just may be destined to find forever happiness in each other's arms, if only . . . *if only* I can make the right moves. I'm trying to work out this triangulated puzzle using reason, but I can't seem to hang onto a thought long enough to take it to any logical conclusion.

I don't believe in destiny, no more than I believe in fairy tales. But I do believe in coincidence. Alex and I are nearly the same age, but I would guess he is two or three years older than me. We grew up in the same city, although it's got over six million people. Those are the basic things we have in common. Who knows if we have ever attended the same concert or rode the same subway? Realistically, the chances we would ever even speak to each other in those situations is infinitesimal.

However, there are two paths I could have chosen in my life which would have resulted in a meeting with Alex.

First, I could have kept in touch with Zoe after our trip. Maybe she would have asked me to be one of her bridesmaids? In that case, Alex and I might have fallen for each other before his wedding ever took place. But our shared betrayal of Zoe and the gulf between our social statuses could have doomed our relationship.

Obviously, I didn't take that path. When I got back to Canada, Zoe and I never spoke again.

The second path is the one that led me to encounter Alex in mid-life. Kate discovered me at my first foray into kickboxing. She owns the gym and she is the most badass and cunning woman I have ever met. By the end of the class, she realized I had a solid left-hand punch, a wealth of pent-up sexual frustration, and a dire cashflow shortage. She didn't need to twist my arm in the slightest.

Over an official dinner at The Keg Steakhouse, Kate outlined her role and also mine. She would solicit the clients, do reference checks, and handle the payments. This meant that she was taking the burden of the responsibility for ensuring that the not quite legal aspect of the business would stay hidden. Kate would make the bookings according to the schedule I would provide on a monthly basis.

I could cancel at any time and I also had the right to refuse any client with no explanation needed.

Kate arranged a photoshoot of me in a champagne coloured under-bust corset. In order to conceal my identity, the images captured my body in seductive poses, but only the lower half of my face, in a saucy pout. Kate advised me on my make-up, tricks of the trade, and how to keep my personal and professional lives separate.

When I asked, Kate admitted that I was one of six girls who worked with her, but I was never introduced to the others. She felt strongly that the choice to reveal ourselves as escorts, or to live behind the wall of our fake identity, was a personal one.

I trusted Kate implicitly from the beginning and that took almost all the fear out of the job, allowing me to hone my craft of providing intimate companionship and profound pleasure to men like Alex. Men like all of my Percys. Married men.

Why do they stray but stay? Why are seventy percent of all divorces initiated by women? Ninety percent, in the case of college educated women. It seems to me that men are not inclined to dissolve their marriage by choice, and I wonder if it's true that men cheat to stay, while women cheat to leave.

Even though I was the one getting monthly checks for sexually transmitted illnesses, I felt that I was part of a team, and it was a huge relief to me to have someone with whom I could discuss the clients: their needs, their desires, and their funny bits.

It was Kate who encouraged me to process my experiences by writing them down and that was easy for me, because I had been recording my thoughts since my father presented me with my first journal, one hundred pages bound in pink leather with a silver lock and key, in the airport just before I boarded the plane to Provence. He gave me a rare smile, pressed my shoulders together with his big hands, and said, "Go make some memories."

I am a very analytical person. Perhaps I should have been a lawyer or a criminologist. However, growing up in a lower middle-class suburb of Toronto with a widower father, a bus driver who drove the same route for forty-one years, I didn't learn how to dream as big as I might have otherwise. I never looked beyond the friendly faces of the people who gave me my education and I chose to follow in their footsteps. Teaching, I find, is rewarding. And supply teaching, in particular, has afforded me the flexibility to pursue a lucrative secondary source of income.

My first one-hour session with the actual client named Percy was a resounding success. He was a middle-aged accountant with four children, and, from the sounds of it, an exhausted wife who spent most nights sleeping with their one-year-old.

He was thrilled when I asked if he would like a back massage. But moreover, he was polite, he was clear about what he wanted from me, and he didn't try to push my boundaries which had been outlined to him by Kate.

After a few more "dates," it became apparent that the physical motions I went through with the clients were not the most interesting or revealing aspect of the encounter. The conversations, simple candid exchanges, blew me away. I believe that, since they were paying for my time and, unequivocally, my discretion, the Percys felt free to say whatever was on their mind. They were confident that I would never be judgmental. They frequently opened up to me in a way most people might only do with a therapist.

Perhaps I had spent too much time trying to decipher the constant babble of my toddler, but what these men revealed to me, through their mundane discourse, struck me as containing profound statements about the human condition.

I became a fly on the wall to hundreds of marital relationships and I was determined to make some sense out of what these husbands were sharing with me, as they unburdened themselves in my guest bedroom.

I decided, why not start a blog about this? *Conversations with Clients,* the name I came up with for my blog and writing about these experiences, was born under yet another alias, *The Curious Courtesan.*

Each week, I transcribed one interesting conversation I had had with a client. I analyzed it, gave my opinion, and invited comments from readers and followers. Sometimes, I found that I was having multiple conversations on the same topic and I wrote them into longer essays such as, *What do husbands think their wives are doing when their husband is not at home?* And, *If you see escorts, are you more likely to be liberal or conservative?* The blog that received the most comments and engagement was when I posed the question, *What do men who see escorts eat for lunch?*

Conversations with Clients has more than two thousand loyal followers who are eager to scrutinize the dialogues and share opinions, and I'm quite proud that I have been the catalyst for this progressive forum.

Meanwhile, Zoe, who always managed to do everything on a larger scale than me, is the sole host of a podcast with over eighty thousand monthly downloads called *Zoe's Green Family.*

I admit it. I google Zoe every few months to determine which of us is aging better. She was one of the first people I searched when I was in my early twenties and it became possible to stalk a friend from your past, especially one whose movie industry father sometimes chose her to walk the red carpet with him.

When googling her name one day produced the announcement of her debut podcast, I just had to click a few links to hear Zoe's voice coming through my phone. I couldn't place the richer, more mature tone at first, until she signed off at the end by saying "*à la prochaine!*"

Each week on her podcast, Zoe interviews a guest who has in-depth knowledge about an environmental topic, and they focus on how it relates to the average family. It's informative and amusing,

CHAPTER FIVE

if you like stories about diapering in the woods and reusable dental floss.

This is how I've been privy to the main events of Zoe's life for the past five years. Happily married with two teenagers, she has a busy social life punctuated by brief forays into environmental activism. Although she seems to enjoy wielding influence, Zoe posts few pictures of herself and none of her family on her Instagram. It's mostly eco-friendly houses and reusable packaging.

I had no idea what Alex looked like, but Zoe interviewed him on her podcast more than once, because his job at the head of a scientific think tank makes him an expert on a plethora of topics. Their conversations told me that he was learned and thoughtful. Zoe and Alex laughed together so easily. I assumed they were happy.

It surprised me that Zoe had became a passionate environmentalist. When I knew her, she reserved all her enthusiasm for boys and self-indulgent pleasures. Zoe was prone to buying new clothes that caught her eye in shop windows without even trying them on. She sampled a different fancy pastry from the patisserie every day. She spent a great deal of time trying to master the art of blowing concentric smoke rings. Of course, we were much younger back then and we were discovering our identities in the same way that we were learning to speak a foreign language, phrase by phrase, trying bits out, adopting elements that resonated with us.

Zoe is still the girl with the magnetic personality who chose me to be her confidante on the first day of class. But I'm sure she must have acquired a few scars since we shared heaping cups of gelato on the ramparts of St. Paul, our shiny hair blowing in the wind, our skin as smooth and unwrinkled as a ripe apple. A span of an entire generation has passed since then, and life takes its toll.

I don't think there's anything wrong with google-stalking Zoe, or listening to her podcast, in order to glean information about her life.

I don't do it because I'm holding onto the jealousy I felt twenty-five years ago.

Someone explained to me once that we all choose one or two people in our lives to use for our baseline data. It's the way our minds work. I can't compare myself to every forty-three-year-old woman in the world to get a feel for how good or bad I look in general, or how successful or unsuccessful my career has been.

Perhaps it was precisely because I felt that our lives were transpiring on parallel lines, that I chose Zoe to measure and compare myself against. We are both still attractive, maybe because we haven't stopped enjoying life. That's the whole truth of it. Or so I thought, that is, until Zoe's husband, Alex, turned up at my door.

I think about Kate, why I got into the escort business, and how I can exit my role as Alex's escort without losing our connection. Could I be content with being a mistress? What if it starts that way and then he leaves Zoe? Would he even do that? Has he ever had an *affair du coeur* before? It's riskier than seeing escorts. From what I know about Alex, he would abhor drama-filled scenes and emotional blackmail. My guess is that he hasn't fallen in love with anyone else since he met Zoe.

Today, I will start reading through the journals of *Just Julia*—one file for each year. I will select the most pertinent conversations for my last, and most ambitious, blog post.

I have determined seven possible answers to the question: *Why Don't Married Men Who See Escorts Leave Their Spouse?* I feel like I'm onto something. Perhaps this endeavor—blog of mine—could serve as the basis for an even longer literary work in the future?

A lot of enterprising escorts manage to find a way to monetize their stories after they retire from selling fantasies. As I examine each of the seven reasons in general, I will also try to figure out why Alex, specifically, is staying in his marriage to Zoe but coming to me for a bi-weekly dose of unbridled eroticism. Then, with careful

CHAPTER FIVE

strategizing, I will devise a plan to persuade Alex to leave Zoe and choose me.

I turn onto my side and grab the pillow where Alex laid his head two days ago. Hugging it, I take slow, deep breaths and mentally check in with all the parts of my body. My brain is sore from so much thinking, but my stomach is quiet, my limbs are calm, and my heart is hopeful.

I can do this.

But first, I need to make a call.

I roll over and reach into my side table drawer for my work phone.

Kate answers after three rings. "Please tell me you changed your mind!"

I pull the phone away from my ear and take a second to turn down the volume.

"Alex, you know, my... last Percy, was really sweet," I admit, grateful Kate can't witness me trying to suppress the smile that invades my face whenever I think about him. "And I could use the extra money during the summer. So... you can keep booking him till September. If he wants to, that is. But just him. Just Alex."

"Oh my god! That's awesome news! But I think something unusual is going on. Is there anything else you want to tell me?"

I wince and wish Kate could speak at a normal volume. I also wish she was less perceptive.

"Nope. I'm good. Thanks. Bye." I end the call.

It's time to start writing my blog.

CHAPTER SIX

Conversations with Clients: 7 Reasons Why He Won't Leave His Marriage:
Reason #1: There's No Place Like Home

AS A NOVICE escort, I recorded copious details about each client's occupation, likes and dislikes, how much time we spent engaging in various activities, and any ideas for sex or conversation that I could come up with for our next session, if he were to book again. But eventually, I realized that mystery and spontaneity are what make my job enjoyable.

Savouring each moment as it comes, open to whatever path *Just Julia* and her current man are inspired to explore. Without a script, we could always find a next level or a sideways trail if we kept our minds focused on the sensations, the vibe and the flavour of the moment.

Before the end of the third month, I was just noting a few personal details and some simple exchanges that struck me right in the heart because they seemed to contain deep human truths. I became fascinated with trying to figure out why men will stay for long decades with wives who bore them to tears in the bedroom.

I know about twenty percent of married men have sex outside of their marriage, but only a small fraction of "cheaters" hire the services of an escort. Why do these men stay married, rarely initiate divorce, and opt to pay companions to fulfill their sexual needs? Here are two examples of one common reason:

CHAPTER SIX

Percy #42

JJ: You sure know how to show a girl a good time.
P42: I wish my wife thought that.
JJ: Have you ever tried that three finger trick you used today? It was a little bit of heaven.
P42: Cheryl doesn't like it when I put my hand down there. She says it's unhygienic.
JJ: Well, lucky me, I suppose.
P42: It means a lot to me to know you're here waiting for me at the end of every month with that pretty smile.
JJ: You're a sweet man.
P42: Thanks. Gotta go. Cheryl's making stew with dumplings for dinner tonight.

Percy #180

JJ: That's a great tan you've got there.
P180: I built a new dock last weekend.
JJ: You were at your cottage?
P180: Yeah, Melissa was having a girls' painting weekend, so my buddies and I went up north.
JJ: Sounds like fun.
P180: Yeah. It's a gorgeous spot. Next year, we're gonna add a sauna and an outdoor theatre.

Sometimes, when you're looking for answers, you don't have to dig very deep. In my opinion, **P42** has stayed with his wife for twenty-five years because . . . he likes her cooking. No, he *loves* her cooking, and food is an important part of his life. Admittedly, there are probably many more things he appreciates about her, and several more things he wishes were different, apart from just their sex life. Maybe they love to cuddle and kiss and, once in a while, it leads to some old-fashioned intercourse? Or maybe his marriage is sexless, but happy? Can a marriage be sexless, but happy? One third of marriages are "happy." Are those the ones where the couple is still having lots of sex? That answer is probably way too simplistic. Or maybe not. I, however, suspect a happy marriage is about having similar expectations in all areas of life, not just sex, as well as having most of those expectations met regularly.

Overall, I think **P42** would rather stay with his wife and break his vows with an escort, rather than risk eating his own cooking for the rest of his life.

P180 gets a great deal of satisfaction from constructing his living space with his own hands and he is proud of his accomplishments. It would crush him to have to start rebuilding his life and his surroundings, from scratch.

I feel that both clients fit into the same category: *There's No Place Like Home.*

Leaving their wife would mean starting out fresh and finding new ways to fulfill the basic needs of food and shelter. They've put on fuzzy slippers and curled up on the squishy couch of life. They are too comfortable, in their physical space, to ever leave.

Last week on *My Green Family*, Zoe's podcast, Zoe and Alex did an episode about all the amazing things you can make using an old bookshelf, from a kitchen island to a coffee table, to a container garden. I'm sure Alex and Zoe's home is a masterpiece of green living. Yet, Alex never talks about it. He has praised my décor, which is minimalist and monochromatic, but with key bursts of colour and texture in every room.

I watch his shoulders relax, his eyelids fall closed, and his breathing slow down when Alex eases his perfect body back onto the overstuffed pillows on my bed. If he left Zoe, we could create a new and wonderful space for me, Alex and Belle.

CHAPTER SIX

A home for a family, not a family home that serves the dual purposes of domicile and business premises. I am not unaware of how crazy that sounds. But the first step of getting something is recognizing that you want it.

CHAPTER SEVEN

September 9, 1999, way later, St. Paul de Vence, Cote d'Azur, France

Chère Diary,

OH MY GOD, I am so drunk! And nobody made me feel like I was a ridiculous girl who can't hold her alcohol, or worse, a troubled girl who drinks too much. The Martins, Madame Gaudet, Pascale, basically all the fifty or so people at the party, were drinking free wine and gobbling squares of pizza garnished with artichokes, or bocconcini, or fried eggs, which was weird, but tasty. They were laughing together and hugging each other and asking us questions in French and listening to what we had to say and telling us they hope we have the time of our lives in St. Paul de Vence. Zoe says that French people understand that true happiness comes from living in the moment and that they don't judge each other for enjoying life, only for not enjoying it. And everyone drinks wine and no one gets uptight about it. Why has this not caught on in North America?

The best part. The BEST part of tonight is that I had my first French kiss! And to be more precise, French kisses, plural! I was looking for Zoe, who had promised to introduce me to some of the sexy kitchen staff at La Cave, and I stepped outside into the private courtyard with tables that you can't see from the street. A boy I

CHAPTER SEVEN

recognized, Raphael, was smoking and talking with two friends. He called me over and introduced me to Luc and Bernard.

Raphael said, in French, something I translated to myself as, "We need a beautiful girl to help us with our argument." Then he reached out and touched underneath my chin, causing an electric jolt to radiate up through the middle of my face from the point of contact. He raised my head so that I had to look him in the eye. Eyes.

Eyes with impossibly long dark eyelashes. Dark skin. Full red lips curved into a sneaky smile with bright white, slightly crooked teeth.

Then he asked, and I understood every word of this bit, "Luc insists that he is a better kisser than Bernard. Would you settle our argument, please?"

He thought my dumb smile was an answer. With his strong fingers still pressing into my cheeks and chin, Raphael angled my head towards Luc, who opened his mouth and ran his tongue across the bottom of his teeth.

I managed to squeak out a consenting moan as Raphael removed his hand and I leaned into the kiss.

I experienced no internal explosions. Luc's lips were leathery and stiff. I was staring over his shoulder at Raphael the whole time.

When Luc stepped back, I spun around and slid right into Bernard's outstretched arms. He did the really wide-opened mouth thing I recognized from Zoe's description, and it felt like he was vacuum sucking my tongue down his throat.

I thought I might gag, but then the two other boys started applauding. Raphael raised Bernard's arm and said, "Le gagnant!" —"the winner." Obviously, my vote didn't count. Oh well, at least I'm at two kisses now.

Soon after that, Madame Gaudet gave a short speech about how wonderful it is to share our cultures with each other. Then everyone said "*Bonsoir*" and started to shuffle out onto the street.

As Pascale and I were leaving, Zoe poked her head of messy curls out of the swinging kitchen door and winked at me. I wonder how many pairs of sensuous lips were in that kitchen. She is probably at ten French guys kissed after this evening. At least I'll get to hear all about it tomorrow.

I walked back home with Pascale. She was in a great mood. She strikes me as an adult who doesn't think she has all the answers, and who doesn't want to tell you what to do. She makes suggestions and leaves the choice up to me. She told me that I should remember that, to these local boys, I am foreign and exciting, and they envy the glamorous life they imagine I have in North America. She said I should act like I don't care what they think and that will make them want me more. I wonder if that's how she attracted Alain? He often treats her like a fabulous prize that he is not worthy of. It's kind of cute, but can't they just be equals? Or does true love need to be a contest of predator and prey?

We took the long way back, along the west ramparts, so we could take in the view of the surrounding countryside from the top of the wall. Pascale pointed out the dark spots in the valley below which, during the day, are rolling fields and forests. Tonight, they were decorated with the twinkling lights of homes and roads with only a few slow cars. Then she described the coastline of the Mediterranean and the sandy beaches being lapped by salty waters only twelve short kilometres away.

Pascale started humming to herself. I recognized it as a melody I've been hearing on the radio several times a day. She taught me the words to "Adieu Deux Fois." It's a popular song by Odette, a fashion model turned singer. Pascale says I look like her, so I've decided to buy a magazine tomorrow and try to copy everything I can about her style. Now, it's my new favourite song, even if it does have a sad ending after the girlfriend finds out her man is cheating on her again, after she gave him a second chance. She follows him one morning and witnesses him kissing another woman under a bridge.

CHAPTER SEVEN

Singing in French, with my freshly kissed lips and swallowing my saliva that now contains the mouth juices of both Luc and Bernard, I feel I am becoming so much more interesting than I was, like a boring stew that's been jazzed up with exotic spices. I'm making memories, like my dad told me to do.

Next Wednesday, Madame Gaudet is taking our class on an outing to some art galleries where we will get to sit and watch the artists at work in their studios. It's a touristy thing to do here and it sounds intimate and exciting. Maybe, with a little luck, I'll find my painting.

CHAPTER EIGHT

ALEX IS A punctual and regular client. I appreciate that about him, and so much more. We are now into our third week. This time, he booked two hours! He wants to arrive and surprise me . . . in the shower.

Everything is set up: filtered natural light, the most flattering for naked flesh, is streaming through the gauzy floor length curtains, the bed is turned down, enticing us to feel the thrill of writhing naked on clean sheets. On a side table, there is a tray with red wine and truffles, as well as a pitcher of homemade iced tea, and, on another table, there is a variety of lubes for different applications, a few fun sex toys—Alex does like to experiment—and some handy wipes and fluffy towels. The bathroom is strewn with flower petals. I am wearing a tasteful, but alluring, amount of waterproof make-up. I have been told that I have sexy eyes, and I know how much glossy red lips add to the mystique.

I've been so excited since I woke up this morning that I've had to hold myself back from indulging in some self-pleasure with my Magic Wand. There is a weakness in my hitherto strong foundation. I've been craving a dose of Alex as much as a junkie needs their next hit.

Kate would not approve. Kate's rule number one of escorting is safety. That's straightforward. Until I met Alex, I thought rule number two of escorting was also a no brainer: Never get emotionally attached. Apart from a few fleeting moments of intense connection,

CHAPTER EIGHT

which arose because something random about each of us inspired a similar emotion in the other, I've been able to maintain a wall that kept me distanced from my clients. That was, until I met this man who made me feel like I had just glimpsed my future, one that's bursting with happiness.

I know how ridiculous that sounds.

I've already bathed, shaved, and scrubbed myself this morning, so I'm standing with my lower back receiving the stream from the shower head, wondering how long the water will stay hot, when I hear his deep voice from the living room, "Julia, I'm home!"

Oh my god! Does he know he said that? Is he playing a game, or does he think of my house as his home? I have an overwhelming urge to run and lock the door and not let him leave until he admits that he has never felt a love like this before.

I move the shower curtain to the side so I can peek at him. He's hurrying to get undressed. I cannot get enough of his naked physique. For ten years, I've seen and touched an average of five different men's bodies per week, and, for the most part, I've enjoyed them, like a physiotherapist who is fascinated by the intricacies of the human form.

I've seen every kind of penis, lots of cute butts, and I never get tired of an honest shy smile. I've appreciated all the kind men who chose me, often for long stretches of time, to take care of their sexual and emotional needs. During our associations, I was happy to share each one with their lady at home and, to be perfectly honest, even though I have many fond memories, there's not a single Percy whose presence in my life that I will miss.

But when I observe this Adonis that is Alex, extracting his long legs from faded blue jeans, I become the greedy child at a playgroup who will not let go of that unique piece of Lego that actually belongs to some other kid. Like Belle's Lego gorilla with its own detachable yellow banana. But I could care less whose it is because I want it and

I'm going to squeeze it in the palm of my hand so hard it can never be pried out.

I close the shower curtain and try to compose myself. Alex will be scared off if he suspects that I have strong feelings for him. He is acting under the assumption that he is buying a fantasy. So, I tone down my smile, and say, "So sweet of you to join me. It's getting pretty steamy in here."

Then he steps under the water and presses my naked wet flesh against his.

"Finally," Alex says into the crook of my neck as he kisses the spot that makes me shiver, and I die a little inside because he has read my mind.

Like the most eager patient, Alex surrenders himself into my capable hands. He doesn't hold back as I wash every inch of his body, even getting him to crouch down so I can scrub shampoo into his scalp with my fingertips. Then I rub a scratchy loofa on his back, legs, and arms while he moans like a happy kitten. Finally, I use the wet water as lubrication to explore the opening of his ass with a soft rubber toy I stick on my finger, and he rewards me by turning around and plunging his rock hard penis into my open mouth.

I'm on my knees, water running down my cheeks, and I'm glad for it, because when I look up to make that all-important eye contact and see something that must be love flash across his face, telltale tears of happiness escape my eyes.

I let him move in and out while I explore his cock with my tongue, then put my hands on his tight ass and direct him deeper into my throat. Too soon, Alex closes his eyes, pulls out of my mouth, and ejaculates onto my breasts. We watch together as his cum travels down my chest and belly, mixing with the rush of water.

After drying each other off, we hop into bed and pause to enjoy a glass of iced tea. I make it myself, so it's not too sweet, and I add fresh mint and blackcurrants.

CHAPTER EIGHT

Alex takes a big gulp, looks at me, and says, "I hadn't expected you to be so . . ."

I'm intrigued. "So what?" I ask him.

"So . . . sexual?" He laughs. "I suppose what I mean is, I hadn't expected for you to enjoy it so much."

I turn away and speak to the window, "What can I say? I love my job."

But this is not normal. I do enjoy sex, and I enjoy meeting the Percys and trying to figure out what makes them tick. Kate told me that most clients are sweet, and she was right. When they come to me to fulfill their needs, it's better than using a casual acquaintance they have no intention of having a relationship with just for sex. I really believe that.

And if they are coming to me because their wife only wants to have sex once a month, but they desire it more often, they can be assured that I have had a recent STI check, unlike many of the girls they might pick up in a bar or online. Kate has stressed that condoms are a must for vaginal or anal penetration and either one of us can request it for oral.

It's not okay to come in my mouth, but other landing sites can be negotiated. Ninety percent of the time, all the Percys want is to lay back, enjoy some erotic massage, and let me ride them until they come. Over the past decade, I've developed powerful thighs and a consistent list of regular cliental. So, yes, I love my job. Or, I loved my job.

I can't say this out loud, but if I could, I'd say, "You're right, Alex. I do enjoy it more with you. I have never been to the places my heart goes when we are together. Like the song says, I never felt this way before. Now, I understand. And when you're here beside me, Alex, I'm thankful for this feeling, but when you leave and go back to Zoe, my guts are crushed like an exploded watermelon flattened by a steamroller called love."

He runs his fingers along my spine.

"I hope that's okay with you?" I say aloud, and add, "That I . . . that you are able to bring me so much pleasure." Then I turn back to face him, because Kate taught me to stay attuned to my Percy's body language. It is more reliable than words.

His expression is calm. "Absolutely. I have to admit, I find it very refreshing."

I put down my glass, straddle Alex, and kiss all over his super intelligent face while I massage the muscles of his jaw and neck where everyone holds tension. "And I find you very refreshing."

I haven't gotten enough of him yet, so I wriggle a bit and wait to feel his penis harden against my vulva, but it doesn't. He opens his mouth as if to speak, but hesitates.

"There's nothing you can't say to me," I assure him.

Alex reaches up and takes my hands in his and lowers them into his lap. Now, there's a puddle of our four hands. I lace my fingers through his and we press our palms together. We lift up our hands to shoulder height, like we're playing a silly game we just invented.

"I noticed a small pair of flipflops at the door today. They're not yours," he says, and I let go in surprise.

Damn. I'm not prepared to have this conversation yet. "Are you saying I've got big feet?" I ask.

He laughs, but his serious face returns. "I have a son and a daughter."

I climb off him and grab my personal phone out of the bedside table drawer. I turn it on and smile back at the cutie on the screen and then angle it so he can see my daughter.

"Her name is Belle and she's eleven years old. I only see clients when she's at school or day camps. After school, she either takes the bus home, or I pick her up. There's no way she could walk in unannounced. I'm also a supply teacher."

"Kate said you only did this part-time. I'd like to hear about Belle," Alex says.

CHAPTER EIGHT

I hate this part. I get confused between what's real and the illusion I'm trying to create. And even though my clients might think they want to know about my personal life, it's never as exciting as they would like to imagine. The conversation usually leads to a quick end of the date.

Alex turns onto his side and gives me his full attention. He looks like he's settling in for a long gab session.

"Well, okay," I say, and I wonder where to begin.

Hardly anyone asks me about my daughter, except my father. He loves Belle like crazy, but, even with his hearing aids, it's almost useless trying to have a proper conversation with him.

Belle's schoolteachers tell me she's a model student, if a little shy. I know exactly what that means. She's a girl who is eager to please and who thinks that by being quiet, she's doing the right thing. She must have gotten that from her father. Or maybe she didn't, I correct myself. I, too, derive a lot of satisfaction from giving pleasure and I also try to do the right thing. It's just so difficult to know what that is at the moment. Am I ready to drag my daughter into this? I know that it's within my power to stop now and tell Alex that I can never see him again. For the sake of his family and mine, that might be the right thing to do.

But my heart won't let me.

Alex is sipping his drink, waiting for me to begin.

"What can I say about Belle? She loves art, especially painting. She's always had a bizarre fascination with insects. Maybe because her world is small. It's only her and me. And my dad."

I search through my photos and choose one of Belle and I standing in front of Niagara Falls.

"She's got bright eyes," says Alex when I show it to him, "And she's tall, like you."

"She was always happy living here, just the two of us. But lately, she keeps asking about her father."

"I'm curious too."

"I told her everything I know. His name was Carlos. He was a bartender I met at a resort in Mexico during a bridal shower vacation for a high school friend. We had lovely sex on the beach at three in the morning. He told me he was from El Salvador." I hold up my hands. "And that's it. I wish I could say more. I wish I could give her a bevy of aunts and grannies and brightly coloured dresses and feasts of empanadas and tamales." Alex waits while I collect the last of my thoughts. "I was convinced that I could be enough of a family for her. But I'm not. She's disappointed in me. That's what hurts the most."

"Don't be so hard on yourself. I know exactly what you mean." Alex expression has that universal look of empathy that every parent gets when they think about the many ways that they, too, have let down their own children. "It can't be easy keeping your two worlds separate inside one house. I'm guessing Belle and your dad don't know about this?" He motions to the table neatly stocked with lube and sex toys.

"I'm not ashamed of what I do," I say, but, for some reason, I feel my cheeks burn like they do when this topic comes up with a client.

The surprised look on Alex's face tells me there was no malice in his question.

It still hurts though, because he brought up the social stigma that eats at me every day from inside—feeling like I have to hide any part of my authentic self just makes me feel shitty.

I find my calm voice and continue, "We almost always go visit my dad at his place. Belle likes to play with his cat. This is my floor of the house, and we keep it very tidy. She knows that she's not allowed in this guest room. Upstairs, Belle has her own bedroom and a little studio that's packed with canvases and sketchbooks. She paints pictures of volcanoes and butterflies, and she says she wants to go to Central America and look for her father. But I can't believe we could ever find him, and, if we actually did, I'm afraid I'd lose

CHAPTER EIGHT

her to a bunch of people who share her beautiful brown eyes. Either way, it's going to be a lot of tears and something I'm not ready for."

Alex reaches out and runs the back of his fingers along my cheekbone. "You're doing the best you can and your love for her will always be enough."

He puts his arm around me and kisses my head. I savour the snuggle for as long as I think is appropriate, then pull back and say, "Thanks for chatting. And for listening. I suppose you want to go now?"

"Well, you suppose wrong then. I paid for two hours today, and there's still forty-five minutes left. What I'd like for you to do now, is to climb back on top of me."

I smile. That conversation didn't scare him off. And he's looking at me like I'm a turbulent ocean and he's trying to see what's at the bottom.

So I slide my body on top of his large, strong frame, and get back to work. It's my job, after all, to do as I'm asked. One day, I'd like to say what I want and watch him do my bidding.

What I want, Alex, is for you to never ever leave me.

CHAPTER NINE

September 12, 1999, St. Paul de Vence, Cote d'Azur, France

Chère Diary,

I'M SURE I was destined to be in this idyllic place at this exact moment in my life. The Dubois are the sweetest family in the world! Pascale woke the twins up early this morning and, when I went down to the kitchen, they served me like little waiters in a restaurant. They tried to speak English, and Georges couldn't say scrambled eggs. Then he started hiccupping and Émilie couldn't stop laughing at him. Pascale was cooking me a Canadian breakfast and she even got sliced bacon and maple syrup from who knows where. Georges spilled orange juice in my lap and Émilie dropped the toast on the floor. I ate it all anyway. My heart felt so full.

Ever since we lost mom to ovarian cancer, it's just been dad and me, and I've never wanted anything else, but being part of this French family is making me realize what kind of life my mom must have wished for our family. I'd like to ask dad why he doesn't have a new girlfriend, like so many of my friends' parents. I think I already know the answer. He loved my mom so deeply and it hurt so much to lose her that he can't go through that again.

This home is like most of the buildings in St. Paul de Vence. It has three floors, the shop on the ground floor, the kitchen and

CHAPTER NINE

living room above that, then the bedrooms on the top floor. Every morning, Alain and Pascale go downstairs to open their shop at eight a.m. These premises have been home to Alain's family's business for over one hundred years. When they started, it was a candle making shop. How cool is that, to live and work in a building that dates back to the fifteenth century? Anything that old blows my mind. Pascale talks about the ghosts in this house like they're nosy neighbours and, if it's windy outside, she tells the twins that *les fantômes* are tapping on the windows.

The metal sign that says "La Maison Dubois" hangs above the arched stone door on the Rue Grande, which is named that way because it goes the whole length of town, about half a mile. It's really just a narrow lane though, a lovely walkway tiled with mosaic stones that look, from an aerial view, like a garland of flowers. The stone walls of the buildings are so close on either side, you could toss a ball back and forth from the upstairs windows.

Nowadays, La Maison Dubois sells locally sourced natural products for the home: olive oil, soap, candles, pottery, and linens, to the two million tourists that visit St. Paul de Vence every year, mostly during the summer. Alain spends a lot of time driving around, picking up products and looking for new ones, while Pascale minds the shop. Pascale said that we're still in the busy season for tourists, but at the end of the month, two weeks from now, there will be a lot less shoppers. The store will close at five o'clock instead of seven o'clock, and that will make life a lot easier for the Dubois.

They are devoted to their children and always take the weekend off. Two old ladies from Vence, which is the larger town outside the walls, work in the store on Saturday and Sunday, because, as Pascale says, "If there are buses in town, the door is open."

But I know that, sometimes, when Pascale and Alain are here together, that they flip the *"ouvert"* sign to *"fermé"* and go upstairs for a quick sex session.

When I got back from class early yesterday and came in the back door, I heard them laughing together on the floor above. So I got busy and cleaned the kitchen. I hope that when I'm in a grown-up marriage, my husband and I will do that too. Shortly, they came down all smiley and Alain squeezed Pascale's butt as they walked down the stairs.

My first au pair chore of the day is to get the twins washed and dressed after breakfast and walk them to school. L'École Primaire is outside of the wall to the north of town through the main gate where all the tourists come in. Along the way, we stop at the Rue des Baouques to pick up Zoe and her little boy, Henri. He's very naughty and they usually make us late because he literally drags his heels and he insists on petting every dog we see, which is quite a lot of dogs. I had no idea how much French people love dogs, especially small fluffy ones.

Next, Henri barges into the boules games of the old men in front of Le Café de la Place. It's a big open area where the ground is packed down soil. It's surrounded by stone sidewalk, so it makes a large sunken in space where several boules games can be happening at the same time. The old men always let Henri throw a few of the silver balls and tell him that he's going to grow up to be a grand champion. People have been playing boules in that spot for over a hundred years, even celebrities.

Boules, or *pétanque*, as I've also heard people call it, is a game that seems to me like every French person thinks they are an expert at. At the very least, they all have opinions about how to play it properly.

Just past the café, Henri says *"j'suis fatigué"* and begs Zoe for a piggyback until she gives in and lets him climb onto her back. This just makes Zoe walk slower, but I can't do anything to help because both my hands are full with Georges and Émilie.

We arrive at L'École Primaire just as the headmistress is ringing a handbell in the courtyard and she gives us a sour look because our three kids are always racing to join the end of the line.

CHAPTER NINE

Today, Zoe made a face back at the old prune and then said to me, "I'm never gonna have kids."

I told her, "Sure you are. Everyone has kids. It's what you do after you get married and buy a house. You fill the empty rooms up with kids."

Zoe said, "I'd prefer hordes of expensive jewellery, closets full of designer clothing, and a sexy husband who refers to me as his Goddess." And I bet she'll get all that too, because she's not afraid to say what she wants out loud.

After class today, Zoe and I did a slow tour of the whole town, trying to decide which house in St. Paul de Vence we would choose if we ever got to live here in the future. I picked the red stucco home over the bakery because it's right beside the tallest palm tree in the village and because it would always smell amazing.

Zoe chose the home called La Miette, a vine covered two story yellow brick building with a private terrace at the back. It's on the edge of the east side of town and must have amazing views of the sunrise. Madame Gaudet told us that house was once owned by the famous French poet Jacques Prévert. We agreed Zoe would host wild parties on her terrace and I would bring the bread.

I love being Zoe's friend. She even noticed how I parted my hair on the side today and she said it looks "chic." I hope we stay best friends when we get back to Toronto, but I can't imagine her coming to visit dad and me. Our house is filled with dad's old *National Geographic* magazines and framed cross stitch embroideries of inspirational sayings like, "Every day is a gift" that my mom made when she was alive. I used to try to imagine her sitting in the living room with one of those circle stitching frames in her lap but the truth is, I don't have any memories of her at all.

I would like to visit Zoe's house though. She lives in Forest Hill, an area which I know is one of the richest neighbourhoods in Toronto, and I can't even imagine how gorgeous her home must be.

September 13, 1999, St. Paul de Vence, Cote d'Azur, France

Chère Diary,

This morning, we met Madame Gaudet and the rest of our class at La Galerie d'Oeufs. There were sculptures of eggs everywhere, on shelves, hanging on strings from the ceiling, or lying on the floor like they had just been laid by a passing turtle. Some of the eggs were whole, while others had creatures like snakes, fish, or birds emerging from broken shells. Some were white and shiny, others were painted different colours or speckled to look real, like something you'd be lucky to stumble upon in nature. There were folding chairs for us to sit on and the sculptor lady, who had long grey hair and was all covered in streaks of clay, said we should call her Sophie. She started by telling us the history of St. Paul de Vence, which I've heard before, but I will write it down now, so I don't forget.

The tiny town is about five hundred years old and, because it's built on a hill, was a strategic military position for France near its border with Italy. It fell into disrepair but was rebuilt in the 1800s. Then, in the 1900s, a lot of famous artists like Folon, Matisse, Picasso, and Chagall either visited or lived in the village. There is the famous Maeght Museum of Contemporary Art outside the walls and a small museum of local history inside. And then there are the art galleries, more than fifty, that people can visit in one day if they want to. It's also a place that movie stars who come to the Riviera like to go to unwind and, well, look artsy.

Next, Sophie explained how to make pottery and we watched her spin blobs of clay into plates and vases. It looked like she was performing magic. We each got to take a turn and make a little bowl, which was messy, but fun. Sophie's going to fire them in her kiln, and we'll go back and paint them next week.

After that, we walked to the Place de la Fontaine, which locals say is the heart of St. Paul de Vence. It's a small square with a fountain that looks like a giant vase. It has four spouts that, I told Zoe, look like water peeing into a large basin. We sat on the edge, listening to the constant flow and laughing as we ate our lunches from home. I had Swiss cheese and ham on a croissant with some figs and a little bottle of pear juice. Zoe had fizzy bottled water and a delicious looking artichoke salad from the kitchen at La Cave.

I asked Zoe how she learned to speak French so well and she said she went to boarding school in Switzerland last year. I wonder how much money that would cost? Her dad is a movie producer, so I'm sure the cost was never an issue. I asked her what she wants to do with her life, and she said, "No fucking idea. Keep travelling until I figure it out?"

I wonder why Zoe wants me to be her friend? I've got no good stories, no cool clothes, no crazy schemes. I just follow her around, listen to her complain about stuff, and laugh at her jokes. I feel so lucky. Like she sees potential in me that I haven't realized yet.

In the afternoon, I saw Raphael again at the next artist's studio. Raphael. Raphael. Raphael.

Best name ever. I get flushed writing it and breathless saying it. Whatever it was the sweet old man, Monsieur Grenier, told us about the different styles of painting, impressionist, cubist, modern, I wasn't able to listen. Raphael is his shop assistant, and he was eyeing all of us girls from behind a counter. I know he looked at me twice, at least. My mind was full of noise, screaming at me to approach Raphael, to speak with him, to kiss him. I need to kiss him. He was at the party last week and he must be part of the French boy's kissing contest, so I'm sure he would kiss me if I let him know that I'm interested.

I can't bring myself to ask, but maybe I can go into his shop and try giving him sexy looks and licking my lips. I mean, he watched me kiss Luc and Bernard. He knows I'll do it.

Raphael looked so good today. He was wearing black jeans and a tight navy wool sweater with the sleeves pushed up. I wonder how he can wear a sweater when it's always so warm here? It probably feels warmer to me than it does to him. After all, he's got Mediterranean blood pulsing through his veins.

Raphael's dark, curly hair almost touches his shoulders. He must have got up late today because he had moustache and beard fuzz. So sexy.

I had to know, so I asked Zoe if she likes Raphael. She said he's cute, but not her type. She likes a guy named Marcel who is a sous-chef at La Cave and makes her special bedtime snack plates with olives and cheese. What a relief! Now that I know where Raphael works, I'll make sure I walk slowly past La Galerie Au Vent as often as possible. If I can see him inside, I'll go in and try to catch his eye.

Maybe I'll drop something out of my pocket and bend over to pick it up.

We didn't get to do our own painting, which was fine because I felt too dreamy to concentrate, but everyone watched while Monsieur Grenier whipped up a watercolour photo of the Rue du Casse-Cou, which means "the street of the broken neck," by looking at a postcard photo of it. His picture was intriguing. I like the idea of a set of uneven stone steps leading up to somewhere I can't see, like a sunlit garden or a secluded alcove, but that's not my picture.

I'm still searching for it.

CHAPTER TEN

IN BED, ALEX is the most playful man I have ever met in all my years escorting. And that's saying a lot. If I didn't love him, I might balk at all the work he makes me do. Not that I don't want to give my clients their money's worth, but Alex puts my skills to the test on every date.

He's got a thing for bondage, he can't get enough of prostate massaging toys, and I've contorted myself more with him than I ever have in a yoga class. He's like a kid in a candy shop who keeps changing their mind about what they want and finally decides to take one of each. I'm ecstatic that we are sexually compatible, but I can't seem to get this to go any further.

A lot of the Percys wanted to spend half an hour per session complaining about their wives, how they never gave a blow job anymore, or always undressed in the dark, but Alex never mentions Zoe and, after that one time, he has never mentioned his children. It would be so much easier to get information if he was overtly frustrated with his family situation.

I sense that Alex is coming to me for a bi-weekly dose of fantasy, every Monday and Thursday afternoon, and it ends there. I feel like he's got his life compartmentalized so well in his big brain that, after he books another date, he probably doesn't even think about me until it's time to drive here.

His head is packed full of scientific information that may as well be a foreign language. I've googled radio interviews he has done discussing the latest research at the think tank where he works.

The hosts described Alex as renowned, successful, and on the leading edge of bioengineering. But about four sentences into his answers to the science questions, I was totally out of my depth and couldn't follow what he was saying anymore. He's a freakin' genius really. But he's a genius who, I know, likes me to nibble on his earlobes. I wonder, how can I wiggle my way into his thoughts?

Most escorts offer a full date experience. Meaning, they go to restaurants, to the theatre, even on cruises. Their clients are often single businessmen who want an enthusiastic companion for the evening, or the weekend, but who don't want the relationship woes that can come along with it.

I follow some professional ladies on Twitter and these escorts frequently post pictures of their gourmet meals, designer gifts, and extravagant holidays, thanking their client who they refer to simply by their last initial, like *Mr. L* or *Mr. G*.

Just Julia, my escort name, has no social media presence. She is all about discretion and keeping her clients' intimate secrets behind closed doors. Still, I dream of the day when Alex and I can sit outside at an outdoor patio restaurant and watch people who are watching us and we know that they're thinking we are the most fascinating couple they have ever seen—that we were made for each other. If there was some way I could get Alex out from these four walls, maybe he would realize that he was meant to walk through life with me at his side.

I have a plan for today. A plan to move this relationship to the next level.

I've got my fingers crossed behind my back as he steps through the door. I almost laugh out loud because he's wearing khaki shorts and socks with sandals. I love all of his outfits, from urban high fashion to backyard campfire. They give me glimpses into a well-rounded life that I yearn to be part of.

CHAPTER TEN

Alex kicks off the sandals and heads straight into my arms. Instantly, his hands begin exploring my lacy lingerie. He buries his head in my hair and inhales for several seconds. I wrap my arms around his waist and start kneading the muscles in his lower back. I sigh as I feel the tension melt under my touch. Then, I let my hands slip into his shorts and feel his round ass through his silky underwear. He's tight here too. I squeeze harder and, as I pull him closer and grind my hips into his, he rewards me with a deep moan.

I was going to ask him why he is dressed like that, instead of in his usual business casual look, but words don't seem appropriate anymore. Our tongues are too busy swirling together in a happy celebration and my trivial thoughts have been usurped by serious passion.

Alex dances me into the bedroom, and then dips me onto the bed.

As he hovers over me, grinning like a kid who got everything he wanted for Christmas, I want to tell him that I love him. I want to scream it and hear it echoed back in his husky voice. But I swallow those words and reach out to pull him back into a kiss. At least I don't have to hold back my lust.

I'm careful today. I orchestrate our sexual activity so that we climax together, both of us panting and shaking on my bed with the sheets strewn on the floor, lube, toys, and pillows in a jumble around us. Still wordless, we remain suspended in a daze of elation, kissing and trailing fingers over sensitive flesh, until I eventually shiver in a cool draft. I become aware of the noise of the traffic outside and check the clock. I've got to do it now.

Our faces are so close, I only need to whisper, "I want to let you know that I went for my regular tests yesterday, and when I get the all clear in a couple of days, I won't ask you to wear a condom anymore."

Alex's thick dark eyebrows squeeze together. "But . . ."

I bite my lower lip. Here goes, "I'll be starting a full-time teaching job in September. I haven't seen any other clients for the past four weeks and I won't be seeing anyone but you from now on."

Alex rewards me with a smile. He's got a few crooked teeth, but they're white and clean and his breath is always sweet, unless he's just had a coffee. "You don't know what I'm doing when I leave here though," he states.

No, I don't, I think, *Tell me! Tell me that you never have sex with Zoe anymore. Tell me that you'll never want to see another escort. Tell me that I'm the girl of your dreams and you can't live without me.*

"Of course, I don't know what you do," I say, staying as close to the truth as possible, so that I sound honest, "but you are all the sex I need right now, and I'd like to offer you the option. It's always your choice, of course."

He smiles again and runs his hand through my hair, lifts it, then lets it fall in slow motion, draping it across my shoulder. "You are a fascinating woman, Julia. And so incredibly sensual . . . Thank you for this opportunity," he says, "I will mull it over."

And now, I want him all over again.

But there's something we need to do first.

"Come upstairs with me," I tell him. "I want to show you the baby robins. They're orange and brown and their bodies are covered with white fuzz like dandelion fluff."

"How many are there? Have they opened their eyes yet?" he asks, hopping off the bed, eyes wide with excitement.

"Three, and not yet," I answer.

As we leave the guest room, we grab towels and wrap them around ourselves, even though no one can see into the house. Then we tiptoe to the upstairs landing and kneel side by side in front of the large window that lets light into the upstairs hallway. Only our upper arms are touching as we watch Mr. and Mrs. Robin fly back

CHAPTER TEN

and forth from my lawn up to the front light, then drop worms into the gaping mouths of their offspring.

"They are both very attentive parents," I say after a couple of minutes of silent observation. "I honestly can't tell them apart unless they're side by side, and then I can see that the male is more brightly coloured."

"There are actually quite a lot of robins in your neighbourhood," says Alex. "It's possible that this brood contains offspring from more than one male."

I laugh. "So you're saying that Mrs. Robin might have a whole flock of admirers?"

I shoot Alex my well-practiced sideways stare.

He nods, looking at me now. "Yes, indeed. She's quite a mesmerizing beauty."

CHAPTER ELEVEN

Conversations with Clients: 7 Reasons Why He Won't Leave His Marriage:
Reason #2: External Forces

SOME MEN, I learned, don't believe they have any options beyond staying in their marriage and secretly seeing an escort for sex. They will stay married until they are parted by someone's death and they are unfaltering in their belief that it is the right thing to do in a conflicted world that was not of their making.

Percy #144

P144: Do I smell like sex? Maybe I should have a shower? But then I'll smell like your soap, or my hair will look different.

JJ: Relax. Go into my bathroom. There are clean cloths and towels beside the sink and some unscented soap. Give yourself a little wash. Then go grab something to eat with onions and no one will ever know.

P144: That's a great idea! My mother was sniffing my jacket when I got home last time. If she thinks I'm coming to you, she'll be angry at my wife for not doing her job.

Percy #253

JJ: Are you going to watch the hockey finals tonight?

CHAPTER ELEVEN

P253: No, I'll be at church this evening.
JJ: On a Thursday?
P253: It's Maundy Thursday, the reenactment of the Last Supper before Jesus' arrest and crucifixion. It's one of the most moving services of the year. I would never miss it.

I have learned that religion, culture, and sometimes the pressures of a career where the simple act of being a divorced person looks like a stain on your character, are *External Forces*. These men knew, when they chose their life partner, that there was no back door. These seem like the most traditional marriages. It doesn't matter how bad they are, they are as solid as the rock of Gibraltar.

It's funny, though, how an itchy cock can betray the vows while the brain remains chaste. Funny, but good. Good for me, and I believe, good for the Percys. Everyone deserves to be happy, and they didn't choose the families and cultures they were born into.

These men justify what they are doing because, even though they surrender to the weakness of their flesh, they preserve the preeminent emotional connection with their wife. They don't allow themselves to develop feelings for another woman beyond the brief physical union with an escort.

Alex is Jewish. Alex asked Zoe to convert to Judaism before they got married. She talks about it frequently on the podcast. I found it very interesting when she explained about *bal tashchit* on her podcast.

It is a basic principle of Jewish law which instructs people to not destroy the environment. Originally, it was used in reference to the common sense idea that if you lay siege to a city, you shouldn't go nuts and destroy any of the fruit trees or you'll regret it later when you're starving. But nowadays, it's been expanded to apply to all of God's creations.

Zoe says that *bal tashchit* is a fundamental principle of their "green" family. I like that sentiment a lot.

One of my Jewish Percys explained to me that technically, a married man does not commit adultery by having sex with a single woman. He is a fornicator, not an adulterer. It is only the married woman who commits adultery by cuckolding her husband. The laws are fundamentally about paternity and seem very outdated, in my opinion.

Is Alex worried about some kind of eternal damnation? I don't think so. Does he feel divorce is impossible? I don't think so either. Alex has never referred to his Jewish religion and he doesn't wear any religious garb like a Kippah or a prayer shawl. In our conversations, however, Alex exudes reason and looks for sound evidence, not scripture, to support his opinions.

I don't think Alex is controlled by a force which is external to his marriage, and I don't see how he can call himself "happily married" when his sexual needs are not being fulfilled. So, if he's not happy, what reason is there to stay?

My mind keeps spiralling. If only there was a magic question I could ask Alex that would point me in the right direction; I want him to be as happy as he can be, every day, not just Monday and Thursday.

I'm certain that he's engaged and enrapt when he's with me. He jokes around, laughs, and even teases me. The more time he spends in my presence, the more animated his voice gets. He gets sillier, and I can imagine what he was like as a carefree teenager. Not that I believe a thoughtful man like Alex was ever free of cares, but I know too well that it erodes the soul to lead a double life, as both of us are.

Lately, when he's about to orgasm, Alex has started letting out uninhibited primal moans so powerful, it can make me climax along with him, even if I'm just giving him a blowjob. More than once, this act of release has brought tears to my eyes.

CHAPTER ELEVEN

I want this every day. How can he not want this every day, too? If there's anything I hold onto with respect to religion, it is that we should honour the beautiful life we have been given and not just plod through our days in obligation, but in ecstasy, because life is a precious miracle and each day we are alive is a blessing.

For me, a sublime intervention happened the day Alex walked into my life.

CHAPTER TWELVE

September 19, 1999, St. Paul de Vence, Cote d'Azur, France

Chère Diary,

EVERY AFTERNOON, I walk past La Galerie au Vent as slowly as possible, pausing to admire the five paintings on little easels in the large front window. One or two paintings get switched from day to day. I wonder if that is to make people think they were sold, or if they did, in fact, get sold? Today, I was looking at a watercolour landscape of the grey city walls descending into the lush valley below, which I think is beautiful, but too expensive, at ninety francs.

Then, my dream came true!

Raphael stepped out of the shop and said, "Salut!" like we were old friends.

I nearly peed my pants, I was so excited. I have daydreamed about him so much that, when he appeared before me in the pulsating flesh, I could barely keep myself standing up. I had to grab onto the wall of the shop and Raphael decided that I must need something to eat.

He was on a break, and we walked together, like a romantic couple, through the narrow streets, to the yummiest little shop in the heart of St. Paul de Vence called Dolce Italia. I ordered a mango gelato cone and he had pistachio gelato in a cup. He paid for them both, so it was a date!

CHAPTER TWELVE

We sat at a small round table outside and I had absolutely nothing to say to him. I kept staring at the stubble on his chin and waiting until he parted his lips to insert the small wooden spoon with heaps of cold pale green gelato into his melting hot mouth, watching him pucker when he swallowed and then lick the sticky sweet liquid off his lips with his tongue.

I know that Raphael doesn't speak much English and all I could think to talk about was the weather or my job, but the French word for twins had flown right out of my head and I was wondering how I could safely bite the cone part when he asked, "Veux-tu poser pour moi?"

It sounded like he had just come up with the idea. Like it had just occurred to him that very moment on a whim that he wanted me to model for him. And before I could stop myself, I asked, "Pourquoi?"

Of course, he didn't answer that he chose me because I'm the most beautiful girl in the world, but what he did say was even better. He laughed and touched the fingers of my left hand that was resting on the table. "Parce que je veux te capturer."

He wants to capture me . . .

I nodded and said, "Oui. Merci."

That would have been the perfect moment for a kiss. With those words hanging in the air between us. He could have lunged onto my half-opened mouth and thrust his tongue down there for the victory and a sweet taste of mango.

But yellow liquid started dripping on my wrist and I had to lick it off. Raphael said he needed to get back to work. Before he left me, he said to come to the back door of the shop on Sunday morning at nine a.m. and not to tell anyone, absolutely no one, where I'm going. There must be some reason why he doesn't want it to get back to his boss, M. Grenier.

This is going to kill me. I don't mind telling Pascale a fib. She keeps encouraging me to immerse myself in French culture on my days off, to hear different voices, to try new things. But Zoe? How can I have this amazing secret and not tell Zoe?

I'll just have to keep repeating it to myself in the mirror, "You are going to pose for Raphael because he asked you to. You are going to sit still for a long time, and he is going to stare at your body and your face so he can capture you..."

Raphael chose me to pose for him. He is, hands down, the sexiest boy in the entire world, and he wants to immortalize me on canvas, an ordinary girl from one of the poorest suburbs of Toronto.

September 24, 1999, St. Paul de Vence, Cote d'Azur, France

Chère Diary,

After breakfast, I told the family that I was going to church. Pascale made an odd face and said, "Prends un pull." Take a sweater. I was disappointed that I had blown the very first part of my plan. Of course, I should have known that jean shorts and a tank top wouldn't be acceptable church attire.

I grabbed a fleece jacket to keep up the charade for no one, and Pascale slipped me a sneaky wink while I was hugging the kids goodbye.

I don't think about my mom very much. In fact, I usually try not to, because it hurts. I doubt she would have been quite as cool as Pascale, but it wasn't my mom's fault that she wasn't French. Whenever I achieve something, like passing a grade or getting my driver's license, Dad says, "Good job!" and "Your mom would be so proud of you." I want to believe that mom might also be proud of me today. I was being adventurous and living in the moment.

When I got to La Galerie au Vent, the back door was ajar, so I entered the cluttered workroom. There were canvases in rows piled against one wall, several easels with stools, tubs of empty picture frames, counters with tubes of paint, brushes and palettes, along with a few upholstered pieces of furniture, empty vases, and fancy dishes they must have used as props.

Raphael was standing with his back to me, so I got to take in his small bum in tight jeans before he turned, looked me up and down, and smiled.

We got right to work, by which I mean, he asked me to sit on a large red velvet chair with low arms that was almost as big as half a bed, but definitely not as comfortable, and look *ennuyée*. That made me laugh, but he really meant it. He wanted me to experiment with arranging my body as many different ways as I could, looking as bored as possible.

He decided on three poses for today; first, me lounging with one leg over the arm of the chair and the other on the floor, leaning my head on the other arm of the chair while staring at the ceiling, with my hair hanging almost to the ground; second, me sitting on the front edge of the chair, slouching forward with my left cheek resting on my left hand, staring up to the right where the wall meets the ceiling; and finally, me curled up and not quite fitting onto the cushion space, my legs elevated and resting against the back of the chair, blood rushing to my head while yawning with my eyes closed. That was the worst. It's very difficult to hold a yawn and not take a break to lick your lips.

I held each pose for about twenty minutes, while Raphael drew on a large sketchpad with different pencils. I tried my best to freeze and to not change my expression or move my body, even though the stillness became almost unbearable after a few minutes.

Raphael was close enough that I could smell his spicy cologne, but I couldn't look at him. I was supposed to look bored, but I tried to make the sexiest bored face I possibly could. I inflated my chest and tensed the muscles of my legs to open just far enough to invite attention down there without looking sleazy.

Raphael said, "Trés bien," twice and "C'est beau, ça," once. Then he told me I could walk around and have a break while he put the finishing touches on his rough sketches which he wouldn't let me see. He said it could influence the way I model, and he won't show me the finished products until they are all done. He wants to try pencil sketches first, then watercolour and oil. He's a very versatile artist and likes to experiment with different media.

Sigh.

This is exactly what I came here for. And yet . . . It's also incredibly frustrating. I pretended to study the other pieces of art in the studio, all signed by M. Grenier, which were either still lives of fruit and flowers or landscapes of local tourist attractions. I was starting to sense that Raphael and I communicate primarily on a deep, creative level. We're part of a larger process that makes beautiful things. The process of Art. I'm sure there is an Art of kissing. And an Art of touching, and an Art of making love. Raphael could teach me all those things.

It started to feel overwhelming, and I realized that it was probably because I had to pee, but I was afraid to go to the washroom and make a tinkling noise that could be heard through the thin wooden door. I was standing with a hand on my hip and my loose hair draped over my left shoulder, feigning interest in a painting of a vase of pink flowers, but actually wondering if peeing sounds could be considered sexy, and that's when Raphael came up and put his hand on my arm and I turned around.

"Tu as bien fait, aujourd'hui. Merci," is what he said. So, I guess I did well. But what part of it did I do well? The being quiet part? The being still part? Or the being ravishing part?

"Oh. Merci à toi. Je l'ai beaucoup aimé," is what I answered, and it was kind of a lie, kind of the truth. I didn't enjoy posing at all, but the knowledge that his breath was wafting over my body from six feet away made me feel like I was on fire the whole time I was there.

CHAPTER TWELVE

I could feel sweet burning aches in my vagina, my nipples, and even in my heart.

We were staring into each other's eyes. We are about the same height. I was frozen to the spot. And then he leaned forward.

And kissed my cheek.

Did his lips linger? I'm thinking they stayed there longer than the polite French peck on the cheek. But I'm honestly not sure. Why are the French always kissing cheeks? Can a cheek kiss be a sexy kiss? I can't ask Zoe. Argh!

Then he told me to come back at the same time next Sunday morning. I basically ran home and peed for two full minutes with Georges asking me through the door if I could help him find his yellow dinosaur.

It was bloody awesome. I have just modelled for three pictures for a fabulous French artist. My life will never be the same again. My bored face and body could become as famous as the Mona Lisa.

Only one short month ago, I was working at a Canadian Tire gas bar, reading university brochures that were at once terrifying and discouraging, and wondering what I was going to do with my life. Now I feel like I'm in a Hollywood movie, but it's real. It's all happening on a different continent and it's fucking fantastic.

Tomorrow is a local school holiday, and we get a break from au pairing. Zoe and I are going to the beach in Nice with Marcel and another boy from La Cave named Bruno, who Zoe promises is cute. She says he saw me at the party and thought I was pretty. I wonder if he saw me kissing Luc and Bernard?

All I can say is, bring on the French boys! I'll play the field, and, who knows? Maybe Raphael will hear about it and get jealous.

CHAPTER THIRTEEN

ALEX AND I are taking a break mid-session, foraging for snacks in my fridge. I pour us each a glass of homemade iced tea flavoured today with lime and a dash of ginger, and Alex dumps a bag of salt and vinegar chips into a bowl. I look over my shoulder at him, tall and naked, leaning against my kitchen counter, eyeing a cluster of chips that he has grasped in the fingers of his right hand, and the image stuns me. I gasp and say, "Why did I just feel like we've done this before?"

"Déjà vu?" He smiles and shakes his head, "Is not a real thing. I'll explain why once I've got you back in bed," and then he stuffs the entire bunch of chips in his mouth.

We carry our refreshments back to our tousled nest of pleasure. I'm breaking all the rules with Alex. No messy food in the bedroom, don't give extras without charging for them, and, of course, do not fall head over heels in love with the Percy.

As time has passed, we've become virtuosos in the minutia of each other's anatomy, while our conversations have remained superficial. We avoid discussions of childhood traumas, crises at work, or family issues. Our pillow talk is about the natural world, the news of the day, funny things, books, movies and television, or our robins. There's a new nest under construction at the moment, and we suspect that Mrs. Robin has a new guy with more pronounced black stripes on his throat than her last mate.

CHAPTER THIRTEEN

Alex positions himself cross legged on the bed with a pillow propping up his back and I climb onto the bottom end to enjoy the view. He's so uninhibited, and so handsome. Have I been fucking men with my eyes closed for the past ten years? Or is Alex truly the most perfect physical male specimen to ever grace my sheets? He takes a long drink of iced tea and explains, "Déjà vu is probably the result of new information getting stored directly into a person's long-term memory instead of their short-term memory."

"So, it never happened before, and my brain filed the information in the wrong place. It's just bad wiring?" I ask.

"Exactly. I hope you don't mind that I've taken the mystery out of it," Alex says.

Alex has helped me to understand black holes, paleomagnetism, particle physics, and the Copernican Principle. I especially liked that one. It's the idea that we are not special. We're small and insignificant, but once we truly understand our modest role in the world, it will feel very significant.

"Please never stop dispelling my illusions and filling my brain with your knowledge. I didn't realize how much I love science until I met you. And now I can't get enough," I tell him. I hope I don't sound like an escort who is simply saying things he'll want to hear.

"You have an analytical mind," says Alex with a grin.

I close my eyes and savour the joy of feeling my heart explode inside my chest. Alex has divulged that he thinks about my mind! He must be referring to the fact that I ask him so many questions about what feels good and exactly how good it feels, about whether he would like me to use more or less pressure, and about how I constantly try to think up ways to lengthen and intensify every beautiful sensation.

"Careful study has been a plus in my line of work," I say. I'm expecting a risqué comment about my job, but instead he replies, "I admire you."

I let that comment hang in the somewhat humid, sex-soaked air of the bedroom, before asking, "You admire me?"

"You have a comfortable house, a lovely daughter, two successful careers, and you've done it all on your own. You know exactly what you want." He bites his lip, then continues, "I avoid making big life decisions, especially when it comes to people." Then he looks down at his hands. "I've always relied on others to do that for me."

"Like when you approached Kate to find me?" I wonder aloud.

Alex nods.

Oh. My. God. I'm getting somewhere. He's opening up! This is our nineteenth date! Our thirty-third hour and finally—finally—he's starting to trust me with his confidences. I take a slow, deep breath and congratulate myself for having patience. Of all my attributes, patience has served me the most. Even Alex, a complex and complicated man, has a code I just need time to crack.

I won't push it. He has to think he's getting to the destination by himself. I'm a good listener. I have to play to my strengths. As much as I want to pummel him with questions, I force my lips closed.

He's ready for sex again now. I reach over and trail my fingers along the inside of his warm leg, from his ankle, to his bent knee, then to his nicely groomed crotch. I like to think he does all this manscaping for me, but I suspect he's just a bit of a perfectionist. Everything about him is neat and tidy. He even hangs my bathroom towels the hotel way.

Alex turns and kisses me on the mouth. Like a wedding kiss. Heartfelt and firm, but no tongue. I let him explore the surface of my lips with his own, pushing back as much as he is pushing onto me. I never break away from his kisses. I let him take his time, and he finally opens his eyes and pulls back a few inches. His gaze is mesmerizing, so I slide down and take his penis into my mouth, just to make sure I don't say anything I might regret.

CHAPTER THIRTEEN

Usually, when I do this for him, he is focused, almost hypnotized, like he's turning off his brain and turning on his passion. But today, he is unsettled. I shift my eyes up to his and send a questioning glance.

"I'm going away this summer," he says flatly, "and I want you to come with me."

CHAPTER FOURTEEN

September 25, 1999, St. Paul de Vence, Cote d'Azur, France

Chère Diary,

THREE! I'M AT three now. And Bruno was by far the best! He kissed my neck first, then my earlobe, then both of my eyes, then the tip of my nose, then my mouth, with lovely warm, soft lips . . . and it was heavenly. I felt like I was floating on the salty waves that were lapping the shore. I honestly wouldn't have stopped him if he had tried to make love to me right there on my beach towel on the sizzling hot smooth stones with about a hundred other people watching.

That might sound crazy, but there was an older couple, like old with grey hair, on the beach, and we were pretty sure they did have sex on the other side of their big umbrella! Either that or they were doing some intense exercise. France is not like Canada. In so many wonderful ways . . .

Zoe and Marcel disappeared behind a bunch of boulders while the four of us were swimming in the ocean, or is it a sea? Zoe told me that Marcel lifted her up onto a rock and went down on her. I've never had someone do that to me, but I saw it in the only porn movie I've ever seen called *All the Way*. My friend Catherine found the VHS tape in her dad's night table drawer, and we watched it at her sixteenth sleepover birthday party. The girl in the movie was

CHAPTER FOURTEEN

sitting on a sofa and she had two guys kneeling in front of her. The guys were both licking her down there at the same time and she was absolutely loving it.

I'll be just fine with one guy, I think.

This was my first ever visit to Nice, which is pronounced like "niece" and was originally named Nike in 500 BC by the Greeks. It's the fifth largest city in France and it's home to gourmet restaurants, fashionable boutiques, and the bluest waters in the Mediterranean, or so I'm told.

Marcel drove the four of us in his father's red Peugeot. It was twenty minutes of hurtling along skinny roads in a tin box, taking corners without slowing down, while the stunning countryside whizzed by, and I couldn't help but lean into Bruno who was next to me in the back seat. Everything has a golden glow here, from so much sun, and I think it makes everyone feel happy. The default state of the French Riviera is a dazzlingly beautiful day.

For lunch, we bought sausage on a bun from a street vendor, and we shared two bottles of wine and two bottles of fizzy water. I got sunburned on my shoulders and, when the blue sky turned to shades of grey, we ate some kind of seafood crêpes in the cobblestone courtyard at a restaurant owned by Marcel's uncle, then strolled hand in hand along the Promenade des Anglais and watched the street performers. There was a super talented band from Australia singing David Bowie hits and we stood there enveloped by sound and hypnotized by their voices, until the horizon turned black. We gave them all the coins we had in our wallets and then we drove back slowly to St. Paul, with the windows rolled down to let in the night air scented with lavender and cypress trees, and with the twinkling stars guiding our way.

I love riding in cars here. Buses and trains make me feel like a tourist, but successfully contorting my long legs to fit into the back of a foreign automobile, where the ashtrays are filled with the butts of French cigarettes and there is a week-old copy of Le Monde shoved under the passenger seat, made me feel authentic. I belong in this historic country filled with lovers and artists as much as I belong in Toronto.

Marcel parked the car outside the walls and the guys walked us to our homes. Bruno and I kissed again for about five minutes out back. I let him go up my top and it was a little awkward because I felt his fingers searching around for my nipple like he was hoping to find a large breast that wasn't there. I let my hands rest on his bum, and he pinned me against the wall with his hips. I don't know what might have happened if Alain hadn't come outside with a bag of garbage and disturbed us.

Bruno is nice. He has wavy blonde hair, and he looks a bit like Leonardo DiCaprio. He's shorter than me, but so is three-quarters of the population of France. Bruno is chattier than the other French boys; he asks me a lot of questions about Canada; what we watch on television, what we eat, what animals we have, and how cold it gets in the winter. And he told me he thinks I look like Odette because I'm tall and slim and I have a big smile.

When I said I had to go inside, Bruno told me to stop by La Cave tomorrow evening for a glass of wine and more kisses.

Things like that don't happen to me in Canada. St. Paul de Vence is truly heaven on Earth!

September 30, 1999, St. Paul de Vence, Cote d'Azur, France

Chère Diary,

I wonder if I am "using" Bruno?

People could see it that way, but I suspect he is "using" me as well, so that makes it okay or at least equal. Every evening since the

CHAPTER FOURTEEN

beach, we sit on the wall and talk about my day with the Dubois family and about his plan to go to culinary school. Then he clears his throat and places his hand on my shoulder. That's the signal. I lick my lips and we start to kiss. Sometimes we go a little further . . . it's pleasant and interesting. I'm fascinated by the way we communicate through touch and the seemingly involuntary reactions of our bodies. But Bruno doesn't make my insides turn to instant lava, the way Raphael does. I know what it is; it's our chemistry, and I'm convinced that it's unchangeable. I could kiss Bruno every evening for the rest of my life, and the volcano would never erupt. I'm pretty sure that there's full on lava flows with Zoe and Marcel. She's so lucky.

On the plus side, I'm modelling tomorrow! It's been easier than I thought to hide it from Zoe all week. Since I don't talk about it to anyone else, it feels like a dream. And whenever I'm at home, I'm always busy with the twins. They're building a dinosaur world in their bedroom out of every craft material known to mankind and a lot of tape and recycling stuff. Georges has all the plant eaters on his side of the room and Émilie has the meat eaters. In between, there is a blue plastic tub which is the swamp and there are green streamers hanging from the ceiling to look like vines. These kids exhaust me, but I love them both so much.

Even if I wanted to spill the beans about modelling, I can hardly get a word in edgewise with Zoe. She is either complaining about Henri, how he won't brush his teeth or pick up his toys, or she's sighing about Marcel. He made her a midnight picnic of chocolate covered strawberries and champagne in the wine cellar last night. I'm so jealous. Marcel and Bruno share a room off the kitchen at La Cave and she creeps down to the restaurant for a sexy rendezvous every evening after her host family has gone to bed. It's no wonder she's always yawning on our walk to school.

I know everything about Zoe now, including that she is on the pill and she has had sex with seven different guys on four different continents. She always makes them wear a condom, and she won't give it up until at least the third date. She said her mother, who is a lawyer, made her promise she won't marry a poor man or an actor. Zoe loves attention and if she's not getting enough, she will either sigh loudly or announce that she will die if she doesn't get a coffee, or a glass of wine, or a chocolate croissant, or whatever else would make her happy. And then she gets it. I feel like the rest of us are holding up a spotlight that is pointed on Zoe at all times.

Marcel and Bruno had to go into Marseilles tonight to pick up some fresh *moules*, which are mussels, yuk. So, Zoe and I decided to visit the cemetery, just south of the walls of St. Paul de Vence. It looks like an outdoor dormitory, with mismatched stone beds squeezed tight together. The headboards all have crosses, and they are inscribed with the barest details, all that is left of a full and vibrant life, reduced to twenty words or less.

It took over an hour, but we read every one of the tombstones. Many of them are decorated with pots of red geraniums or random items like small toys or greenery that the visitors, mostly tourists, must have plucked from the hillside. Marc Chagall, the famous painter, is buried there, and his tomb is covered in loose round stones. Zoe and I agreed that the saddest grave is the one that translates to, "Here lies Francine Malamaire, born Guiji, died the 16th of December 1913 at the age of twenty-seven."

So, we know she was married, but we want to know more. She must have been a daughter, but was she someone's sister, someone's lover, someone's friend? How did she die? Was it an accident, disease, or suicide? They gave her a huge headstone, but they should have taken the time to carve a few more words to tell us what it was that made her life matter.

There were no other people in the cemetery, so Zoe and I sat together on the foot of Francine's eternal bed, keeping her company,

CHAPTER FOURTEEN

and looked out at the rolling hills and a sliver of the sparkling blue Mediterranean we could see in the distance.

Zoe told me that I was the coolest friend she ever had. She said I was great to talk to because nothing seemed to shock me. It didn't feel exactly like a compliment, but thinking about it now, I think she meant that I'm different because I'm naturally curious about all kinds of behavior. I don't judge people who might choose to do things that are out of the ordinary.

Then Zoe made me promise that I would always be her friend and that we would meet in St. Paul de Vence again in our lifetimes.

"Even if we're ancient, like fifty or sixty years old," she said. "We will meet back at this very spot and tell each other how our lives turned out."

Zoe wrapped her baby finger around mine and we both said, "Pinky swear!"

Then she shushed me and told me to close my eyes and we agreed that we could hear whispers coming from Francine's grave.

October 14, 1999, St. Paul de Vence, Cote d'Azur, France

Chère Diary,

Wow! Two weeks have gone by and I haven't written in my journal. I finally understand what it means to live in the moment. Days go by when I forget to think about my old life. I'm going to have to leave one day, and I know I should write down my experiences so I won't forget the details. But how could I forget any part of this new life that fits me like a glove?

I dream in French now. I watch *Une Famille Formidable* on television with Pascale and I know all the characters' names and backstories. I am developing a proper Provençal accent and I'm not getting the "Oh, she's just a tourist" look in the shops anymore. I know where to buy the best espresso and which shopkeepers will have gossip. I don't just drink wine anymore, I order *un jaune* which is a liquorice flavoured alcohol meant for sipping. Bruno is impressed that I truly love the flavour. I haven't told him it's because my dad always has a tin of anise flavoured candies on his dresser, and I've been sneaking them for as long as I can remember. I wonder if Dad actually buys those candies for me?

I have modelled for Raphael two more times, and he said that tomorrow will be our last session. He has some finishing touches to do, and then he will show me his Bored Girl collection. That's what I call it anyway. Raphael said it's called *Une Belle Fille en Repose.* A Beautiful Girl at Rest. Why does everything sound better in French?

October 15, 1999, St. Paul de Vence, Cote d'Azur, France

Chère Diary,

Worst day of my life.

After I finished modelling this morning, Raphael kissed me for real. He sat down beside me in the red chair, and he told me I did a fabulous job and the pictures of me could make him famous. He said that my natural beauty inspired him to do great work.

"Merci, ma belle," he said and then kissed me on the lips. My body was electrified with waves of passion. Lava started to churn in my loins. My hands started to shake. The spicy scent of his skin rushed up my nose and I felt I would collapse. The joy I felt made me love being in my own body in a way I have never experienced. No doubt about it, best kiss ever.

Then he broke away and told me that he is going to frame my pictures and I could come back to see them next Sunday.

CHAPTER FOURTEEN

I said, "D'accord," and then I left because he got up and started to look busy.

I floated all the way home.

When I got back to the house, Alain told me that my Aunt Sarah had called and said I needed to phone her as soon as possible. Alain helped me place the call and watched as Aunt Sarah told me that my dad had suffered a heart attack. He's not dead, but he's very ill. I have to go home. I was supposed to stay for four more months. Aunt Sarah bought me a ticket to fly home tomorrow morning. She said it's the right thing to do.

When I hung up, I was sobbing, so Alain hugged me. We stood in the hall and I cried in his arms. I was so sad that I would have to leave France; so much more sad than I was for my dad, and that made me feel like a horrible person.

And then I felt his hand slip down between my shorts and my underwear. He was feeling my ass through my panties.

I pushed him away, ran downstairs and out the back door. I wasn't sure where I was going. Maybe to see Bruno or Zoe, or both. I was headed towards La Cave. But on the way, I had to pass La Galerie au Vent. I stopped at the rear entrance and decided to go for it. If I had to leave, I wanted see Raphael one more time and maybe he would hug me and take away the nastiness Alain had put on my body.

I flung the door open only to witness Zoe jump off of Raphael, who was sitting on the red couch. Her long blonde curls covered her breasts, but the rest of her naked body was on display. I think they had been having sex. Raphael was pulling up his pants. He looked angry or upset.

I started to choke and I felt like I couldn't breathe, so I ran out onto the road.

I still don't know what hurt the most. That Raphael preferred Zoe to me? That Zoe must have lied to me when she said she wasn't interested in Raphael? Or, that neither of them came after me?

St. Paul de Vence felt like a house of horrors, so I ran down La Rue Grande, under the archway and out of town beyond the walls. After a couple of minutes, I got off the main road, followed a path, and hid in a grove of olive trees in the valley.

When I was finally alone, for the first time in six weeks, I couldn't cry or scream. I lay there on the hard ground, breathing, letting all the feelings leave me and flow into the earth. It was too much to feel for one day, and I let myself turn hard.

I only came back to the house because I needed to say a proper goodbye to Georges and Émilie. When I got here, Pascale told me that Alain had to go visit his brother in Toulon for some obviously made up reason.

The twins are holding onto my legs as I write this. They insist that we will all sleep together tonight. If I start thinking about how much I will miss them, I will break. So I'll just cuddle them and pretend they're little dolls that I can keep forever.

Au revoir, Diary. And this is the end of my au pair experience.

CHAPTER FIFTEEN

"YOU WANT TO take me away?" I return my gaze to Alex's crotch and repeat his words back to him as a question, still holding his semi-hard penis in my hand.

"My family is vacationing this July in a little town in southern France called St. Paul de Vence. We have been there many times over the years. It's one of our favourite spots." I hear him swallow hard and I can tell he's got more to say, so I just stroke him idly, waiting. "I can't spend a month without you," he admits. I'm certain that I detected a note of desperation, at least longing, in his voice.

"That sounds lovely, but . . . dangerous. Are you sure you want me that close to your family? And I would have to bring Belle."

"Kate will take care of all the arrangements. We can still meet twice a week, on the days when I would normally go golfing. We could arrange supervision for Belle. There are so many great art programs for kids in St. Paul. She would love it. The French Riviera is the most beautiful place on Earth, and I want to experience it with you."

I did not expect this. It wasn't part of my plan. I begin slowly licking the length his penis to give myself time to think it over.

Most escorts love this kind of thing. They brag online about their first-class flights and five-star hotels, spa visits and yacht excursions. They get to mingle in the world of high society by doing the humblest and most fundamental of jobs; making someone else feel good. I do want to travel more, but the irony of returning with this man to the place, that was at once so dear and so painful to me, is frightening to say the least.

But, I would get to take Belle to France in a style that I could never afford on my own. Plus, I would be able to spend quality time with Alex—to build and strengthen our relationship by moving it outside of my home. I've dreamed of that every night and every day for the last ten weeks. And honestly, even though I would be absolutely vigilant and never slip up, if Zoe somehow discovered that Alex wasn't actually going golfing twice a week, she might decide to divorce him.

Is Alex taking a risk because he wants to be found out? Maybe he's tempting fate because he can't escape the confines of marriage by himself? Could I end up with everything, instead of leaving France with nothing, like last time?

Alex is quite hard now. I expertly place a condom on the head of his penis, pinch out the air from the tip, and unroll it all the way down. I climb on top of him, lower my butt into a squat, and we sigh in unison as I slip his cock inside my soaking wet vagina. I am excited about this.

I lean forward, place my hands on either side of his head, and kiss him deeply, our tongues dancing together. When we are connected in this way, my mind blurs, I let go of reason and I imagine that our bodies are melding together. I want to do everything in my power to make Alex happy, to make us happy.

I pull back and savour the taste of his saliva as I swallow. "You are the kindest, most generous man and there is nothing I would enjoy more than doing this with you on the Riviera."

"Oh, Julia. I can't believe I found you."

I stay on top the whole time and let Alex bask in his dreams, his beautiful head resting against my satin pillowcase, a transparent look of pure pleasure on his face.

CHAPTER FIFTEEN

After he ejaculates inside me and opens his eyes, he surprises me by saying, "I'm curious about that picture by the door of the woman sitting on a chair."

He cranes his neck to look around the room. "Well, I guess it's the only picture in here. I love how the woman's eyes are closed, and her curly hair conceals her breasts, like she has something to hide, but her legs are wide open, and she's only wearing underwear. There's such a contrast between what's hidden and what's revealed."

"I've always liked that picture, too," I say.

Alex is not done talking. "And there's something else. I know it's just a sketch, but there's a realistic quality to it that fascinates me. I feel as though I know the girl in the picture. Do you know who the subject is? She's not you?" he asks.

"No idea who she is," I lie. "I don't even remember where I got it."

CHAPTER SIXTEEN

MY PHONE RINGS and I push a button to answer it as I'm driving in my car.

It's Kate.

"Can we talk now?" she asks.

"Sure," I say.

"Are you kidding me? Alex wants me to book you and Belle on a trip to the Riviera! I've got to admit that I never saw you as a sugar baby," she says as I pull into the school parking lot. "This arrangement is costing him a shitload of money. It's not going to last," Kate continues.

"It's not like that," I tell her. And I want to believe it. I hope, with all my heart, that what Alex and I have is more than an arrangement where he pays me and gives me gifts and, in return, I act like I'm his girlfriend and heap praise on him for being the most generous and special guy in the world.

"Well, then what is it like?" Kate sounds earnest and it's unnerving. "I'm afraid you're going to get badly hurt. They never leave their wives. You know that, don't you?"

"This situation is different," I say.

"No. It absolutely is *not* any different. Alex is not special. He's an ordinary guy who likes to fuck more than his wife likes to fuck. And you are a fabulous escort who swore to me three months ago that she's over it now and wants a civie job."

CHAPTER SIXTEEN

"But Alex is—"

"An awkward, plain looking man who will be asking me to book him with one of my other girls as soon as you stop fooling yourself."

"You've met him in person?" I ask.

"I've also met his wife and kids. Give up, friend. Quit while you're ahead and go find someone who is actually available."

"Where did you—"

"That's confidential. I do have a life of my own, you know."

Alex is awkward? Plain looking? This is crazy.

"I've got to go, Kate. I'm picking Belle up at school. She'll be out any second. Email me all the details, please."

And I hang up.

The old brown brick building with its moat of grey pavement looks tranquil and deserted. I spy a lonely soccer ball hiding under a large pine that's putting out a new set of pale green needles. My car is uncomfortably warm and stuffy. The arrival of summer is imminent, and I've hit a fork in the road. One way or another, I'm certain that my life is heading in a new direction.

The school doors burst open and a horde of children run out into the yard. Belle stops and squints into the sun. Her silky black braid is pulled forward, hanging past her waist, and her slender hands clasp a large sketchbook against her navy blue school uniform. I watch her until she catches my eye and waves.

I wave back.

Belle opens the back door first, tosses in her backpack, then climbs onto the passenger seat beside me and shows me her sketchpad.

"I drew some ants that were hanging around the garbage outside at recess," she says.

"They're fabulous, Belle! The shading is great, and I love how the broken cookie looks good enough to eat." She smiles and my heart melts. She's going to be so excited when I tell her.

"Buckle up, babe! We're going to go to the mall before we go home. I have some wonderful news, and we need to buy you a suitcase."

"Really?" Belle starts bouncing in her seat. "I knew it! We're going to El Salvador!"

"No baby, we're going to . . . France!" I put on my most excited face. Like, who would ever want to go anywhere but France? Obviously, France is the coolest place ever!

She sits back and eyes me. Her face scrunches up. Shit, she's gonna cry. "You've already been to France. I've never been to El Salvador. We always do what you want to do," she says and crosses her arms in front of her chest.

She didn't add, "It's not fair," because she's heard my lecture about that phrase too many times to try that one again. But her eyes said it, and now she's looking out the window.

I start the car and pull out onto the road. It's easier to talk to her when I'm driving. "The place we're going is called St. Paul de Vence. It's basically a town of art galleries. You can do art classes and go to the beach and eat gelato. We can practice speaking French. I promise you that we'll go to El Salvador, but not until you're older. Right now, people have to exercise a high degree of caution in El Salvador due to the high crime rate. That's serious stuff. It's too dangerous for an eleven-year-old girl and her mom."

"I'm almost twelve. Have you ever tried to email my father? Or ask anyone at the hotel? We could go to Mexico and talk to people. Why do you think he wouldn't be at the hotel anymore?"

"Because he told me he was only working there for the summer."

Inwardly, I sigh. We've been over this so many times. I bite my lip and focus on the road.

"You're never going to try to find my father, are you?" Belle presses.

"I love you, Belle. And we're going to France in two weeks. You can choose to enjoy every moment, or you can choose to waste your time being angry. Believe me, you'll regret it if you don't make the best of every opportunity in life."

CHAPTER SEVENTEEN

Conversations with Clients: 7 Reasons Why He Won't Leave His Marriage:
Reason #3: Show Me the Money

Percy #88

P88: You are so hot, baby. You want me to fuck your ass, don't you?

JJ: You didn't pay for that. If that's what you want, talk to Kate about it first. That costs significantly more than what you paid.

P88: I paid a lot of damn good money for this.

JJ: I have to do more preparation for anal. Time is money for me, just like it is for everyone else.

P88: You women are all alike. You try to make guys fork out for every little kiss like they're fucking gold.

Percy #174

P174: I almost shit myself when your girl called and asked for me at work.

JJ: Every reputable escort service checks references. It's for our safety.

P174: How do you get anyone to come when you make us give you a work number and you actually call it?

JJ: You're here, aren't you?

CHAPTER SEVENTEEN

P174: You can't just take our word for it? Even after we pay the deposit?
JJ: Kate needed to verify that you are who you say you are. It's for our safety. She would never leave a reason for why she was calling.
P174: How do I know that you are who you say you are?
JJ: You don't. I didn't make the prostitution laws.
P174: Sorry, I get that it's for your safety, but I work with my father-in-law. He owns the company and it's his cash that's paying for this afternoon. If my wife found out, that'd be the end of it, and I'd never be able to afford your prices again.

I told my agent that I would never see **P88** again, and that also ensured that no other escorts in the agency would be available when he called. There are sufficient clients to go around, and no one needs to have to entertain an asshole like that. Safety is rule number one.

P174 became a regular for five years. I understand how nervous many of them are the first time. They anticipate that the whole deal will take place in the dark and it comes as a shock to realize that a legally tricky operation run by women can be grounded in good business practices and will hold their clients accountable for actually being who they claim to be. The first concern of every Percy is about preserving their anonymity. This is understandable, but they also sometimes need to be reminded to consider the unfortunate reality that there are people who try to hassle and harm escorts.

Both of these Percys would not leave their wives because divorce costs money and, after a divorce, there is always less money to go around. Sometimes, like in the case of **P174**, wealth was a huge motivation for their marriage in the first place. Other times, they fear that their spouse would rob them blind in a divorce. These men love the comforts that money brings even more than the comfort of a warm bed. If they will submit to reference checks and wear a condom, they can rest assured that they can buy that too.

Thanks to the ease of doing business online, over half the escorts I know of work entirely for themselves, no agencies, and, thankfully, no pimps.

But these enterprising ladies don't have anyone watching their back on a daily basis, so checking references is an absolute necessity. Any girl who doesn't do it is putting herself in tremendous danger. The escorts who last, and thrive, are careful and calculating. And when they feel safe, they can, to the surprise of many who would rather believe it's not possible, find huge satisfaction in their job.

They love it because they do important work, and they work very hard. Even if the majority of people in the vanilla world choose not to see the truth that lies just under the surface of their daily lives, those of us in the sex industry know that we are the cake that holds up the sweet icing veneer of polite society.

How much money does Alex have, I wonder? How much would he lose to Zoe in a divorce? Do they have a prenup? How important is wealth to Alex?

I know their families knew each other socially from when they were children. Zoe explained on her podcast that she was a childhood friend of Alex's sister. They both came from wealthy families. I won't hold that against him. He talks about ideas, not things—although he does dress very well, and he drives a brand new Tesla. This is a difficult one that I can't completely rule out, but my gut tells me that true love would prove stronger than money to Alex. And he's not stingy. He is paying for Belle and me to fly to France, to stay in a gorgeous B&B in St. Paul de Vence. There will be $2000 added to my bank account each week to cover our expenses. Kate will get her cut on top of that.

I'm fairly confident that Alex is not a man whose primary motivation to stay in a less than happy marriage is money.

CHAPTER EIGHTEEN

"WHAT'S WITH THE giant sunglasses?" asks Belle. "Are you trying to look like a movie star?"

"Got to protect my eyes from the sun and all that," I tell her as we step out into the sea of cabs outside the walls of St. Paul de Vence.

And I don't want Zoe to recognize me. Before we left, I studied a picture of myself from twenty-five years ago against a selfie I took in the bathroom. They say you get a new face every seven years, but mine is basically my eighteen-year-old face with creases extending from all of my features like a poorly folded sheet. My body is the primary asset of my business, so I do what every smart escort should do, and I always invest part of my earnings back into myself. I have regular facials, eyebrow waxes, peels, and I've been going to Kate's Fitness religiously for the past decade. I only weigh ten pounds more than I did when I first went to France.

The biggest difference is the look in my eyes. That teenage girl was blissfully naïve, and rightly so. But when I examined the selfie of present day me, I didn't see a vague romantic longing, I saw a mature woman on a mission, determined to win her soulmate from the clutches of a rival who couldn't possibly love him as much as she does, I hope.

I will have to be on constant high alert to not physically run into Zoe. St. Paul de Vence is smaller than most university campuses and we could bump into each other at any corner or in any shop.

I purchased the large sunglasses, along with big sun hats and some flowy peasant type dresses that are not at all the usual form fitting and flattering styles I would normally choose. I'm wearing my hair pulled back into a braid, which I never did in France when I was trying so hard to impersonate Odette.

I also bought a couple of unflattering coral lipsticks to wear instead of my signature cherry red. I'm going full tourist, and I'll be with my attractive daughter whose inquisitive personality draws a lot of attention herself, so I'll try to hide in her shadow.

Belle never refers to me by my first name—"mom" is a wonderfully generic title—and I will make an effort to speak quietly when in public, in case my voice carries to Zoe's ears and whisks her back to the past.

But at the end of the day, Zoe only knew me for six weeks. I left and she must have chosen another girl from the group of au pairs to fill the best friend void, to follow her around, to flatter her, and to envy her beauty and charm for the remaining four months.

As the years went by, if Zoe were to have googled my name, she would have found absolutely no hits that bore any resemblance to me, and I wouldn't flatter myself into believing that there was enough space in Zoe's brain to cling onto memories of a brief friendship with a lower-class girl who was less beautiful and much less charismatic.

There are two old men leaning against the thirty-foot high wall, smoking strong French cigarettes. Instead of stepping away from them, like I would back home, I inhale the thick, fragrant smoke and let nostalgia well up inside of me.

"He's going that way, Mom," Belle says, tugging at my flowing sleeve and bringing me back to the present.

Belle and I each grab a suitcase and walk towards the familiar archway through the stone wall, dodging tourists to stay within view of our driver who is maneuvering our two other cases over the cobbles with practiced ease.

CHAPTER EIGHTEEN

Why have Zoe and Alex returned to this tourist mecca multiple times during their marriage? Surely, they could find a more tranquil locale off the beaten path and immerse themselves in authentic French culture, instead of dealing with the inflated prices, constant noise, and jostling crowds of this village in the summer? I don't remember Zoe having a particular interest in art and I can't see any connection between this place and her eco-friendly family podcast.

Perhaps it's the charm? There really is no place on earth as quaint, and the views surrounding this perfectly preserved gem of Medieval history are magnificent.

Or is it something else, or someone else, that brings her back?

Once inside the walls, I pause and feel a soothing embrace. It's like the town is sad about the way I left and is thrilled to see me again. I look down at Belle. Her mouth is agape. She is looking all around, at the narrow fairytale laneways paved with round stones to look like a fixed field of flowers beneath your feet, at the ancient yet pristine stone buildings with trendy shops and eye-catching art that line the inviting maze of streets, and at the enveloping cloudless sky that is the happiest shade of blue imaginable.

Belle's free hand slips into mine and grabs hold. "It's way more beautiful than you said it would be, mommy."

I squeeze her hand in return.

"You're so right, sweetie," I say. "I forgot about the magic."

CHAPTER NINETEEN

I'M IN THE bathroom of La Vie Douce, our B&B on the Rue de la Petite Sellerie, grateful for the rustic charm of this functional room where I am likely to be spending an inordinate amount of time over the next three weeks. I'm alternating between willing a text to pop up on my phone screen and gazing out the window at the southern view that overlooks the cemetery outside the walls and extends all the way to the not too distant Mediterranean Sea. I don't want to be on my phone in front of Belle, so I will keep it close to my body, set to vibrate, and check it only when I'm alone.

I've only got one phone now, and I've entered Alex's number under the name Alexis Smith. He's got me as Julien Jones on his phone. We've agreed on several coded messages to convey basic information or to request a phone call within the next hour. But we've also made detailed plans for our first meeting in two days' time, which I have memorized, so no other contact should be necessary. This forced abstinence, when I know he is in such close proximity, is intensifying my craving to see him again. I wonder if it's doing the same thing to him?

The scant details Alex shared with me are that his family is staying at the Hôtel du Faucon on the Rue des Verdalettes near the east wall, that his wife is a middle-aged woman with curly blonde hair, and that they have two blonde teenagers, a fifteen-year-old boy and a thirteen-year-old girl. He still hasn't told me their names. The more

CHAPTER NINETEEN

I think about it, the more this seems like a Shakespearean comedy in the making.

It's dangerous for Alex to have brought us all together in the same little town. I asked him what to do if I somehow meet his family socially and he said that his children will spend most of their time at the beach, tennis lessons, and horseback riding, and that his wife is usually with them, so it's very unlikely.

Is he keeping me in the dark because he doesn't trust me? Of course, he is operating under the assumption that Zoe and I are strangers, but still. I feel rather like a pawn in his game. Does he get a thrill from taking risks and flaunting his mistress beneath his wife's nose? Or, could Alex simply not handle the prospect of being away from me for a month and he was willing to risk it all to hold me in his arms twice a week? The answer to that matters very much. If I only appeal to Alex because I'm a bad girl, his affections won't last if Zoe finds out that he is cheating on her. I need him to desire me for who I am, not for what I represent.

The worst case scenario is that Alex loves me, but he finds out how I kept important information from him, and he ends our relationship.

The best case scenario is that Alex loves me too and understands how, every step of the way, I've had no choice but to play the game according to his rules, and how that necessitated deception about my past.

Who am I kidding?

The worst case scenario is that Alex doesn't love me and never will.

I put myself in his shoes. What if he loves me and he's afraid I don't love him? What if he is unsure about his feelings and he brought me here to figure it out?

I decide to throw some hints his way to show him how much he means to me, without scaring him off. And I need to make it clear that, while I don't derive any pleasure from participating in subterfuge, I am willing to do whatever it takes to be with him, at least in the short term.

I dream of the day I no longer have to hide my true self from the world. Everyone tells a few fibs when they're young, like I tried to do with Pascale when Raphael told me not to tell anyone about the modelling. However, my deceitful life began in earnest when I concealed my escort business from my family, from my friends and colleagues at work, and then from my daughter. Over the span of the next decade, I became proficient in living a double life. All those lies culminated in the moment when I didn't tell Alex that I had deduced his identity, and that I was, briefly, a friend of his wife.

But it was just business, until it wasn't.

I look again at the screen in case I've missed a message.

"Are you ever going to come out of there, mom? You said we could walk on the walls before dinner!" Belle has too much energy for a girl who hasn't slept since we left home yesterday evening.

I stow my phone in my oversized rattan tourist bag—which I figure I can use as a physical barrier to conceal my identity if necessary—and step out into our lovely suite. It's decorated in the classic Provençal style; ornate mouldings and heavy wrought iron, combined with finely crafted antique furniture, set against a colour palette of ivory with touches of pale blue and green. Alex really splashed out for this place and I'm grateful. It reassures me that he must think I'm special and it's going a long way towards calming my frazzled heart.

Belle is kneeling on a stack of pillows, studying the sketches of local wildflowers that are arranged in three rows of three on the wall behind the king-sized bed we will share, just like we did for the first four years of her life. I couldn't bear to have her in another room when she was little, but finally, she insisted. And she was right. I could never stop her from growing up.

CHAPTER NINETEEN

I laugh with happiness and relief that she is excited about this vacation. I drop my bag and gather Belle into my arms, thankful that she's never unhappy for long. I'm proud of the amazing individual Belle is becoming and I hate lying to her. Hate it. Hate it. Hate it.

I promise that one day I will beg her forgiveness for every false and misleading word I have ever said to her.

Still holding onto her slight shoulders, I lean back to look into her deep brown eyes. "Do you know that you were born on a beautiful day like this one? You have always been my ray of sunshine and I love you more than anything. I'm so grateful that we are here together and that I can share this town, which has a special place in my heart, with you. Let's really try to speak French all the time, and, as soon as we get home, I promise we're going to start learning Spanish together; so we'll be ready for our next trip."

"D'accord!" she says, bouncing down and pulling me off the bed. "Allons-y!"

I grab a floppy hat and we head out, waving goodbye to Camille and Solange, the lovely couple who run the B&B, and start our self-guided tour. Belle is holding onto the map of St. Paul de Vence and repeating the name of each street we turn on to.

So much of it is familiar, but it's like a book with a new cover and I only read a few chapters the first time I tried it. With every step, I feel like I'm walking backwards, to youth, to hope, to romance, and then forward, to love—to Alex, and to a dazzling reincarnation of *Just Julia*.

CHAPTER TWENTY

BELLE AND I sit in the breakfast nook of the B&B, facing out the window at the narrow street, watching as tourists begin filing into town. Seven days a week, they arrive in buses, taxis, and private cars, spend a day in this idyllic artists' paradise, then scurry out of the walled enclave as the sun sets, loaded up with paintings, sculptures, and bags full of souvenirs of Provence.

The salt-scented air off the nearby Mediterranean touches our cheeks through the open window as we eat boiled eggs, warm croissants with raspberry jam, and drink freshly squeezed orange juice.

"Are you excited about the charcoal sketching workshop at La Foundation Maeght?" I ask.

"Yeah. But is everyone going to speak French there?"

"Mais oui, mademoiselle. And you'll be amazed at how easy it gets. I'm sure after a couple of weeks here, you'll be dreaming in French."

Belle gives me a smile that shows off her big white teeth. She's wearing a bright red beret I bought for her yesterday, along with her favourite jean skirt and smocked peasant blouse. She places her hand on top of mine on the solid oak table and I'm taken aback for a few seconds. Her fingers are longer than mine. "Merci beaucoup, maman, pour ces vacances," she says.

And just like that, whatever was said before, whatever Belle

CHAPTER TWENTY

thought about my motivations or the unjustness of life, is forgotten. I'll never let her be rude to me, but I'll let her change her mind and I won't rub it in. She'll never catch me gloating that she came around to seeing things my way and she wouldn't gloat either if I had been skeptical about something she suggested and it turned out well. Like the time she insisted on putting peanut butter on her hamburger and I had to eat my words. It was delicious. I was thirty-two when Belle was born, but she and I have grown up together in many respects, and the love we share is the most precious thing in my life.

I'm not sure how I taught her to be grateful, or if maybe that's something she got from Carlos. I thought it would take until she was eighteen for me to feel secure that she knew her own mind and that I'd done my job. How did it happen so fast? I'm certain now that Belle and I will go to El Salvador together one day and, no matter what happens, that it will be okay. I'm also convinced that I need to be more open and honest with her going forward, or she will catch me out in lies that I will sorely regret.

Belle stands up and pushes in her chair. "I don't want to be late to my first class. Depêche-toi, maman!"

We wave goodbye to Camille, who is refilling the silver trays of quiches and strawberry tarts, and head out into the dazzling sunshine, down the length of the Rue Grande and under the archway, dodging tourists as expertly as any of the locals.

On the Route des Serres, I slow down as we pass by the La Fontette primary school and the fenced in courtyard with little slides and teetertotters.

"This is the school where I brought the twins every morning when I was an au pair."

Belle is fascinated. "How old were you?" she asks.

"I was eighteen. Somehow, twenty-five years have flown by."

"So, now the kids you took care of are . . ."

"Thirty-one. Wow. That makes me feel old," I say.

Belle giggles. "You are old. You're a mom. Do the twins still live here?"

"I don't know. I noticed that the store, La Maison DuBois, isn't there anymore, but I'll ask around about the twins' mom, Pascale. She was very kind to me."

I attempt to give Belle a wistful smile, but the thought of Alain's hand slipping into my shorts still makes me nauseous. I should have said something to Pascale before I left. But what? I was sick with worry about my dad and brokenhearted about Raphael. And I had never experienced anything like what Alain did to me. Well, not from an adult anyway. It was all very confusing, and I thought I had erased it from my mind.

We walk the rest of the way in silence, each of us soaking in the sights, scents, and warmth of this affluent suburban area that is northwest of the old town. When we reach the grounds of the museum of modern art, the elaborate building, the tall, manicured trees, and the plethora of random outdoor sculptures, all combine to make a striking impression. Belle gives me a quick hug and slips in with a group of about a dozen kids as they follow an instructor through the ivory-coloured latticed metal entrance. She doesn't even look back to watch me wave goodbye. It makes me sad, but I shake it off. My daughter is confident and courageous. She is independent and determined. She is in a fabulous place where she can learn and grow, and now I have an entire day to myself in St. Paul de Vence.

I'm almost skipping on the way back into town. The boules court in front of Café de la Place hasn't changed a bit in twenty-five years. It's like the old men soaking up the sun and drinking their café au lait have been caught in a time loop. The years start falling away from me like too many warm layers on a hot day and I keep glancing over my shoulder.

I can almost hear Zoe's loud snorting laugh and I imagine her saying, "I dare you to ask the first guy under thirty who we see

CHAPTER TWENTY

smoking a cigarette to give you a light," or, "I'm positive Madame Gaudet doesn't wear underwear with her stockings, and I bet she wears those high heels to bed. All the French ladies do, you know." And then I think to myself, "I wonder if Alex is hoping I'll show up in stockings and high heels today?"

"Ow!" I stub my right foot in its practical Birkenstock on the curb in front of the Hôtel des Rêves and hold onto the garden fence, waiting for the pain to subside. A few tourists walk around me as I pause to calm my breathing. I look up at the three-story façade and, for the first time in my career as an escort, I feel uneasy about what I'm going to do.

I'm about to have sex with someone else's husband.

Discovering Zoe with Raphael all those years ago hurt like hell. I blamed Zoe for a long time even though, in my heart, I knew I had no right to be angry with either of them for what they did. If anything, it was my fault because I had never found the courage to admit that I was falling for the sultry artist. Zoe had no idea, and she had even been kind enough to introduce me to Bruno.

I'm well aware that Alex is a married man and that he is therefore considered, by common consensus, to be "out of bounds." How would it feel to find out that your husband has been seeing an escort? And why has it never occurred to me before to ponder this question? I always assumed that I was doing the wives a favour, taking over a chore they no longer had any desire to perform themselves, like ironing, or washing the windows. The wives were never fully formed people to me. Not like Zoe, with her rich girl boldness and impish grin.

But Zoe didn't run after me when she saw how shocked I was at discovering her liaison with Raphael, and she never even said goodbye. She must have known that I went back to Canada because of my dad's heart attack. Madame Gaudet would have told everyone. But Zoe didn't try to contact me afterwards. She's the one who said

I was the coolest friend she had ever had, and then she forgot about me in less time than it takes to put on a fresh coat of make-up.

I look up again at the white stucco building with rows of shuttered windows. I can't help but love the fascinating man who is anticipating my arrival in one of those rooms. Perhaps this makes Zoe and I even? Or, just maybe, this time I'll get to come out ahead.

The cruel irony of this situation is not lost on me. For the first time in forty-three years, I have fallen head over heels into a pot of piping hot true love and it is with someone else's husband—one who shows absolutely no inclination to leave his marriage.

My sore toe is not bleeding. I suck up the pain and enter the hotel lobby. Safely inside the subdued ambience of this space, I remove my big hat, stuff it in my bag, and swap my large white sunglasses for an unremarkable black pair.

I approach the front desk and, before I can utter a word, the receptionist hands me a hotel card with the room number 303 written on it in blue ink. She says, "Bonjour, Madame. Votre ami vous attend en haut." My friend is waiting for me upstairs. She said it matter-of-factly, like she has no clue about the nature of my business and no intention of remembering any details about me five minutes from now.

I find the stairs, avoiding the elevator, and count the steps as I ascend, trying to slow down my racing heart as I move towards my prize. When I reach the upper landing, I stop.

There's a short hallway with four rooms, two on either side. Dark brown doors punctuate the white stucco walls and the carpet has a large green and gold floral pattern. There is a painting of the bridge of Avignon between the two rooms on my right, and one of a vineyard between the doors on my left. Three pot lights provide dim illumination to the quiet passage. Hanging from the handle of room 303 is a sign that says, "Ne dérangez pas, s'il vous plaît." Please, do not disturb.

CHAPTER TWENTY

But I know the sign is not meant for me. Under this shapeless purple and grey print dress, I am wearing a brand new lacy black bra and thong. For the very first time in our relationship, Alex is waiting for me on the other side of a door, and I will get to make an entrance. I love how the tables are turning.

I tiptoe to room 303, knock softly, and the door swings open. We see each other and squeal like jubilant spies.

Aaaah! It worked!

I surrender myself into Alex's arms and we lock lips and undress each other at the same time. Then we fall onto the bed and, for a moment, it occurs to me that these sheets feel different, that the duvet is thicker, that the air is more humid and it has a salty tang. And then those thoughts are erased by the sheer joy of being reunited with this human being who is so dear and so perfect to me.

Alex flew to France before Belle and me. So, it's been two weeks since our last date. And now we're on the other side of the world, continuing this tale that I hope will become an epic love story.

While I walked Belle to her art class this morning, Alex was kissing his family goodbye as they piled into a taxi to Nice. Hook-ups like this happen all the time in France, they happen all the time in the whole goddamned world. But this one is different. It's my first date in France with the man of my dreams. And now I'm in his arms and there are no words yet, we have so many missed kisses to make up for.

For the next hour, I feel like a glass of fine wine that Alex is savouring on his tongue for as long as possible until he swallows each measured sip. This is his place, and he is running the show, guiding my body through waves of pleasure like a sexual magician. I can barely feel the pull of gravity. His touch, his kisses, and his slow deep rhythm hold me suspended on a plane of ecstasy like a fluffy white cloud in an azure blue sky. And just when I don't think I can ever come down, he ejaculates inside me, without a condom, for the very first time, and I get to feel the sticky joy that I, someone who has had so much safe sex with so many different partners, experience as a delightful novelty. I smell it and gingerly taste it and playfully anoint my stomach and legs and breasts with it until he asks me, laughing, to stop making a mess.

"And you may want to have a shower," he suggests with a wrinkled nose expression, his head propped up on his elbow, observing me as I lay beside him on my back.

"Maybe tomorrow," I tease, and dab some on the sensitive tips of my erect nipples. "This was really a wonderful surprise."

"Hmm. Did you know that when people are surprised, their brain releases dopamine?"

"You're so attentive to my dopamine levels," I say slyly.

Alex chuckles and brings his leg in between mine, massaging the inside of my left thigh with his toes. I roll onto my side and press my body tight against his, trying to create the maximum connection of skin to skin.

He continues, "I had the full set of tests before I left, and I got the results last week. I'm clean and my wife is, well, not very interested in sex anymore. Especially when we're in France. I guess because we're with the kids full time and the days are long and busy. I'm not sure, really."

That was a lot of words about his wife. However, he hasn't even told me her name yet. It must be easier for him to manage his emotions if he refers to her with a generic title.

"Thank you, Alex. I know it must seem to you like I would have a policy for every situation, but I'm new to this kind of arrangement, too. I've never been on a working holiday, I've never been exclusive with anyone, and," I drape my leg over his back and grind my hips even harder into his, "I want you to know that sex with you is completely unlike anything I've ever experienced," I say. I stop at that. He should be able to decipher the hidden message if he's interested enough to go looking for it.

CHAPTER TWENTY

Alex kisses my forehead and his lips linger there, like he's making a wish. Then he mumbles, "There's something I'd like to get off my chest. I feel the need to tell you this. Because . . . I don't want our relationship to be based on half-truths." The long pause that follows puts me on edge. I wait and try to hold space for whatever he is going to tell me.

Alex rolls away and looks at the ceiling. "I saw three other escorts before you. You were going to be my last attempt to find someone compatible."

"I'm glad," I say, right away. "I'm glad that you reached out for something you needed to have in your life. And I'm glad that you gave it one last shot and found me to your liking." In my own head, I add, *And I'm thrilled you wanted to share that information with me.*

He lets go of a big breath. Oh, how I love the seductive smile, curly hair, twinkling eyes, and generous lips of this man who Kate referred to as "plain looking." I love his strong body, his brilliant mind, and his willingness to investigate, experiment, and reflect. I want to tell him those things, but he's not ready. So, instead, I will attempt to kiss him in as many new places as I can until our time is up for today.

CHAPTER TWENTY-ONE

Conversations with Clients: 7 Reasons Why He Won't Leave His Marriage:
Reason #4: Glory Days

Percy #276

P276: Today is my anniversary.

JJ: Oh.

P276: So, you're probably wondering what I'm doing here.

JJ: It's definitely not something I hear very often.

P276: When I see you, I always have a good day. When I get home today, my wife and I will go to a dim sum restaurant and talk about our wedding day, like we always do. We got married on the Great Wall of China eight years ago. Both of our families and our best friends flew there to be with us.

JJ: Wow! That sounds awesome.

P276: It was a great day. Not too hot, and the air was so clear you could see for miles. It's so beautiful. The wall twists and turns up and down the tree covered mountains. Last year, my wife put up a huge photo of us on our wedding day over our bed.

Percy #119

P119: Deb and I were high school sweethearts.

CHAPTER TWENTY-ONE

JJ: You've been married a long time?
P119: Forty-three years next month. We got married on Valentine's Day. She was the prettiest girl in school, and I felt like the luckiest guy in the world.
JJ: She had a lot of male attention?
P119: Well, she was the only daughter of the richest family in town. And she was the hottest girl any of us guys had ever laid eyes on. My rep went up a notch when I let on that she'd put out for me in the back seat of my dad's truck. Like, I didn't fuck and tell, but they all knew. We had a high school reunion last year and those pervs were still drooling over her big tits.
JJ: And you, I hope you were still drooling too.
P119: Hmm. Things change, you know. Those days are long gone.

These marriages are stuck in the past. They started out well, then fizzled, and now the excitement is just a rose coloured memory. But reminiscing cannot quell physical urges, so the husbands find themselves on my doorstep in need of immediate release. Perhaps they're too stubborn to admit they made a mistake. Perhaps the past looks a lot more attractive, from the vantage point of time, than it actually was. Do they long to recreate the best version of themselves that was that guy from the past? Are they searching for something they thought they had back then? A glittering jewel that has been misplaced under the haystack of work, responsibilities, and mundane tasks? What are the odds of winning the lottery twice in one lifetime? Better to share stories about that time when what they had was everything they desired, than to risk it all by seeking out something new.

Zoe must have been a stunning bride. Long curly blonde hair pulled back to accentuate her pretty cheekbones with just a few stray wisps to highlight her sparkling eyes and ruby lips. Alex would have stood beside her, proud and tall and even leaner than he is now, in the best tailored suit money could buy. Big bouquets of exotic flowers, a five-piece band, and a ten-course meal. I bet that was some party. It probably made the society pages somewhere.

Glory Days has to be an absolute no. Alex has hinted that marrying Zoe was not exactly his sole choice. He may have had a push from his parents or even from his grandparents. He also revealed sadness about the fact that he hasn't been completely honest with Zoe. No one likes to fail at something that they, at one point in their lives, set out to do with the best of intentions. But the man who made love to me today was not pining for yesteryear.

To recap, what's keeping Alex with Zoe is likely not religion, not his actual home, not nostalgia, but maybe money? That's where I am, so far. There are still three more possible reasons he won't leave his marriage.

CHAPTER TWENTY-TWO

I AM THE first to leave the Hôtel des Rêves. I slip through the quiet lobby, emerge outside in the bright sunshine, and I still can't feel my feet touch the ground. The street is full of people and I let myself get absorbed by the passing crowd. I don the big hat and white sunglasses and proceed to the nearly three-hundred-year-old building I briefly thought of as home a lifetime ago. The same metal rail protrudes eight feet above the ground from the granite wall, but the sign no longer says La Maison DuBois. Now, it says Les Champs de Lavande. Peeking in the front window, I see a haven of everything lavender, dried stalks in baskets, oils, soaps, candles, china, linens, and countless pouches and little ornaments full of potpourri. There's a woman with sleek dark hair pulled back into a ponytail, who looks faintly like a young Pascale, placing a hoard of souvenirs into a purple paper bag for a smiling tourist. Almost all the doorways in St. Paul de Vence have a rounded arch entrance. It makes every shop feel like a hidden cave, a serendipitous discovery for a lucky globetrotter.

I push the door open and pause to enjoy the sweet fragrance that fills my nostrils—until I glance down, and a shiver runs up my spine. The modern fixtures in the store are all new, but the floor is the same honeyed hardwood, and the narrow stairway behind the cash counter still beckons me upstairs, to the former home of an attractive French family who drew back the curtain of formality and welcomed me into their lives.

I peruse the shelves and decide to buy one small item now and bring Belle back later to shop to her heart's content.

After the customer has left, I select a bar of soap with grains of lavender pressed into the surface and approach the cashier.

"Bonjour, Madame. Six euros, please," she says.

I hand her the cash and ask, "Can you tell me what happened to the owners of La Maison DuBois that used to be here? I stayed with the family many years ago. I was an au pair."

"Ah, oui. The au pair still come to our town every year. And I do know about the lady."

She reaches under the counter and pulls out a worn business card. It says Savon de la Chèvre Brune and there is a picture of a brown goat in a field of lavender. Pascale's name is on the card, along with Georges. "The soap you bought is from this farm."

"May I take a picture of that?" I ask, pointing to the card.

"Certainement," she answers. So I pull out my phone and snap a photo. The address is in Courmes, a village not far northwest of here, and there is a phone number I will call when I have a moment to think and decide what I want to say to her.

I slip the pretty soap into my purse and head down the Rue Grande. There are two other places I need to visit on my own, La Galerie au Vent, in case Raphael is still working there, and La Cave. I did check online and both businesses are still in operation under the ownership of descendants of M. Martin and M. Grenier, respectively. Aside from these people, I doubt very much that anyone else here in town would remember me, likely not even Raphael himself. If the au pairs never stopped arriving in St. Paul de Vence each August, he probably had several conquests a year among them, until he either settled down or started to get paunchy and the young foreign women no longer found him appealing.

Remembering this part of my past still makes me feel like there is something inherently wrong with me that makes me unlovable.

CHAPTER TWENTY-TWO

I swallow a lump in my throat to force back the tears. It's not easy to come to terms with the fact that a relationship that rocked your world could be considered trivial and entirely forgettable to the other person involved. It's a cruel life lesson, one I hope that I am not repeating at this very moment.

I pause to take a few breaths beside a florist's outdoor display of fragrant pink peonies. There is a bush of these behind my dad's house. They are the only flower that survives in an otherwise neglected patch of weeds he calls the back garden. He rarely even mows back there, but he babies that peony bush because my mom planted it over four decades ago. At forty-three, I'm ten years older than my mother ever got to be.

I stroke the fluffy petals and the sensation tugs me back to the present. My stomach growls and I realize that I'm long overdue for lunch.

I grab a quiche to go and a San Pellegrino and try to look inconspicuous, leaning against the window frame out front of the Galerie au Vent, peering out from underneath a plain navy baseball cap that I have swapped out for the big hat. After ten minutes, I have witnessed three employees interacting with eight customers and I'm satisfied that, if Raphael does still work here, he is not here today. I ponder the idea of phoning the shop and asking for him, but my name could come up on a display, so I find a recycling container, toss in my empty pop can, and proceed to my last stop.

I only ate at La Cave that one time, the party where I kissed the two boys in front of Raphael. Zoe never wanted to hang around there in case Henri came downstairs and started bugging her to play with him. I wonder how Zoe managed with her own children? She wasn't what I would call a "natural" with toddlers. I wouldn't be surprised if she herself had taken on an au pair to help her around the house. But I must admit, from listening to her podcast, Zoe is as proud of her teenagers as I am of Belle. They volunteer at the Humane

Society and the food bank and do odd jobs for the elderly in their community.

From the outside, La Cave looks like it's had a restaurant makeover. There's a fine dining menu posted beside the ornate gold-trimmed front door and, stepping inside for a quick glance around, I can tell from the crystal glasses and linen tablecloths that the new operator must be after the big spenders—tourists with deep pockets. But I am being well paid for this summer job, so I decide to make a reservation for Belle and me.

I am discussing a suitable time for dinner tomorrow evening when a man in a brilliant white chef's outfit approaches the maître d'. My mouth drops open and I nearly choke on my own saliva before I can pivot away from his brown eyes. Thank goodness, he is obviously concerned about a work issue. He hasn't registered my presence at all.

It's Marcel. Zoe's Marcel. He has the same chiseled cheekbones and aquiline nose, much less hair, and what's left of it is grey. But, for sure, this man was the boy who caught Zoe's eye—or one of the boys, at least—twenty-five years ago. Along with Bruno, the four of us sat together on the western ramparts and watched the sunset, we went to the beach in Nice several times, and, in an effort to find privacy in a town that was saturated with tourists, we explored the woods outside the walls. There, we consumed quite a few bottles of wine in a secluded clearing among the cypress and pine trees on the steep hillside.

Marcel laughed at me because I could never drink directly from the bottle without splashing the wine all over myself. Does he still carry that memory around in his now balding head, I wonder?

I calm down when I remind myself that, at the time, Marcel only had eyes for Zoe. However, if Marcel is still in St. Paul, then maybe Bruno is too?

This is risky and I debate whether I should cancel my reservation, but I have the advantage of foreknowledge, of being able to disguise

CHAPTER TWENTY-TWO

myself, and I'll be careful. Coming to terms with the past is going to be necessary whenever this whole charade blows up and Alex finds out I am not a stranger to St. Paul and I knew all along that he was married to my old friend Zoe. If we are in love by the time that happens, I'll have a better chance of not losing him. The more information I can find out now, the less chance there will be of a surprise revelation throwing a wrench in my plans.

I tell the maître d' that six o'clock will be fine for dinner and I slip out of La Cave. That was close, but overall, I feel that this has been a productive day. The best part was when Alex kissed me goodbye in our Provençal love nest. I had started to walk away, but he pulled me into the tightest hug we've ever shared and held it for at least thirty seconds before letting me go.

I'm analyzing that moment in my mind as I stroll through the suburbs at three in the afternoon, on my way to pick up Belle. I'm feeling satisfied and even a little smug, when I hear, from the other side of the street, a man's voice shouting, "Julia! Julia!"

I panic, my eyes darting every which way. The only cover is other people, so I hurry to jump in with a family walking ahead of me. Could that be one of my clients? Could Kate have asked someone to find me here? They are still raising their voice and saying something in French I can't make out.

My feet are moving forward, but I can't resist turning around to look. Everyone's heads are looking ahead or down, except for a young couple who are embracing at the previous intersection.

I stop and let my crowd of people move ahead. I'm all sweaty and there's a sour churning in my stomach. I vomit on the sidewalk before it even occurs to me that I'm about to. The next person to pass by me turns up their nose, and I stumble away from my shame before this moment can get any worse and someone really recognizes me.

CHAPTER TWENTY-THREE

OUR DINNER COSTS two hundred euros, including a generous tip. But it is worth every penny to listen to Belle try to pronounce each item on the menu, to hear her funny impressions of all the patrons, to feast our eyes on each meticulously arranged course for a full minute before devouring it with glee, and to discover—through a quiet conversation with our server while Belle is in the washroom—that Marcel is the head chef and that no one named Bruno has worked at La Cave for as long as our server can remember.

"I'm going to be full for two days," I tell Belle, as we exit the restaurant in the humid twilight. I love walking around town at this hour. The tourists have departed, and the darkening sky creates shadows that suggest wonderful things could be happening in secluded corners.

"I'm not!" she says, "I left room for gelato. Please can we get some?"

"As long as I don't have to watch you eat it, or I might be sick." I almost add "like I was yesterday." All over the sidewalk.

I steel myself for the millionth time in the past week. I need to be strong. I have moves to make, and I need to make them in the correct order, or this plan will not succeed. I have to navigate the thin line between exposure and secrecy, while exploring Alex's evolving emotions. I pray that the magic of St. Paul has got us under its spell and that our love will be nourished within its walls.

CHAPTER TWENTY-THREE

I couldn't wear the big hat inside the restaurant tonight, so I opted to fashion a large navy blue scarf into a pretty head covering tied into a dangly bow over my left shoulder. This conceals all my hair. The grey linen dress with an empire waistline is doing a good job at distorting my figure and I'm wearing the black sunglasses—which may look odd, but which are an absolute necessity. I cannot risk being recognized by Marcel, or by anyone else who knew me twenty-five years ago; because anyone who knew me also knew Zoe. I'm sure they would be thrilled to pass along the news that her former friend was back in town.

Belle and I zigzag through the maze of short streets in the centre of town, taking our time and peeking inside the windows of a few art galleries and every shoe store. She is fascinated by the stunning array of footwear on constant display in St. Paul de Vence and she has a goal to buy ten unique pairs of sandals, in a variety of sizes and styles, the more straps and bling the better, so she will have a stock of French shoes to last until her feet stop growing.

Nearly every third store sells gelato, but Belle wants to go to her favourite, La Belle Fraise, because she likes to see her name scripted in neon red lights.

As we walk down the incline of La Descente de la Castre, we can hear the musical trickle of the water before the rotund form of the stone fountain takes shape in the semi darkness. Nearby shops and homes throw splashes of yellow light into the small central square.

And there she is, showered in the golden glow of a streetlamp. Pictures on the internet told me she was still beautiful. But to be honest, I'd have to go further and say that she is beguiling.

Zoe's perfect posture and white designer sundress exude poise and elegance. And, because she is Zoe, there is a crowd around her, smiling at her conversation. But these aren't groups of lustful French men, or enrapt fans of her podcast, studying her vintage fashion style. This group is her son, a tall lanky boy, her daughter, who has her colouring, but not her sparkle, and her husband, the most desirable man on the planet and the reason I am standing frozen to these cobblestones at this very moment. Yesterday, that fascinating man kissed me with trembling lips like I was a sacred thing, but, at this moment, it feels like he is a heavenly body orbiting in a different sphere. He is as unattainable as an A list actor on the big screen.

I sense Belle's impatience, so I reach into my bag and pull out a ten euro note. "Here you go. How about you go into the shop, and I'll wait for you here." I manage to shuffle a little closer to the dark windows of the closed bakery beside us.

Belle takes off like a shot into the gelaterie.

I am transfixed. There is an invisible forcefield connecting the figures of Zoe and Alex. They are about fifty feet away from where I'm hiding in shadows like a calculating thief. He is standing much closer to her than I am comfortable with. He's looking at her when she speaks. He's laughing at something she is saying. He throws his head back and puts his hand on his stomach as he laughs.

Now the two of them are observing a conversation between their children. When that ends, they look like they're about to leave the square. I want to lasso Alex and draw him towards me, away from his flock. But instead of intuiting my presence and meeting my perplexed gaze, he lifts his hand, delicately places it on Zoe's shoulder, and oh so gently redirects her to face the Rue Grande.

When Belle emerges with a huge scoop of pink gelato and an ear-to-ear grin, I have to turn my head to brush away the single tear that has worked its way out.

I will not be defeated. Of course, he cares for Zoe. Of course, he is attentive to her. Of course, he is considerate of her. He is a loving person. He is a thoughtful person. He is the kind of person who doesn't want any harm to come to his wife and children. That's why, when he realized his life wasn't going to be complete without some wild and crazy sex, he chose the path of discretion and decency.

CHAPTER TWENTY-THREE

He hired a safe, mindful escort to attend to his needs because she wouldn't tell anyone, she would get medical tests and not give him any diseases, and she would be sensible enough not to fall in love and complicate what is ultimately a simple business transaction.

I watch the four of them amble down the street until they disappear around a corner. Then I step out of the darkness. "Hey, baby girl," I manage to say with a feigned dash of enthusiasm. "Stand underneath that sign, and I'll take a picture of you with your name."

CHAPTER TWENTY-FOUR

"OH! I WANT to see what he's drawing," says Belle, pulling me towards a man kneeling on the ground just outside of the walls. We are on our way to her second workshop at La Fondation Meaght, Faux Stained Glass.

"Okay, but just for a few minutes," I say. I don't want Belle to be late, but I don't want to be late either. I don't want to miss a minute of my two precious hours with Alex. It's been three days since we made love in the hotel and two days since I glimpsed him at the fountain.

This wiry looking man with a full head of shiny black hair is engrossed in sketching with what looks like chalk or pastels. There's a white grid in an area of about eight-by-eight feet on a recently washed section of pavement and he's drawing irregular blue shapes and filling them in, blending the blues with white.

"Wow! I think that's the sky," Belle says.

"Maybe it's the Alps, or the Arctic?" I suggest.

"How long do you think it will take him?"

"I've seen chalk artists like this before. It usually takes about a day. We can give him some money on the way back this afternoon." I motion to an upside-down hat at the corner of his work, already containing a handful of coins.

"I'd rather give it to him now," says Belle, "so he will have encouragement to make it as beautiful as possible."

CHAPTER TWENTY-FOUR

"You're so right." I kiss the top of her head, which seems to be growing closer and closer to mine every day. I hand her a twenty euro note and she tosses it into the hat.

The artist, who is wearing ripped jeans and a tight grey t-shirt, turns his head, winks a golden brown eye at her, and says, "Mille fois, merci, mademoiselle."

Belle replies, "De rien, monsieur. Merci pour l'inspiration."

The man doesn't go right back to his work—his eyes travel past Belle, to me. I feel, momentarily, like the dress I am wearing is no longer there, like the hat is gone, and my hair has tumbled out of its braid. Then he motions to his drawing and says, "J'espère que ça va te plaire." *I hope it's going to please you.*

"Tu as beaucoup de talent," I reply, and I get a little flutter in my chest when he smiles back at me with bright white teeth. What is it about me and French artists? I chide myself. But I was telling the truth. His obvious talent is very impressive and something I can't help but respond to on a physical level.

Belle catches on right away. "Oh, he likes you, mom!"

I lower my voice. "It's just a bit of flirting. If someone does something that makes you happy, let them know. It's a good way to live."

Belle laughs and grabs my hand, presses her head against my shoulder, and squeezes her eyes shut, "You make me happy, mom."

I'm so in love with this girl, and everything about this moment. And I'm well aware that I owe it all to Alex for bringing us here. I feel that I'm spending his money wisely. I wish he could see the joy he has brought to my child, as well as to me.

I quickly snap a picture of Belle with the artist, who tells her that his name is Omar. I'm eager to show Alex my photos of the trip so far, a few hours from now, when we're lying in bed, sated from sex and languishing in the sounds and smells of Provence that waft in the open windows.

Belle is still holding my hand as we leave Omar and his growing crowd of admirers behind.

"Are you looking forward to your class?" I ask.

"Yeah. Daria is going to be there, but Rico is in Cannes today. I'll see him next week, though."

"I'm so happy that you've made friends here," I tell her.

"Me too." She looks down. "I was scared at first."

"Everyone is a little scared when they meet new people," I tell her.

"Is that why you don't have any friends?" she asks, then adds, "Apart from me, that is."

I'm confused. "I have lots of friends."

"I don't think Grandpa counts."

Hmm. It seems that I have found a new way to fail as a parent. "When we get home, I'm going to throw a party and invite all my friends to meet you. My gym friends, my work friends, and my university friends. I've been too busy with work. I know that, and I promise it's going to change. You'll see."

"Ooh! I love parties. Can we get a karaoke machine?"

"Maybe," I laugh, and she runs ahead to meet up with a tall girl with red hair standing outside the museum.

After I watch Belle enter the building, I jog back into town. I wonder if Alex is going to take charge in bed again, but whatever happens in our box of Cracker Jacks lovemaking session, I feel it's time to tell him expressly that my feelings are growing stronger. It's time to tell him the truth—or at least as much of the truth as I think he can handle.

I'm glad I saw Zoe two nights ago. It was tough to witness their happy family in action, but I know that there's something rotten in the state of Denmark, or rather, the state of Matrimony. If Alex's marriage was everything he could ask for, he wouldn't be seeing me.

Or would he? Were his expectations for his marriage always just to find a good mother for his children?

CHAPTER TWENTY-FOUR

What if he left Zoe and married me? Would he still want to see escorts? How would I feel about that? I'd like to say I would be okay with it, because I know that sex is very different from love, especially to a man.

Who am I kidding? What I observed looked like a man who loves his wife and family. I've met a lot of very disgruntled husbands. I can't place Alex among their ranks.

And yet, he brought me here for a reason . . .

I don't need to marry Alex. I've never yearned to be in a marriage, to have the needs of another adult person exercise a kind of control over my life. I just need Alex to be single, to be fully available to accept my love. Alex's marriage may end because of his involvement with me, but it won't end simply because of me. I didn't start the crack in his marriage. But I desperately want to be around to pick up the pieces.

Today, I will dip more than just my toes in the water.

I'm out of breath when I get to the hotel. I approach the desk clerk and reach out to take the room card from him, but I get a confused look instead.

"Uh, mon ami. Uh, he is waiting for me," I say feeling like I've just outed myself as an idiot. Should I mention his name?

I'm met by another sour faced look just as my phone vibrates inside my purse. I pull it out, hoping for a quick resolution to my dilemma.

Alexis Smith
What's up?
Shit.
That's code for *I can't make it.*

CHAPTER TWENTY-FIVE

THE ROOM IN our B&B is ten paces long. I found that out after lying on the bed became unbearable. I'm waiting for Alex to text me *Hey*, which means that he is available to chat.

Waiting around sucks. It means that I'm low on his list of priorities. I want to come first. But I'm also terrified that someone is hurt, or that we've been found out. I debate calling Pascale to pass the time, but Alex's text has thrown an obstacle in the path of my thoughts that I cannot circumvent.

I decide to attempt a bubble bath while I'm waiting. There's an antique clawfoot tub that looks like the best chance I have to ease the tension in my shoulders. I turn on the water and look out the window at the stunning southern view, over the cemetery which only has a few visitors at the moment.

Two days ago, Belle and I left a bouquet of dried flowers on Francine's grave. They are still there and—that has to be Zoe. She is sitting on the edge of Francine's eternal stone bed, hunched over, with her face in her hands. That mane of tumbling ash blonde hair is unmistakable, and her shoulders are heaving.

I sidle over and turn off the taps, keeping my eyes peeled out the window. I check my phone. Nothing. No text.

How much do I mean to Alex? I was ready to tell him that I love him today. Meanwhile, he's in an unknown location doing something he doesn't want to share with me while his wife is crying

CHAPTER TWENTY-FIVE

by herself in the cemetery. So, he probably has access to his phone, and yet he has not texted me.

For ten years, I have been the centre of attention during all my interactions with men. I called the shots, and my actions were almost always greeted with exuberant appreciation. I understand that Alex has a full life apart from the short time he spends with me. I get it, but it hurts.

I need to know more about what's going on and I can't let this opportunity pass me by. I was going to have to come face to face with Zoe eventually. I was hoping I'd have several more weeks of lovers' trysts with Alex under my belt, and possibly, mutual declarations of love, but if he's going to cancel me at the drop of a hat with no explanation, I may as well roll the dice and see where they land. If I approach Zoe, instead of having her discover my presence by accident, there are still some things I can control.

I change into an off the shoulder lemon yellow mini-sundress with puffy sleeves that shows off my strong arms and long legs. Then I brush out my hair and apply a swipe of cherry red lipstick. No hat or glasses this time. I'm going to visit Francine with my head held high.

I almost walk right into Solange in the hall with a basket of laundry.

"Oops, excuse-moi," she says, turning her back to the wall to make way for me to pass.

"C'est ma faute," I apologize. "I need to pay better attention."

"You look lovely today. Do you have a date?"

"Just meeting an old friend." I smile, feeling rejuvenated as I bounce down the stairs.

I've got no idea what I'm going to say to Zoe. But I'm a master of small talk, if that's what it takes. She will be surprised to see me. I'll say I came here with my artistic daughter because it's the perfect place for Belle to pursue her interests. Then I'll try to get Zoe to open up about why she is upset. This could work out fine.

Oh my god, I think I figured it out! When Alex discovers that I know Zoe and that it's not my first visit to St. Paul de Vence, I'll say that I didn't have the heart to tell him that I had been here before because he was so excited to be taking me on a trip. He never *asked* me if I'd been to the Riviera. He knew I didn't do outcalls, and he knew I was a single mom. He probably just assumed I don't travel much. That's true. And, when I was here before, a lot of shit happened that I'd rather not remember. Alex may feel hurt, but not justifiably angry. As far as he knows, Kate has never even told me his last name. There are volumes of information that we haven't yet shared with each other.

I exit the B&B, sprint across the road, and slip through the Porte de Nice gap in the walls to the south. The entrance to the cemetery is right there and as I walk through the wrought iron gate, I easily locate Francine's grave because the headstone looks like a cross on top of an elegant A line skirt. There are about a dozen tourists here now, but I also see Zoe. She's standing up. She's close enough to me that I could throw a stone and it could hit her.

I freeze in mid step as a man approaches her. He grabs her hand but drops it right away like it's on fire. He takes a step back. They both look quickly around, then return their gaze to each other. I can't see Zoe's eyes, but it's obvious that the man is enrapt. Zoe says something, the man nods, and she turns and walks toward the end of the row of graves.

He doesn't have his chef's uniform on today, but there's no doubt about it, that is Marcel. He waits until she disappears into a large group of cypress trees and then turns to follow her.

What the hell are those two up to? There's no fence around that end of the cemetery. It drops down into the thick woods that cover the steep hillside for about five hundred feet down to a narrow creek. Apparently, Zoe and Marcel haven't forgotten about the secluded clearings either.

CHAPTER TWENTY-FIVE

I resist the urge to follow the sneaky couple and see if I can uncover the mystery. But I'm dressed more like a crossing guard than a spy at the moment, and I think I can put two and two together by myself and get four. I'm almost disappointed that it's so simple. They must be having an affair. Did Alex find that out today?

There's nothing to do but go back to my room, wait for a text, and review my plan.

I return the pretty dress to the closet and examine my figure in the oversized mirror that leans against the wall. I'm wearing three hundred dollars worth of lingerie. There is no hair and no tan lines on my body. My skin is so soft, I can't resist running my hands over my silky ass. But, despite these features, I am well aware that I am losing the battle. Should I get a tummy tuck? A facelift? I try to smile without making lines appear on my cheeks and around my eyes. Would an unlined face and a flat stomach be enough to lure Alex away from whatever is commandeering his attention today?

I remove my pink satin corset, go into the bathroom, and finish filling the tub. I ease my body down into the fragrant bubbles. The liquid caress of the water is mildly soothing. I imagine Zoe, lifting her skirt in a shady thicket and welcoming her lover. Her heart must be racing with the thrill of forbidden pleasure as she offers herself to a man who makes her feel like she did when she was a sex-crazed nineteen-year-old.

I give my head a shake. I'm turning into a fan girl all over again. Sulking in the exquisite aura of Zoe's tragic beauty. What is wrong with me? I should be elated that Zoe is fucking up her own marriage. This could leave Alex available without us having to reveal our liaison.

But, at this very moment, I am alone, while Zoe has Marcel, as well as Alex.

She also had Raphael. He drew her like the proficient seductress she is, whereas my body inspired an artistic study of teenage tedium.

I sit up and check my phone. Still no message.
I sink back into my now lukewarm bath with its diminishing film of lavender bubbles.

CHAPTER TWENTY-SIX

BELLE RUNS INTO the immaculate stone courtyard of the Foundation Maeght to greet me at the very same moment that my phone vibrates. I ask her to wait for me as I step inside and use the bathroom.

Hey

My hand is shaking as I stare at his text inside a stall in the public washroom. Has it really come to this? I'm hiding from my daughter, texting my client from a public cubicle where the walls are scratched with the initials of transient tourists. Am I a highly paid professional escort or a disillusioned middle-aged whore with more wrinkles than good sense? I am at Alex's beck and call like an obsessed groupie. It doesn't feel good.

Hey
I'm sorry I couldn't make it today.
I was getting worried.
Something came up. I'll be there next time for sure.

I appreciate the apology. I note the lack of explanation. I can't live like this. Our next scheduled date is in four days.

Can you meet me tonight at nine at the Place Neuve? It's dark there. Just for a few minutes.

I'll try.

"Hi mom! I decided to go too," Belle's voice echoes in the large cement room as I grimace at my phone and stow it back in my purse. "What does the chalk drawing look like now? Is it a meadow?" she asks.

I remember that on my way here, there was a crowd outside the walls. I did not investigate. I can think only of myself, it would seem. "It's awesome. You need to wait for the surprise," I say.

I let Belle talk for the entire fifteen minutes of our walk. People think she's quiet, but she just needs an audience of one to be able to let it all out. She tells me stories about her friends, thirteen-year-old Rico from Spain who also loves to draw insects and twelve-year-old Daria from New York who insists that Belle visit her there for her thirteenth birthday. Belle has their email addresses, so they will be a part of each other's lives forever now. If technology had been like this twenty-five years ago, Zoe would not have been able to fall out of my life without even a whisper.

Belle makes her way into a circular crowd. "Oh, mommy! It's amazing!" she cries, and I step up behind her and do a double take. The pointed snout of a great white shark is leaping out of the sidewalk. Its jaws are open wide, exposing fleshy pink gums and rows of horrifying chiseled teeth, while its fierce beady eyes appear to be stalking its next victim.

Omar is collecting ten euros apiece from tourists who are lining up to have their picture taken, standing on a marked spot, leaning at an angle with one leg lifted off the ground. This makes it appear as though they are tumbling towards certain death inside the mouth of

CHAPTER TWENTY-SIX

the shark. A family nearby shows us the terrifying—yet hilarious—pictures of them on their phone, and we are sold.

After a twenty-minute wait, we arrive at the head of the line, and I stand on the mark at the front of the chalk drawing. Omar touches my elbow, indicating that I should lean back and lift my right leg, "Comme ça." He's so close, I feel like we're dancing. Then he moves away, leaving a hot sensation on my arm and says to Belle, "Maintenant!" and she snaps several photos before I lose my balance.

I take photos of Belle falling prey to the shark and finally, Omar takes my phone from my hand and photographs both of us clinging to each other in terror as we tumble to our doom.

Walking away with my arm still pulsing from Omar's touch, Belle says, "Just think, if I did something like this on the sidewalk in front of our house, I could raise money for our trip to El Salvador!"

"You're so good at bugs, you could do a giant 3D spider or maybe a hornet! I'll find out where to get that special kind of chalk for you," I tell her as we step into the welcome shade under the archway into town.

I wonder why I never thought to bring Belle to Europe before. I suppose I always felt there would be lots of time, but she's turning twelve in ten days. She wants me to let her be more independent, to go to the mall with friends, to stay at overnight camps, and she wants to get a dog and take it for walks by herself. My influence in her life will become less and less until I'm just that person she needs to remember to call and wish a Happy Mother's Day. Which, I suppose, is as it should be. As long as there is joy in that call, and pride, and tons of love.

"Let's sit on the wall for a bit," I tell her.

"Can we get a crêpe?" she indicates a vendor who has set up her cart nearby to take advantage of the crowd.

"Sure."

Treats in hand, we perch ourselves on the stone ledge.

"Today I learned that the walls around St. Paul were built in 1540," says Belle, patting the hard uneven surface.

This place is getting into her heart as well. "If you know so much, what city is that over there?" I point to the east.

"Nice."

"And what are those mountains behind Nice called?"

"The Alps."

"And why are these crêpes so delicious?" I take a bite, then wipe the oozing chocolate off my chin with my hand. "So yummy. This will be our new Sunday morning breakfast back home."

"Can I have a birthday party with my new friends next week?" Belle blurts out.

"Oh, that's a fabulous idea! Absolutely. What would you like to do? Maybe the beach or the perfumerie? I'd have to speak with their parents first."

Belle is bouncing up and down now. "Ahh! It's gonna be so fun! I'll chat with them tonight on the iPad and we'll make a plan, okay?"

"You bet."

We continue eating in silence, listening to the happy cacophony of tourists from all over the globe who are not taking any notice of the contented lady with her beautiful daughter.

I'll never get a better moment than this.

"Belle, there's something I want you to know about me," I say, keeping my voice as even as possible.

"What? Are you a spy? Or a witch? Are you pregnant?"

I nearly choke with laughter. Then I suck the last bit of chocolate off my fingers and look directly into her sweet brown eyes, "No. None of those things. I want you to know that I had two jobs while you were growing up. I was a supply teacher, and I was an escort. Starting in September, I'm just going to have one job. I'll be a full-time high school French teacher."

She's not asking me the question, so I continue, "An escort is

CHAPTER TWENTY-SIX

someone who gets paid money to go on dates with people—in my case, men. I went on dates with men, and they paid me."

Her head is tilted and she's giving me a pursed mouth look. "I didn't know people could do that."

"Well, most people don't do that. Most people go on dates because they want to have a long-term relationship with a person. I didn't want a relationship. I wanted money." Her face hasn't changed. "Oh, I'm not sure I'm explaining this very well. I'll leave it for now. I just wanted you to know that escorting used to be my job and, like any job I do, I always tried to do my best. It's not my job anymore, though. Please let me know if you have any questions at all and I'll answer them, no matter when you think of one."

"I have a very important question," she says, and I brace myself.

She leans her chocolate smeared face into mine and says, "What's going to happen to the shark?"

I relax my shoulders. "Great question. I don't know. If Omar is still there tomorrow, you should ask him."

We pop off the wall and head towards to our B&B. While we're walking, Belle says, "I thought of another question! If Omar said he'd pay you to go on a date with him, would you say yes?"

CHAPTER TWENTY-SEVEN

I LEFT BELLE with her iPad in Solange and Camille's living room, watching Mamma Mia in French. They were happy to keep an eye on her and I'll not only be leaving them a huge tip, but I'll write an excellent online review as well. I told Belle that I was going to meet an old acquaintance for a glass of wine, and I'd only be gone for an hour. That was an outright lie. Every time I do that, I swear it will be the last.

There is scant night life in St. Paul de Vence and few humans wander the narrow lanes after dark. The ever present fifteen-foot-high walls offer a solid curtain of secrecy and a plethora of darkened corners after the sun sets. I can hear the faint taps of my shoes on the cobblestones as I traverse the length of the Rue Grande like a prowling cat, avoiding the scattered pools of light from streetlamps and bright windows.

The Place Neuve looks empty when I arrive, but then Alex steps out of a shadow. "Julia! Over here," he calls.

When I catch his smile in the moonlight, I want the earth to open up and for the two of us to fall into a hole and disappear until I've had a lifetime of cuddles.

He takes me into his arms, dances us both into an auspicious corner, and we kiss for the first two precious minutes. Our lips are locked in passion, our tongues delighting in the pleasure we were almost denied today.

Alex breaks off and says, "Is everything alright?"

CHAPTER TWENTY-SEVEN

"I was going to ask you that," I say.

His hands are exploring under the sleeveless satin top I'm wearing. It's reassuring that he can't resist touching my flesh when we're together.

"There was a mess at work with the funding proposals that I had to sort out. It took all day."

"Oh." I wasn't expecting that. So, Alex was busy with work and Zoe was crying in the cemetery with Marcel? It's too much to ponder right now when I'm more than halfway to drunk on the proximity of my lover.

Alex undoes the front clasp of my bra and pulls me tight against his chest. He whispers in my ear, "I was thinking about you all day. The way you smell. Your hot mouth on my . . ."

I stop his words with my lips. I recognize my own frenzied desire in this man. He's leaning against the wall now. I squat down and unzip his pants as he slides them over his hips.

From somewhere comes a message to my brain. *You've got about half an hour left.*

If someone were standing ten feet away, they would see nothing. We have found the darkest crevice, the deepest black spot in the corner of ancient stones. We can barely even see each other, so I close my eyes and let touch take over.

The cobblestones are hard against my bare knees. His legs have a downy layer of hair, but his round ass is smooth and firm. I open my mouth and take his engorged penis into my throat, over and over, until a deep moan escapes his lips and I am filled with the most urgent desire.

Alex helps me stand up, puts an arm around my stomach, and eases my ass in towards his hips. I lean forward and the rough blocks of ancient stone graze against my outstretched fingers. Alex flips up my skirt and enters me from behind as the humid breath of the night air caresses our bare flesh.

There is an ethereal tone to this night. I lose my sense of time and space, my psyche slips into the realm of sensation. If someone were to glance our way now, they might think they had just seen the ghosts of all the forbidden lovers who have met in this very spot to fulfill their carnal desires over the last five hundred years.

I can tell that Alex holds back so that we arrive at our climax together, our stifled voices sounding like a bizarre owl.

When our rhythm subsides, I am aware of the flood of sticky hot fluid between my legs. I stand up tall and turn for a quiet kiss to seal the moment as a slow squish of semen exits my body and falls onto the hard ground. I reach out and hold onto Alex's silky shirt, lay my head against his chest and hear, as well as feel, his beating heart, while he threads his long fingers into my hair, and we try to hold onto the magic just a little longer.

Every time Alex and I are together, another door opens onto a deeper connection, putting us in a constant state of discovery, like endless linked tunnels through the network of our veins.

I was going to say *I love you* today, but right now, I am overwhelmed with relief and joy. Those three little words don't seem sufficient to express all that is in my heart.

"Time to go," Alex mumbles, and I hear his zipper. The irony of his three chosen words pokes at my heart.

"I'll see you Monday," I say. It comes out sounding like a question.

He leans in for one last kiss. "Absolutely. This was . . . fantastic. As usual."

He leaves and I feel like my soul has been strewn across the courtyard. I need a moment to come back to myself. There's a bench under a large leafy tree on the other side of the Place Neuve, and I stumble there, unsure of my legs, still weak with emotion.

I have had sex with hundreds of men. Some of them turned me on. Some of them touched my heart. Not a single one made me feel that absolutely everything about them was perfect. That I would

CHAPTER TWENTY-SEVEN

never want to change a single thing. That I could spend every minute of every day with them and never ever feel anything less than amazed that they exist.

Ah, love. I know what love is. I love Belle. And I love Alex. And if I don't find a way to make Alex a part of my everyday life, not just a regular hook-up, I will never get to experience the depths of romantic love that, until a few months ago, I had scoffed at as much as miracle cures. I would regret that more than I regret all the lies that have brought me to this bench in a foreign land in a tiny town that always sets me on an emotional rollercoaster.

I look up at the sliver of a moon hanging in the sky like a silent watchman over the sleepy village, smiling at what it witnessed here tonight. Then I check that I still have my small purse that slings over my shoulder with a long leather cord, and I pull out my phone. No messages. That's good. But I've only got eight minutes to make it back before ten o'clock.

I let the aura of our lovemaking, like the magic that stays in the air after an outdoor concert, carry me back along the length of the Rue Grande to the south walls, where I turn right, see the light on in the window of the B&B a few steps away, and smash into a human being.

"What the fuck?!"

"Zoe?" I touch my pained chin that just rammed into something hard.

"Jade? What the fuck?!" Zoe is rubbing her forehead.

I start laughing. Zoe starts laughing. Then Zoe, still laughing, puts her arms around my waist and her head against my shoulder and squeezes me like a stuffed teddy bear. I can hardly breathe.

Zoe pulls back and looks me up and down. "I can't fucking believe it! Jade Matthews is back in St. Paul. How long has it been?"

I am relieved that she has asked a question that I can safely answer, "Twenty-five years."

"Holy shit, Jade! It's so good to see you. This is crazy. I had the crappiest day today and I was out walking. I was actually thinking— Man, I need a friend to talk to—And I literally run right into you."

I can see that Zoe's hands are shaking. And, close up, she has a bit of a saggy neck and lines running from the sides of her nose to the corners of her mouth. Her hair is long and wavy, but maybe also dry and over-processed. We aren't teenagers anymore, but we just laughed together exactly like we did back then.

"Are you staying here?" Zoe motions towards La Vie Douce.

"I am. With my daughter, Belle," I answer.

"Oh, such a pretty name. I have a daughter too, Miriam, and a son, Noah."

I am very aware of the time. And I am afraid if I stay here too long, she might realize that I smell like her husband. "Belle is waiting for me. I should go in."

"Of course, but Jade, I meant it when I said I need a friend. We had a laugh back then, didn't we? And I'd love to get together if you're staying for a few more days."

Zoe's eyes are puffy and it looks like she has smeared mascara on her cheeks that won't come off without proper make-up remover. Belle's words to me from this morning still sting, "You don't have any friends."

I'm not even supposed to know Alex's last name. And he has no idea who Jade Matthews is. He thinks I'm "Just Julia." Even if I arrange to meet with Zoe, I have done nothing wrong. I'm juggling a lot of balls, but I can't lose my nerve now, or they could fall anywhere and roll away out of sight.

"I'm taking Belle to Cagnes-sur-Mer tomorrow, but Saturday is pretty open."

Zoe takes a deep breath and smiles, "Excellent! DM me on Instagram. I'm Zoe Green now."

CHAPTER TWENTY-SEVEN

I nod, because I can't trust myself to make any comment about that. "I've got to go. It was good to, well, run into you." Our ensuing laughter fills an empty space in my heart that I didn't even know was there.

I move to the front step, but I pretend to be distracted by the scent of the bougainvillea that frames the oak door until I've watched her walk away. She's going towards the west ramparts, but I know that her hotel is on the east side of the village.

When I step inside, I'm only three minutes late and no one has noticed. They are at the wedding scene. Belle is midway through a chocolate éclair and, of course, she doesn't want to leave. Camille says, "Why don't you join us for a bit?"

I squeeze myself into the loveseat with Solange on the other end and Belle in the middle. I'm content to gaze blankly at the screen because I am very aware that my heart is beating through my chest.

Belle looks up and asks, "How was your old friend, mom?"

"Oh," I force a smile, pleased that I don't have to lie again. "She was very happy to see me. And well, she looked older, I guess, but so do I. We had a good laugh."

"What's her name?"

"Zoe. She used to be Zoe Carlisle, but her married name is Zoe Green. We only knew each other for six weeks when I was eighteen, but we had a lot of fun together twenty-five years ago."

CHAPTER TWENTY-EIGHT

Conversations with Clients: 7 Reasons Why He Won't Leave His Marriage: Reason #5: Fear

Percy #378

P378: My wife says she's going to live with her sister.
JJ: Oh. How do you feel about that?
P378: I don't want her to go.
JJ: Did you tell her that?
P378: She knows. She doesn't really mean it. She'll go for a week, then come back. She always does.
JJ: Have you thought of counselling?
P378: We don't need that. She just needs to remember that she misses me when we're apart. It'll be fine.

Percy #224

P224: I hate lying to my wife about coming here. She thinks I'm having physiotherapy on my knee. I don't know why I came up with that story. Now I have to limp all the time and I forget which leg it is.
JJ: Have you ever thought of telling her the truth? I truly believe that what we're doing here is a kind of therapy. It's something special for you. It's what you need.

CHAPTER TWENTY-EIGHT

> P224: No woman would ever accept that. It would ruin us if she ever thought she wasn't enough for me. I could never do that to her.

These husbands are afraid of many things, but mostly, of opening up and facing truths which might cause pain, hurt, or loss. The status quo must be maintained, even if it's total shit. Too much uncontained emotion bubbling over the cauldron of life is to be avoided at all costs.

I think these people were conditioned from birth to accept—not to question or to push boundaries, not to ask too many questions, and to leave well enough alone. They are completely unprepared to face the consequences of leaving their marriage: the pain, loss, and loneliness that would most likely ensue and therefore, they are frozen in place.

I've never been married, so I can only imagine what a nightmare shit show it would be to find out that your partner has been unfaithful. I've heard it's one of the main reasons for police being summoned to households: to squash the riot that erupts between two people who once declared undying love and who now sit on opposite sides of an ugly schism.

And there is no guarantee that anyone else will come along to fill the void. Endless hours spent scrolling through websites, evenings spent alone with no one to share a thought or a story with, only an empty bed on a cold night.

Is Alex afraid of change, loss, pain, or loneliness? He'd be crazy if he wasn't. And, from his perspective, if I am the balm which can heal his wounds, how much of my time could he reasonably afford to pay for after a divorce? Furthermore, I told him that I'm leaving the business in order to pursue what escorts refer to as a "vanilla" job.

If Alex were to divorce Zoe, he needs to do it because his life would be better off without her than it is with her. Period.

Zoe is a vibrant, intelligent, dynamic person. I have always known that. I saw it again tonight. But she is also very possibly in love with someone else.

Their marriage cannot be a bed of roses. If fear is holding Alex back, I can let him know, in no uncertain terms, that I will always be there for him. I seem to keep getting to this resolution, but then I back down from expressing my undying love.

It never seems to be the right time.

CHAPTER TWENTY-NINE

BELLE IS CRAFTIER than I thought. She has brought me to Cagnes-sur-mer under false pretenses.

"I do want to see the museum," she insists as we step off the public bus, "but I'm following Omar on TikTok and he said he'd be here and you want to ask him about the special chalk, right?"

"Good try. If you found him online, I could have just sent him a DM asking him, couldn't I?"

"We're here now. I wonder what he's going to draw today?"

I laugh. "Do you know what a groupie is?"

Belle gives me the twisted mouth look and pulls on my arm, "Hurry up! Why do you have to wear high heels everywhere? Aren't you tall enough already?"

"I like being tall. I can see everything from up here."

"And I can see all the tiny creatures on the ground that you always miss. You realize you just squished a beetle, right?"

"I am sorry about that. I'll try to be more careful."

Belle always notices the little details that I tend to miss, pretty buttons on a sweater, a custom manicure, or the chocolate at the bottom of an ice cream cone. I've been practical, preoccupied with getting on to the next thing. Or at least I was, until Alex made me stop and appreciate the vast potential for joy that is contained in every single moment.

We arrive in front of the Grimaldi Castle Museum, an impressive squarish looking structure, obviously designed as a medieval keep, but which is functioning today as a tourist museum and gift shop. Omar is hard at work on what looks to be a child-sized lily pad with inquisitive orange and black fish poking their heads out of the water all around it.

Belle runs up to him. "Bonjour, Omar! C'est formidable!"

He looks up, "Ah! C'est la belle Belle," he says laughing, and my daughter blushes. But she holds his gaze and smiles, not looking down in the way I'm used to seeing her do when she receives a compliment.

"Wow! It looks like you're at it again," I say to him. "Your work is so impressive. Do you only create art outside?"

"Non. I did an earthquake crater in a shopping mall last year. And an underground zombie world in the Paris Metro. Google 3D chalk art by Omar."

I can't take my eyes off him. Life is a hustle for this man. He chose a creative, nomadic, follow the crowds and the sunshine kind of occupation. I respect that. I know how it feels to make your money by putting a smile on someone else's face. To take cash from the hands of strangers. It's a grind, but it's exciting too.

Omar looks like he's eager to get back to work, but Belle asks, "Where can we buy those pastels?"

"My brother Ari has an art supplies shop on Le Chemin Fontette, near La Fondation Maeght. Sometimes you might find me there, too." Omar winks at her and reaches into the back pocket of his faded jeans that look like a second skin. He pulls out a worn looking business card that says Pour Mon Art and places it in her hand.

And again, like last time, he flashes me a smile that says, *If we fucked, it would be amazing.* Or maybe it doesn't say that? Maybe it's just a random thought that is stuck in my mind.

* * *

CHAPTER TWENTY-NINE

Belle and I spend a fairytale afternoon in Provence. We do the self-guided tour of Grimaldi Castle, imagining what it would feel like if we lived there. Strolling from room to room, we discuss which of the vast stone chambers with ancient fireplaces would be our bedrooms, where we would locate our living room, and what the views would have looked like outside of our windows in 1309 when it was constructed by Lord Rainier Grimaldi on the site of a ruined Greek fortress. In the great hall, we decide which tapestries we like and which ones we would get rid of, and who we would invite to our balls. I'm glad that my little girl doesn't see herself as a Cinderella. Her vision is that she would rule her subjects wisely and she would give everyone a puppy.

When we're done, we walk across the road and buy artichoke pizza for me and mushroom pizza for Belle from an actual hole in the wall on the street.

We sit on the edge of a cooling fountain and watch Omar collecting money from tourists who are having their photo taken sitting on his lily pad. Biting into the thick cheesy slices, with aromatic herbs and sauce that tastes like a fresh ripe tomato, we both moan in unison.

"This is the best pizza I have ever eaten," I say.

"Mmm hmm," she agrees, and we take our time, savouring the perfect balance of dough, tomato sauce, fresh basil, and cheese.

"You said I could ask you anything, right?" Belle asks, in a smallish voice.

"I said it and I meant it. Ask away."

"Did my dad pay you for the date when you got pregnant with me?"

"Oh." My heart crumples inside my chest.

"Did he? How much did he pay?"

"I wasn't an escort back then, Belle. No, he didn't pay me any money. It was . . ." I swallow back tears. "It was a spontaneous thing that happened because I was feeling happy and I wanted to connect with someone, and he was very kind and handsome. And he told me I have beautiful eyes."

She looks up at me and forces her eyelids to open as wide as possible, "Do you think he would think my eyes are beautiful, too?"

"Absolutely. Your eyes are like his. Big and luminous and framed with ridiculously thick eyelashes." I touch underneath her outstretched chin and lean down to kiss her bare forehead.

"Did my dad look like Omar?" She gestures at the wiry man who is gingerly helping a toddler to sit cross-legged on the lily pad.

"No. He didn't. He looked somewhat like you." I really want to change the subject, so this seems like a great time to bring up my news. "Hey, my friend Zoe has invited us to go on a hike with her and her children tomorrow morning. Would you like that?"

Belle nods. "Yes! That's so cool. How old are her kids?"

"Noah is fifteen and Miriam is thirteen. That's not too much older than you. Zoe does a podcast called *My Green Family* because their last name is Green. And well, it's an eco-friendly thing. She says her kids love the outdoors and I know you do, too."

"I hope they'll like me," says Belle.

"Oh baby, you don't have to try to please anyone. Not even me. Be yourself and if they are nice kids, they will like you."

"Okay," she smiles. "Maybe we'll get to see a mouflon sheep or a wild boar!"

And maybe I'll discover what Zoe's been up to, what her marriage is really like, and how I can position myself to inherit the husband she appears to be letting slip through her fingers.

CHAPTER THIRTY

ANOTHER PERFECT DAY in Provence. No wind, no rain, just a permanent golden heat that compels you to close your eyes and offer your face to the sun for its blessing.

"When you got out of the cab, I got the weirdest déjà vu," says Zoe.

"Me too," I answer, my voice light, with the youthful playfulness I recognize as something I buried over two decades ago. It has come back to haunt me since my return to France. "You and me, and three kids on a walk. Just like old times. I bet you're relieved you won't have to carry any of them."

"I don't care if he was only four years old, Henri was an asshole."

I laugh because it's true. "I bet he makes his wife get on top all the time, because he's too tired." I mime the floppy look that Henri used on Zoe every single day we took him to school. "Your real children are lovely, though. They were so sweet with Belle, asking her how she's enjoying her holiday and telling her about the trail."

"Ha! Belle is the sweet one, with those big brown eyes that dart everywhere, and she's so full of energy. Don't be fooled by my sometimes well-mannered children. They will be generously rewarded for their good behaviour today."

I'm puzzled. "What do you mean?"

Zoe pauses to remove her small backpack. She's wearing form-fitting black bike shorts, a pale pink tank top, and ankle-high hiking boots. Her hair is coiled into a sleek rope that hangs over her left shoulder. She's got a generous amount of make-up and dark sunglasses on today, so I can't tell if she's been crying. It still throws me to be this close to her. She's played such an important role in my imagination for the past three months that I keep having to stop myself from reaching out and touching her to make sure she is real.

Zoe checks her phone, then answers, "I had to promise them they could go ATVing tomorrow if they were polite to my friends."

"I admire your resourcefulness, but isn't that dangerous?"

"It's far less dangerous than a hotel room with two bored teenagers."

I nod, agreeing. "I can understand that."

The three kids are walking about fifty feet ahead of us on the Baou des Blancs trail, a nine-kilometre loop. It meanders up green hills strewn with craggy white rocks and it's adorned with whimsical wildflowers like feathery purple allium and butter yellow snapdragons. Provence was definitely allotted much more than its fair share of natural beauty. Kind of like Zoe, I muse. It's no wonder she likes it here so much. She is a reflection of her surroundings.

Belle applauded my sensible shoe choice today, a pair of grey Toms, but the trail is uneven and I'm being cautious. There are a lot of pokey rocks camouflaged with moss that jut out of the ground just enough to stub an unsuspecting toe.

I realize that this is a moms' date disguised as a kids' date. Zoe has orchestrated our reunion in such a way that we can talk about personal matters; however, the presence of the children ensures that we won't let things get too dramatic.

We've completed the first leg of the trail, a strenuous uphill which made it uncomfortable to chat. It's flatter now, and the cloudless blue sky is stretching wide as far as the eye can see, just out of reach over our heads like in the pictures Belle used to draw when she was little. I try to realign my thoughts in such a way as I would have been feeling if I had never met Alex. As if we were a single mom of one

CHAPTER THIRTY

and a married mom of two, catching up on each other's lives after a twenty-five-year hiatus that was caused by a series of unfortunate events.

And so it begins. "It's good to see you again, Jade. I felt awful when you left St. Paul all of a sudden. Madame Gaudet said that your dad had a heart attack. Did he.." she pauses.

"He survived. And had another heart attack five years later, but he survived that one too. He's okay. I mean, he's all I've got so . . ."

"That's really good to hear," Zoe nods and cuts me off like an interviewer and she slides into some polite inquiries about Belle. I give her the abridged version of my journey through motherhood and she tells me hers. Uneventful pregnancies and births, one colicky baby followed by an easy one. These memories represent a phase of our lives that we didn't share, and which no longer holds much interest for either of us, but we both recognize it as a safe topic.

Zoe pauses under one of the few trees on the trail and we enjoy a moment of welcome shade. I still can't see through her sunglasses, so it's making me uneasy. I'm good at reading the truth behind people's expressions and I enjoy connecting with someone eye to eye. But Zoe's obvious guard speaks for itself.

She finally says, "And I suppose there's another thing we need to talk about."

Her words hang in the air like the scent of the wild thyme that we've been crushing underfoot. What is there to say about the day when I intruded on her and Raphael?

I've carried this embarrassment around with me since the day it happened, playing on repeat in the background of my brain, distorting into something more grotesque with each iteration. In this haunting memory, I'm the epitome of the loser—my mouth is gaping in shock, and I'm choking with sobs from the perceived betrayal. How could I ever think I had a chance with the gorgeous, talented

Raphael? It turned out that I was so insignificant, such a paltry bored little girl, that fucking me never even crossed his mind.

But I had never realized, until this moment, that Zoe could be feeling even more shame about what happened that day than me.

When I don't respond, Zoe starts walking again. It's difficult to stay side by side on this part of the trail, so I gratefully relinquish the lead as we edge around a large boulder. We walk in strained silence, listening to our shoes shuffle against the packed earth, until the path starts winding down into a protected river valley. The kids are in view, but well out of earshot. Miriam looks like a reluctant magnet, following a few feet behind Belle who is flitting everywhere like a capricious butterfly. Noah is trudging along behind Miriam with his head down and his hands shoved in his pockets.

I'm watching Zoe's slim legs and hips bounce down the zigzagging path. Her butt is not as cute as it was back then. I would know. But, if I'm being honest, she started life with the body of a Barbie doll and two and a half decades have left only cursory marks on her form. From the perspective of an escort, however, I know that allure is as much a state of mind as a state of body. Men want women who are excited to be in bed with them and who get turned on by the sight of them naked. I'm never going to beat Zoe in a beauty contest, but this is not a beauty contest. In fact, it never was.

"Raphael," I say, and his name feels rough in my throat.

I haven't spoken it aloud for twenty-five years. I feel like I'm talking about someone who now resides in a stone box, bereft of fresh air, unable to affect the world except by eliciting memories of ages past; someone lost to us, like Francine. I check in with my heart and there is no ache in my chest, and no tears threaten to tumble from my eyes. I inhale, fully expanding my lungs with fresh air, and shed the last layer of tension I'll ever have to carry for that man.

Zoe freezes, blocking the path, and turns to face me from higher ground. She has always been a fashion aficionado and the fine details

CHAPTER THIRTY

of her outfit are starting to grate at my nerves. The double Gs on her Gucci sunglasses are made of little diamonds, her immaculate boots are a creamy buff suede. The hair tie on her twisted flaxen rope is pale blue satin, and I know, if she would remove the sunglasses, that it would perfectly match the shade of her eyes. She bites her lower lip, somehow not disturbing the rosy gloss in the process, and says, "I didn't know that he was drawing you, too."

I nod.

"I'll never forget your face when you saw us," she says. Her voice is flat and low. "It must have been a shock. Raphael said he didn't understand why you were so upset because it was you who walked into his studio. You know, Jade, he was using both of us. I was just a little sluttier."

"Have you seen him since?"

She shakes her head. "No. I heard he went to Marseilles."

"And Bruno?"

"That's a sad story."

We are interrupted by the flash of Belle, the leader of our little troupe, brusquely turning around, throwing out her arms like a crossing guard, and then placing a finger over her lips.

Zoe and I catch up to her children and then the four of us proceed cautiously and crowd behind Belle, holding our collective breath. She is pointing to a clump of grass from which a sleek brown head with small round ears and alert black eyes is frozen, watching our every move.

"It's a marmot," whispers Miriam.

"No, it's not. It's a meerkat," says Noah.

"There are no meerkats here, stupid." Miriam glares up at her much taller brother.

"You're stupid," snaps Noah. "You don't even know what a meerkat looks like."

"Well, you don't even know what your face looks like!"

"What the . . .?"

Zoe snaps her head toward her son to cut him off.

"Why couldn't we go white water rafting today?" mumbles Noah under his breath. Then he gives his mother a look that says, *Life is so unfair.* I know that look, and I get it. I'd rather not be doing this either. I'd rather be back in l'Hôtel des Rêves with Alex, basking in the heat of his embrace, feeling his sweet kisses on my neck.

I'm starting to think that Belle is the only person who really wants to be here, and I wonder, yet again, what the hell I'm playing at? Did I come here to witness Zoe's parenting woes? Will this make me feel less awful about breaking up her family?

At least I can attempt to thaw the icy tension. "There, I got a good picture," I announce after snapping a close-up of the animal whose identity we can confirm later. "I think we should move on and leave it alone now."

Zoe lets Noah walk in between the two groups because Miriam is doing a decent job of acting friendly towards Belle and, I'm sure, because she doesn't want her kids to start World War Three in front of us.

"He's a good boy," says Zoe. "Just doesn't feel like he fits in sometimes."

So far, Zoe has been very open about her children. I'm dying to ask about "her husband." It would seem like a logical progression of the conversation, but I'm afraid to go there. It might make sense for me to ask her why she was upset two nights ago, because she admitted as much when we met on the street, but I hold back. I'm also reluctant to inquire about Bruno's sad story. I still feel badly that I left all those years ago without saying goodbye to him.

"I tried to Google you once," admits Zoe. "Sixteen years ago. It was our first visit to St. Paul and it brought back memories. I couldn't find you."

"I'm not surprised. I'm not easy to find." I don't elaborate. I've

CHAPTER THIRTY

finally found a way to change the course of the conversation. "So, this isn't your first time back?"

"I've lost track," says Zoe. "Maybe the eighth?"

"What keeps bringing you back to Provence?" I try to keep my voice light.

"It's the prettiest place in the world, isn't it?" She shrugs her shoulders, but then wrings her hands, possibly aware that her answer sounds trite.

"Do you do your podcast here in the summer?" I'm afraid it must sound like I'm interrogating her, but she doesn't seem to notice. She always liked being the topic of conversation.

"Oh my god, no!" she's laughing like I suggested she poke herself in the eye. "You know I'm a fraud, don't you?"

"What do you mean?"

"Let's just say I don't really care as passionately about the environment as I let on."

"Wow. You could have fooled me. Belle and I listened to an episode last night. The one about cutlery you can eat. You were so funny."

"The podcast was my idea. You know how much I love to talk. But the theme was courtesy of my husband, Alex. He's a scientist."

So here is my segue, yet I can't bring myself to ask her anything. Not, *What's he like?* Not *What do you think about marriage?* Not even *Tell me about how you met?* Instead, I'm dreaming about running upstairs in my house with Alex and counting how many eggs have been laid in our new robin's nest.

And the opportunity is lost.

"Miriam looks so much like you," I remark, jumping back onto a safe topic.

"Hmm." Zoe is pursing her lips. "She's a smart girl, but she's a pain in the ass to her brother sometimes. She's been that way since she was born, trying to push Noah out of the spotlight. Of course, she's a daddy's girl."

I wonder if Belle would have been a daddy's girl, and then I decide that that is a creepy expression, and it should never be used. This conversation is not going as I'd hoped. Poor Zoe. Belle and I have our moments, but for the most part, it's been straightforward and easy with the two of us making our way through life together.

"Are you alright?" I ask Zoe.

"Not really."

"Do you want to talk about it?"

"Not really."

But she didn't say "no."

I can't admit how I saw her crying in the cemetery yesterday or that I know that her husband is seeing an escort, so I'll circle back to the beginning.

"It's okay about Raphael. I don't blame you for what happened. And I'm sorry I didn't tell you I was leaving St. Paul. I was worried about my dad, but, if I'm being honest, I was more embarrassed than anything. I wish I had reacted differently, but, really, we were so young."

We're back to walking side by side now and I catch her giving a wistful smile.

"How did the rest of your au pair time go?" I ask.

Zoe's shoulders drop and she lets out a big sigh. "Hey, let's take a rest here," she says pointing to a large, flat rock.

I look ahead to the kids and Zoe pulls out her phone. "We'll catch up. I'll text Miriam and tell her to wait for us. Let's sit for a minute, please?"

She's got that look I recognize from teenage sleepovers that means she is about to bust out a secret. We sit, almost touching, on the pockmarked slab of limestone, and Zoe pushes her sunglasses up onto her head, revealing her striking blue eyes. "Soon after you left, I started sleeping with Marcel every night. It was bizarre, like we were a young married couple living in an older married

CHAPTER THIRTY

couple's space. The Martins didn't give a shit where I was sleeping, as long as I was doing my au pair jobs. By day, I took care of the little brat Henri, with much more patience than he deserved. And, not only did I clean the Martin's house and restaurant, but I started helping out in the kitchen when Marcel was working. I chopped vegetables and washed dishes. When we weren't working, we spent every minute together, usually in the woods south of town. We must have fucked at least two times a day, every day, for five months."

I shake my head in a combination of disbelief and envy. "Wow. Just wow." Nineteen-year-old Zoe was in a class by herself. She saw opportunities and grabbed them with both hands.

I make a mental note of two things from this disclosure. First, it doesn't sound like Zoe made another close friend from the group of au pairs. Second, I sense that there is something big she has chosen to omit.

"Didn't Marcel share a room with Bruno?" I keep my voice light. "Wasn't that a little crowded?"

She giggles, and the old Zoe is back. She gives my knee a little slap and says, "Bingo, Jade! You never disappoint me. I always admired your ability to think outside the box. I can't tell you how refreshing it is to find you again." She leans in closer. "Bruno was in the next bed, and sometimes, he was in our bed, too."

"Have I said 'wow' yet?"

"Too many times. Try to think of something else."

"Okay," I take a deep breath. "What the fuck? Was it amazing? Was it awkward? Was it like the movie *Summer Lovers*, but with two guys and a girl instead of two girls and a guy? How did you come back to Canada and just carry on? You were only nineteen." I pause to gather my thoughts. "I guess Marcel and Bruno weren't much older than you. It must have been really hard for you to leave here and leave them behind. Or did it all fall apart somehow?"

149

Zoe is glowing. As much as I try to resist the sidekick role, I think she deserves the attention right now. She has the guts, or at least she had the guts, to explore her desires. Heck, I've had sex with over six hundred men, yet I've never had a threesome—the idea has never appealed to me—but I applaud her willingness to experiment.

Zoe's phone pings with a text. She reads it and makes a sour face. "For fuck sake! Miriam says Noah took off."

CHAPTER THIRTY-ONE

ZOE AGES TWENTY-FIVE years right in front of my eyes. Her hands clench, her eyes roll up in frustration and her mouth forms a tight line. She starts jogging on the trail and I keep up behind her.

We cross an open field, skirt a group of pine trees, and spot Miriam and Belle up ahead. They are jumping around and laughing, doing some sort of improvised dance. As we get closer, we hear their voices accompanying "Voulez-vous" by ABBA, which is being broadcast from Miriam's phone.

"What's going on?" demands Zoe, stepping in front of her daughter who is performing an exaggerated jazz square and waving her hands in the air.

"Whaaat?" slurs Miriam, regarding her mother with her eyes half shut like she just woke up and has no idea what has transpired.

"Where is Noah?"

Miriam stops dancing and shapes her lips into a tight rosebud. "Funny you should ask . . ." she says, enunciating each syllable, "I just texted you that I don't know where Noah is."

Zoe ignores the attitude being heaped upon her. "Did he go ahead on the path?"

"I think he went over that hill," says Belle, pointing in a perpendicular line to the trail through a minefield of boulders.

"Will you stay here with the girls?" Zoe asks me.

I turn my sternest teacher face on Miriam. "I'm sure we can trust you two to stay put."

Then I take my phone and a bottle of water out of my pack and toss the bag to Belle. "Stay with Miriam and eat a sandwich."

I put my hand on Zoe's shoulder and say, "I'm coming with you. At least until we know he's safe." And, with more certainty than I feel, I add, "He couldn't have gone far."

"I'm sorry about this," Zoe says when we're out of earshot of the girls, picking our way through the bumpy terrain. "Noah's having a hard time this summer. It seems like he doesn't want to be part of our family anymore. It's a teenage thing, I guess." She wipes her cheek.

"Who would want to be a teenager again, eh?"

"Me," Zoe replies without hesitation. "I'm not sure I should be responsible for other human beings."

"You're a great mother, Zoe. Because you care. It's obvious. As a high school teacher, I've met my fair share of disgruntled teenagers." I reach out and touch her arm. "Noah will be fine."

"Do you know what he's up to?" she asks. Her stride is purposeful, matching my own, but her voice is cracking.

"Let's see," I muse. "How about smoking pot, watching porn, skipping school, swearing, talking back, drinking, sneaking out, taking risks, and generally preferring any form of technology to meaningful interaction with his family?"

"You are good." She gives me an appreciative nod.

"He's also a really nice boy who told Belle a joke to make her feel comfortable, he asked me intelligent questions about my camera, and he volunteers for the food bank and your local trail association."

"You must have listened to a few podcasts."

"Belle loved the one where your kids explained how they grew giant pumpkins on their uncle's farm and sold them to grocery stores to use as displays. Then they donated all the money they raised to

CHAPTER THIRTY-ONE

plant trees in their schoolyard. Belle's adamant that next year, our front garden is going to be transformed into a pumpkin patch."

Zoe smiles. "You have to order the seeds online. Those pumpkins were amazing. The stores paid five hundred dollars each, which is a fair price for something that generated so much attention from customers. Our whole family camped out in the pumpkin patch the night before they were harvested."

"Who actually does stuff like that?" I throw up my hands. "Your kids love you, Zoe. And Noah is just trying to figure out who he is. That's all."

We crest another hilltop and Zoe gasps, "Oh my god, it's him!"

About a hundred feet down a rocky incline, Noah is hunched over, clutching his right leg.

Zoe gulps and hesitates, so I reach him first.

"What happened?"

He looks up at me. His pale eyes and wide cheekbones strike me as familiar. His face is flushed, and his mouth is a thin line of pain, but he answers, "Tripped over a rock."

"When it happened, how badly did it hurt, on a scale of one to ten?"

"Uh, eight?"

"Point to where the pain is."

Noah touches the soft part of his ankle, underneath the bone.

Zoe arrives and crouches down beside her son. "Is it broken?"

"I don't think so, but a sprain is just as debilitating. He should have an X-ray anyway, and he'll need help to walk." I recall what I need to ask next from a first aid workshop. "Can you get up by yourself?"

He shakes his head.

"It's okay," I say, "I'll help you."

I squat down, ease my shoulder under his arm, and we rise up, leaning our weight into each other. Zoe is on her phone and says,

"I'll get a taxi to meet us at the exit. We're almost there, Noah. Once we get back to the trail, there's about one more kilometre. Do you think you can make it?"

"Yeah," he says through gritted teeth.

Noah is as tall as I am, and Zoe must realize she wouldn't be much help trying to support him. I'm happy to be of use. I've had a glimpse inside Zoe's head, and it's a tinderbox, with no rain in sight for the foreseeable future. But right now, I can be a buffer between this confused boy and his distraught mother.

Apart from his injury, Noah has the strength and coordination of a natural athlete, and together, we're able to make decent progress. At first, he's just hopping, but as we start to leave the accident site behind, his tension eases and he is able to put a slight bit of pressure on his right foot which is enough to get into a steady forward motion.

Zoe gets ahead and when we meet back up with the girls, it looks like she has managed to subdue her daughter.

"Hey bro, you didn't have to do that just so I could beat you in a race for once," Miriam says with no hint of sarcasm. Then she gets up and offers Noah her seat on a flat rock.

Belle hands Noah a tuna sandwich and chocolate croissant, the last of our picnic which I thought would have been enough for all of us, but has somehow disappeared, and I resign myself to downing the last of my water.

It's mid-afternoon by the time we reach the end of the trail. I've been making small talk with Noah to keep his mind off the pain. We've established a common appreciation of Ironman, the Blue Jays, and hazelnut gelato. I'm sticky with sweat, beyond hungry, and my left shoulder would appreciate a deep massage.

The girls cheer for us as we hobble off the trail and onto the gravel parking lot next to the road.

Zoe clasps her hands in front of her chest. "I'm so grateful to you, Jade! You took charge like a paramedic. My husband is coming here

CHAPTER THIRTY-ONE

in a taxi to go to the hospital with us. I called another one to pick up you and Belle and take you back to town."

"What?!"

Shit. I blurted that out and Zoe looks puzzled.

"A taxi, well, I figured you wouldn't want to spend any more time . . ." she says.

Noah is still leaning on me, and I almost drop him as a yellow taxi pulls up, the passenger door whips open and Alex, his face looking drawn and flustered, lurches out.

"Noah, how are you . . ."

Then he sees me. Really sees me. We've never met outside before, in the light of day. I am totally out of context for Alex. No lingerie, no bottle of lube in my hand, ready to spread it on private parts that ache to be touched. I am a disheveled looking meddler who has insinuated herself right into the heart of his tight knit family.

"Ju . . ."

"Jade!" I interject, raising my free hand in greeting. "I'm an old friend of Zoe's."

Alex's eyes open wide and, realizing how that must sound, I add, "Zoe and I reconnected a couple of days ago. We bumped into each other, literally, just outside of my B&B."

He is gaping at me. I've never seen his face with this look that I admit could be called "panic."

Zoe is glaring at her husband who still hasn't spoken an entire word. Even the kids are all strangely quiet.

"It's nice to meet you, Alex?" I say his name like I'm not quite sure I've got it right. "I'll let you take over now."

I help Noah take three steps towards the taxi, and Alex thankfully comes to his senses enough to start helping his son into the back seat.

CHAPTER THIRTY-TWO

Conversations with Clients: 7 Reasons Why He Won't Leave His Marriage:
Reason #6: Love

Percy #155

P155: My wife is my best friend.
JJ: That's so sweet.
P155: I know she's done with sex, though.
JJ: How do you know that?
P155: I watch her. She doesn't talk about it. She doesn't like to undress around me. The handful of times I tried to initiate something physical last year, it just didn't work out, and I love her too much to ask her to do something she doesn't want to do.
JJ: I wonder why she doesn't want to do it?
P155: She has body issues. I tell her she's beautiful, but she just doesn't feel beautiful anymore.
JJ: Beauty is not a prerequisite for sex.
P155: Love isn't either, I suppose.
JJ: So true.

Percy #429

P429: My wife is perfect. I'll never know why she chose me.

CHAPTER THIRTY-TWO

JJ: Tell me about her.
P429: She has a successful career, she's wonderful mother, a great cook, we both enjoy our home, we give each other emotional support, and we have great sex once a week.
JJ: Is there a certain day?
P429: Saturday night, nine o'clock. I never miss it.
JJ: Just like you never miss Thursday morning with me.

These Percys won't leave their marriage because they are in love. A date with them is usually dull and focuses on the physical act of sex. Hot sex, slow sex, kinky sex, dirty talk, whatever it is that they don't get with their wife.

No one can provide every single thing another person needs and desires in a partner. Everybody compromises in a variety of ways in a marriage. However, some men find it extremely difficult to compromise when it comes to sex.

These loved up Percys suffer more than most from an affliction known as guilt, which is dangerously close to shame because, yes, most of them are "cheating." But life and relationships are so much greyer than they are black and white. These Percys realized what they needed and sought it out with me in a safe, respectful, transactional way. I know that many people would disagree with me about that, but it's likely that those people haven't seen the self-loathing on the faces of these men.

Some of the most pleasant, straightforward dates I ever had were with Percys who were in a loving "open" marriage, often one in which the wife described herself as asexual. I frequently received messages from these wives, thanking me for being a crucial part of their happy relationship. Some even sent presents for me along with their husbands: home baking, jam, and gift cards. A few asked for a meeting so they could thank me in person, but I always declined.

My agent had taught me that mystery is a major factor in my allure and that it's as delicate as a pair of silk stockings. I felt it was better that these wives not witness how their husbands interacted with me.

Does Alex love Zoe? He's never said that to me, but he hasn't said that he doesn't and I'm going to assume that he does.

My own feelings toward Zoe, with whom I have actually spent less than two months of my life, waver between envy and empathy, but are always mixed with an undeniable dose of fascination. She makes me look at the everyday in a new way, pushing me to see things from a different perspective and she makes me feel valued.

Just like on the first day we met, when she recruited me to be her cheer squad, Zoe still needs people, and she's not afraid to admit it. After twenty-five years, she swung the door on our friendship wide open again and welcomed me into her life with an open heart. Zoe doesn't pretend to have it all figured out and that makes me want her to succeed. I truly want her to be happy.

And yet, I also want her husband.

CHAPTER THIRTY-THREE

"WAKE UP! WE'RE going to the beach with Miriam and her dad!"

Belle's distorted face is inches from mine. "I've got sunscreen on already and I had breakfast with Solange: scrambled eggs, raspberry yogurt, and some kind of melon. All the healthy stuff." She puts her hands on my shoulder and shakes me. "Why are you so sleepy?"

I'm sleepy because I didn't sleep. I was flopping from side to side in bed, clutching my phone, waiting to feel the vibration of a text from Alex. When I finally got a message at 2:30 a.m., it was from Zoe. She thanked me for my help and said that Noah's ankle is sprained and he's got to take it easy for a few days. She also told me that it was great to reconnect and that she hopes we can get together again soon, just the two of us.

I suppose she wants to dive into the nitty gritty of her wild nights in the little sex den off the kitchen in La Cave twenty-five years ago. And maybe she's going to tell me about her present-day affair with Marcel?

I am tantalizingly close to confirming my suspicions and that should make me feel like I'm succeeding in my mission, but it doesn't.

If Alex does leave Zoe, it doesn't mean that he will fall in love with me. I was hoping that, over the course of this three-week vacation, Alex would get glimpses of the way I live my life, my close relationship with my daughter and my genuine appreciation of his kindness. But now, my vision of an incognito vacation with Belle, interspersed with passionate dates with Alex, has morphed into a G-rated family retreat, complete with kids and organized activities. Whose idea was this?

"We're going to the beach?" I mumble into my pillow, sidestepping Belle's query.

For the next hour and a half, I fret about what I'm going to say to Alex. Belle selects my outfit, a sunny yellow one-piece bathing suit with a white crocheted cover up. Camille arrives with a tray of fruit, coffee, and pastries, and I am instructed to hurry up and finish every bite. Finally, I am escorted to the taxi stop where I'm squished in the back seat with Belle and Miriam babbling the whole time like excited pigeons.

During the entire half hour ride to Cannes, Alex does something on his phone while the driver taps along on the dashboard to a radio station playing obscure English oldies. I stare at the nape of Alex's long neck as it descends from his recently shorn, curly hair to the top of his navy-blue polo shirt. The soft tanned skin is less than a foot from my face, and I am remembering how I bit too hard there once and he tickled me until I said I was sorry.

We pull up on the Rue La Croisette in a line of taxis. Alex pays the driver, and we are drawn out of the car by the energy of two exuberant young ladies.

They ask me what I want to do at the beach today, but I just shrug. I still can't bring myself to talk. It feels like the last bite of strawberry tart is stuck in my throat as we march with swim bags in hand across the golden sandy beach to the Baleine Beach Club. We install ourselves on a row of four plastic lounges with rust red cushions, each one shaded by a brilliant white parasol.

Grateful at least for the fact that our children didn't conspire and choose a day of touring the shops, I lay back and retreat behind closed eyelids while Alex and the girls discuss water safety and the rules of the club.

CHAPTER THIRTY-THREE

The three of them decide to venture into the water and leave me to guard our stuff on the lounges. I wave them off with as much enthusiasm as I can muster, then watch, mesmerized, as the three figures dive and splash in the ocean. I drink a full bottle of water, hoping to clear my head and settle my stomach, but it makes me feel bloated and more muddled.

What the hell happened to my plan? How did I fuck it up so badly? No text at all and Alex hasn't even said ten words to me this morning. We got along so much better when we were naked and alone. Reality has pulled a veil over our fantasy world and, without the promise of an illicit encounter, we are left to play the role of awkward strangers.

Eventually, the attractive trio emerges from the ocean, and I watch them talking as their dripping bodies dry off in the hot sun. I can't help but wonder how I would feel if these beautiful people were all members of my family. What if I could live a life with no secrets where I express my love and have it reciprocated? But, after yesterday, I'm so far from Alex. I know he doesn't trust me now. But did he ever?

The girls seem to have spotted something on the sand, probably one of the funny yellow ghost crabs with black eyes on raised antennae, and they drop to their knees. Soon, they start digging with pails and shovels that were lying around. I'm sure they are eager to distance themselves from Alex and myself. I imagine they're coveting a bit of privacy so they can chatter about cute boys, music, stuff they want to buy, and, of course, annoying parents.

Alex joins me and grabs one of the emerald green towels provided by the beach club. I resist the urge to stand up, take the towel, and dry him off myself. Rubbing his firm body through soft fabric is such a turn on for me, as well as for him.

I steal a glance at his crotch. He is definitely not finding me irresistible today.

"Belle is a great girl," Alex says politely, without meeting my eyes.

"Thank you. Your kids are awesome, too."

"They have their moments, but we are very proud of both of them."

I'm hoping that Alex didn't glimpse my involuntary flinch. Did he say "we" on purpose? That tiny little pronoun jabbed into my heart like a razor-sharp knife.

"So, you've been here before?" he continues, in a voice that could be either suspicious, hurt, surprised, or all three.

I answer coolly, "For six weeks, as an au pair when I was eighteen years old."

"And you know Zoe?"

"We hung out together while I was here. But I had to leave the program early because my dad had a heart attack. Zoe and I never kept in touch."

"That's quite a coincidence, Julia, that you have a history with my wife. And I'm still puzzled that you never thought to tell me that you'd been here before."

"To be fair, you never asked. And please, drop the charade. It's Jade now, Alex."

He runs his hands through his hair and sits down on the edge of his lounge, like he's not interested in staying there for long.

"This has thrown me for a loop," he says, and I'm scared that he's been pushed too far. There's an iciness to his voice that makes me choke back a sob.

"Me too," I protest. "Every minute since you stepped out of that taxi has felt surreal. Like I've lost half of myself. After a brilliant ten-year run, *Julia* is finished. I never realized how much she meant to me. She made me feel powerful, and special. Now I'm ordinary Jade, with an ordinary life. I feel confused and just plain shitty right now."

I feel shitty mostly because I haven't told him that I realized who he was on the first day. I'm not innocent in this. He shouldn't trust me. If I hadn't known Alex's identity, I would still have gotten to this

CHAPTER THIRTY-THREE

place in time, but I'd be able to act authentically shocked about the whole coincidence. So I'm still keeping secrets, only there's one less because I don't have to be two people anymore.

I reach down over the arm of the lounge, scoop a handful of warm sand, and release it slowly back down to the earth. Then I rub my fingers together, feeling the fine grit of powder it has left behind. "Au revoir, Julia," I mumble as I pull my knees in and curl up on my side, facing away from Alex.

I can sense him leaning in closer to me so that his voice won't carry. "I'm not going to lie. It was much simpler when you were Julia," he says in a tone I've never heard before.

"Please stop saying her name," I repeat.

"I should have known you were too good to be true."

I flip back over to look right into his frosty eyes. "What the fuck? Of course, it wasn't true. Dating an escort is living in a fantasy. How could you actually think that someone named *Just Julia* was real?"

"You're saying that the woman I had sex with last week in the Place Neuve wasn't real? It felt pretty fucking real to me."

"Of course, it was real. Having sex with you is amazing. But . . ."

I can't continue. I am afraid if I initiate any more dialogue right now, I will regret whatever it is that comes out of my mouth.

"Mom! Come and see our castle!" calls Belle, rescuing us from further conversation. I stand up, slip the cover-up off each shoulder and wriggle out of the garment, letting it fall to the sand. I step out of the puddle of clothing and proceed to the water, knowing full well that the whole time, Alex is staring at my half-covered ass.

The girls are wet and happy, smiling at an unsymmetrical conglomeration of sand structures that is being eroded on the south side by the gentle swell of the Mediterranean.

It crosses my mind that if I could somehow stop wanting Alex for my very own, I would likely stay in touch with Zoe. Then the girls could continue making memories like this one and their lives would intertwine like a long braid of hair. Or, if by some miracle Alex would fall in love with me, they could become sisters in the legal sense. As they grew older, they would find it important to keep in touch and discuss not only the fun stuff, but the tough stuff as well, like accidents, illnesses, and deaths. They might decide to raise their children in the same city to support each other, and the paths of their lives would become strikingly parallel.

If Zoe were to find out that Alex was seeing an escort named Julia—me—Miriam and Belle would likely be forced apart by anger and mistrust. They would simply be two ships that crossed paths, with names that would be difficult to recall two years from now. Unless they keep in touch between themselves, starting a private correspondence, well, texting, I suppose, in which they demonize their wanton parents who were responsible for breaking up Miriam's happy family.

I just walked away from him, but I don't want Alex any less right now than I did on the first day we met. When I brought Belle to St. Paul, I opened a pandora's box. My intentions were to find a way to take something that wasn't mine. I'm not proud of this, and yet, I feel that if I don't continue to act selfishly now, I will spend the rest of my days drowning in my own regret and that surely won't help my child who has only one parent to help her navigate through life.

They are still smiling like a pair of toddlers waiting for some praise. I kneel in the warm sand and inspect their work. "You know I always give an honest opinion," I say to Belle. "And therefore, I will say that this castle is complex and ambitious, but it looks like it doesn't have a strong foundation. It's lucky for you two that I am a seaside building expert!"

Miriam hands me a yellow plastic shovel, and says, "Your mom is cool, Belle. Unlike my mom, who is basically a psycho." Then she gives me a surprise fist bump and we all get to work.

CHAPTER THIRTY-THREE

I have to bite my tongue and stop myself from defending Zoe. It's not my business and I wouldn't doubt that Belle has used similar words to describe me over the years. Instead, I say, "First, we've got to transfer the whole project over there," and point to an open spot near the lounges.

This puts us close to Alex, who is dozing, or pretending to doze, in the hazy shade of the parasol with his hat concealing the top half of his face. I can see beads of perspiration glistening on his upper lip and, when I catch the odd breeze, I detect the familiar smell of his sweat. I don't know if he is sleeping, observing me through a crack, calculating his next move, or just wishing for this day to be over, but his presence is a comfort to me, nonetheless.

One hour later, the castle is fully relocated, we've added an underground passageway, a couple of flying buttresses made from sticks and a fully functioning drawbridge that used to be a discarded flipflop.

"Hey daddy, what do you think about Le Château du Soulier?" Miriam asks.

The hat comes off and Alex, back in dad mode, grins and pulls out his phone. "It's fantastic! I'd like a picture of this Castle of the Shoe. Smile, ladies." And I hope I look good, or happy at least, because this is the only picture of me that Alex would have to look at, if he ever wants to remember my face. Kate has pictures that she sends to prospective clients, but, like all the photo shoots she arranges for her escorts, my face is blurred out and I am wearing seductive lingerie.

I look like an object, a Barbie doll you may or may not want to play with. I never asked Alex if he chose me from my picture, from the accompanying blurb about how I cater to curious husbands who want a discreet, mature encounter, or just from Kate's recommendation. But it's unimportant now. Alex will have a picture of Jade on his phone, the woman who thinks that life is better than any fantasy because he is in the world. The woman whose heart aches to be pressed against his own, where, she is still certain, it was always meant to be.

"You must be hungry," Alex says, pointing to our picnic lunch.

"Oh! Let us do that!" says Miriam, grabbing the wicker basket and placing it on her lounge.

"That sounds great to me," says Alex.

Miriam is obviously besotted with her father, and I can't say I blame her. She hugs him and says thank you for bringing us all to the beach. She takes his outback style straw hat and places it on her own head of matted sandy blonde curls and he laughs, then agrees that it does look better on her. Their conversation is affable and cheery, free of the teenage angst that she brandished during the hike with Zoe.

Belle is delighted with Miriam, and they proceed to take our orders and prepare our plates with the delicious charcuterie provided by Camille: cured meats, slices of cheese, olives, nuts, dried fruits, baguette slices, and jellies.

Belle is obliging her by following her complicated instructions about how to arrange the food.

After we eat, we collect all our belongings and walk out to a more secluded, rocky point. I can tell that Belle has also fallen under Alex's spell. Walking beside her, he is explaining the life cycle of the tiger mosquito with all the details of a university lecture, and she is hanging on his every word.

On our own private peninsula of the beach that nobody else seems to want to roost on, we stash our bags in between the rocks and splash together like a happy pack of otters whiling away the beautiful afternoon. Alex praises Belle and Miriam's strength and dexterity as he lets them climb on his shoulders, attempt to balance there, and then dive off, if they can manage, or else flop ungracefully into the water.

I swim out towards the horizon. Enjoying the effort, kicking, propelling myself with my arms, blowing out all my bubbles, then

CHAPTER THIRTY-THREE

tilting my head up to the sun and breathing in a fresh stream of air. When I know I shouldn't go any further, I turn around, swim back and rejoin the group.

"I think we should head back now," I say, knocking water out of my ear and noticing that the beach is starting to empty. I don't want Zoe to get the idea that I enjoy her husband's company too much, because it is the absolute truth.

"I'll call a taxi," says Alex, heading toward the beach.

"Noooo!" the girls beg in unison, but I insist and we all head to the outdoor shower and change rooms to rinse off the salt water and slip on dry clothes.

"Can we please get ice cream before we go?" asks Belle.

"Sure," says Alex and he hands Miriam some cash, turns to me and asks, "Would you like ice cream?"

"No, thank you. Hurry and get it, girls. The taxi will be here soon."

We watch them run to a nearby gelato shop on the pedestrian walkway and line up behind a large family.

Alex's shoulder is inches away from mine.

"This turned out to be an okay day," I venture.

"It did," Alex agrees.

"Tomorrow is Monday."

"Monday is a day I usually go golfing."

"And Belle has a watercolour workshop," I add.

Alex shakes his head. "But I'm not going golfing."

I hold my breath.

He continues, "I want to spend some time with Noah."

I swallow the hurt and take advantage of the precious seconds I have left. "I miss being alone with you, Alex. You mean a lot to me. I care about you and I'm sorry for . . . well, I'm just sorry."

"I need to think about this."

"Of course. But, I want to make it very clear that if you see me now, it's not a business transaction anymore. I'm going to tell Kate

167

to stop forwarding your cash to me. I'm completely out of the escort business."

He purses his lips and gives a slight nod. "That's a whole new ballgame."

"I only want what's best for you. I hope that turns out to be me. But if it doesn't, well . . ."

"Thank you . . . Jade, for being open." He looks into my eyes, and I force my face to look as transparent and honest as possible. We are so close right now. Is Alex remembering our dates? When we were together, it was like we were doing a slow tango for an hour, never leaving the enchanted aura of each other's personal space.

His face softens into a tiny, sad smile. "All I can tell you is that I don't want to say goodbye right now."

"Okay," I whisper, but I want to scream. He didn't end it with me! It may just be because he's afraid of what I'll do if he rejects me. Perhaps he thinks that if he scorns me, I will tell Zoe all the sordid details. Of course, I would never do that. But for the moment, I will take any lifeline of hope I can grab on to.

The girls are still at a safe distance, placing their order, but Alex lowers his voice further. "Is there anything you can you tell me about Zoe? I feel like she's not been herself since we got here. She's completely on edge."

It's too soon to tell him about her affair, but this might be an opening. "Are you asking me to spy on her for you?"

He shakes his head. "That's not what I meant. I'm just having a lot of difficulty understanding my family right now. At least Miriam is up front about what she wants, and if she's unhappy, she tells me what the problem is. Noah has been steadily growing more distant, and Zoe is perpetually upset—one minute she's snappy, the next she's sullen. I try to take care of things . . ."

"I see. You're trying to figure out what everyone else wants. But what do you want, Alex?"

CHAPTER THIRTY-THREE

"I want work to phone and ask me to handle something I'm good at."

I give a little chuckle. "Oh, you're good at more than work." I try to make my voice sound light, "It could just be nothing. You never know. Or maybe Zoe senses that you've been seeing an escort?"

"I really don't think it's that. Let's give it a few days, okay? Maybe keep our meeting on Thursday? There's a lot to think about."

I know I wouldn't be attracted to a man who acted impulsively, without considering the feelings of his family. I can wait. I can help him to get to where I want him to be. I look into his beautiful smokey grey eyes, and I tell myself that this will work out in the end. I need to be strong enough to be patient.

Then I feel his hand on my elbow, propelling me to walk towards our children who are returning with their dessert. This is the same motion he made with Zoe by the fountain last week. I'm sure he's unaware that he is doing it. I like this dance. It means that he is including me in his life. I will fall asleep tonight clutching the spot on my arm that is reverberating beneath his fingers.

I look up at Alex, wanting to reassure him that he's doing the right thing. "If I can help Zoe, I will. And I promise that I will never betray what is between us."

He drops my elbow and takes a step back. "The picture," he says, narrowing his eyes. And I wait for the inevitable conclusion. "That sketch in your bedroom of the naked girl in the chair with the long hair. It's Zoe, isn't it?"

"Yes."

"How did you get it?"

"It's a long story, but I promise I'll tell it to you someday soon."

* * *

Alex returns his attention to his phone on the taxi ride back to St. Paul. When Miriam and Belle start to doze off, I pull out my phone and text Kate.

> Hi! Everything is good here, but I want you to please stop accepting payments from Alex. Take whatever he owes you and don't put any more money into my account. Thanks

It's just after lunch in Toronto. Kate texts me back promptly, as usual.

> Alright. As you wish. But are you really okay? That was a pretty short career as a sugar baby.

> I'm really okay. And I was never a sugar baby.

Or was I?

> Fine. Bring me back some macarons, only pistachio flavoured. They're the best.

CHAPTER THIRTY-FOUR

BELLE AND I arrived early for drop off today, so I could introduce myself to Rico's and Daria's parents who have agreed to let me borrow their children to attend Belle's party two days from now. I had a great idea last night, made a few phone calls, and it was all arranged.

Pascale was stunned to hear my voice, but was delighted I wanted to bring my daughter and three of her friends to visit their farm. She said that Georges will give us a farm tour and soap making demonstration and she will prepare lunch for everyone, all for a fee of two hundred euros. Belle had insisted that Miriam celebrate her birthday with her, and Zoe said that she would like to come along and let Alex spend the day with Noah, whose ankle should be well enough by then to go kayaking.

On Wednesday, I will hire a taxi van to take the six of us to Courmes, a village in the countryside northwest of St. Paul. I can't say that I wasn't disappointed to have Zoe's company instead of Alex's, but I'm really looking forward to seeing Pascale, and I know that if I have any chance of having a future relationship with Alex, he needs time to process all this information that I have been aware of for three months.

I promised Belle I would pick up some gifts to give to the children in a party bag, which I will do in the time I have to myself before I meet Zoe for lunch.

Instead of returning directly to town from the museum, I go around the corner in the direction of Omar's brother's store, Pour Mon Art. I pull the bent card smudged with blue pastel out of my pocket to check the address, and smile.

We've only been in France for ten days and so much has happened. Life seems to be on fast forward and half speed at the same time. I'm whirling between trying to forge my future one minute and then taking slow sips of fine wine while contemplating stunning vistas the next. My body and soul are on high alert, every moment here counts and I'm always a little breathless, like during the last two minutes of passion.

Belle and I are scheduled to fly home on Saturday. Only five more days. How will I feel when I'm back in Toronto? No longer hearing lively voices greeting each other in French, not feeling the sultry kiss of the Mediterranean sun, not smelling lavender and olives everywhere, not being surrounded by art at every turn.

Whatever happens here, I will be restarting my life in Canada. Will it be with Alex, or just Belle? I'll no longer be an escort and I no longer wish to sleep alone. I want to snuggle against Alex for an entire night, and then again the next night, and the next, until we can't get to sleep without the reassuring sound of each other's breathing. Does Zoe really want to be married to Alex? Would she still say "I do" today? Or has their marriage become a ritual of uncertain significance? That is what I need to figure out this afternoon.

I step through the glass doors and marvel at the collection of art supplies arranged on pale wooden stands in geometric displays that are themselves works of art. "I'm glad I didn't bring my daughter here. I'm sure I'd never get her out. What a great store!" I say to the man who looks like a an older, less Bohemian version of Omar.

"Merci, madame! How can I help you?" he asks.

Fifteen minutes later, I'm loaded down with paints, pencils, papers, the special pastels for sidewalk art, as well as bags, ribbon

CHAPTER THIRTY-FOUR

and some nail and body art pens and hair chalk which I'm sure will contribute to an excellent party.

Feeling like a good mom, I say, "The kids are going to be over the moon! When you see your brother Omar, tell him Jade says thank you for recommending your store."

"Why don't you thank him yourself? Omar is in Monaco for a few days, but he will be drawing in St. Paul again on Friday."

"Oh, my daughter will be thrilled," I say and step outside before he can see me blush.

Back in town, I drop the bags in the B&B, then proceed, with all the conviction I can muster, to my next stop. I step up to the familiar stone arch on the Rue Grande and push on the door of the Galerie au Vent. A bell jangles and my footsteps echo on the worn wooden floor. Some things never change, I think, just as Monsieur Grenier emerges from the back room.

"Bonjour, madame! Puis-je vous aider?" the grizzled old man greets me like a stranger, as I'd hoped.

"Hello!" I say, ignoring his offer of assistance like an uncomprehending tourist. Then I look down and pretend to be interested in the bowls of small souvenirs on the counter.

How do I tell this man that I stole a picture from his premises when I was eighteen years old? That, an hour before I boarded the taxi to take me back to Canada to tend to my ailing father, I entered his studio through the back door. I knew it never quite locked and needed only a good push to open because Raphael had demonstrated how to do just that during my first modelling session.

I had been a bit frantic, looking for what I thought was, by rights, mine. A picture of me, with long, straggly hair, wearing ripped shorts and a tank top with no bra, leaning back in an oversized armchair, looking bored . . .

But, as I had flipped open the large portfolio where Raphael kept his sketches, my eye was caught by something truly well done. Zoe, seated on a simple wooden chair. Her nearly naked body curved in all the right ways, she had shed her polite veneer, closed her eyes, and had given herself over to the artist. And somehow, with simple strokes of his pencil, Raphael had laid her desires across the page; the backward tilt of her head, the laxity of her shoulders, the extension of her hand that was resting on her knee, subtly beckoning someone to bring her the release she craved. A simple charcoal sketch on a single sheet of art paper, larger than a regular sheet, but small enough for me to roll up and conceal in the cloth bag I used as a carry on.

Was Raphael upset when he realized his work had gone missing? How much would it have sold for? Most of the money I am about to hand over should go to Raphael, but Zoe says he's gone for good. So I pick up a keychain from the counter. It's a red wooden cicada and costs two euros. I take out five twenty euro notes and place them on the counter.

Monsieur Grenier looks at me and cocks his head. "Madame?"

"Keep the change," I say quickly and leave before he questions me further.

That felt good. My conscience is heavy and anything I can do to lighten the load is a help.

I'm still early for lunch, so I pause in the Place Neuve. It's bustling with tourists in the light of day, but I find a spot on the shaded bench where I sat, my body still pulsating with the aftereffects of a powerful orgasm, four nights ago. Today, I am sandwiched between a grandpa who is sitting still with his eyes closed and a woman reading an Italian novel. I need to think again. Think and breathe. Plan and prepare. I'm afraid I've missed something, and I might take a wrong turn.

How much of the love that I feel for Alex, how much of his desirability, is based on the fact that I have been jealous of Zoe all my life? I have had sex with hundreds of men in a room with a picture of her on the wall, for heaven's sake. How much of her blatant sexual

CHAPTER THIRTY-FOUR

abandon was responsible for the titillation of my clients? If Alex were a single man, or an ordinary Percy with a nameless wife whom I had no reason to envy, would I crave him as much? I admit I'm a driven individual. I've always wanted to see the next best thing and I have said yes much more than I ever said no. Dad has told me all my life that he is proud of me because I excel at whatever I undertake. Am I simply trying to get a front row seat for the downfall of Zoe? Will I still want the prize once the competition is over? Or, is my love for Alex as pure and unique as any great love? Could it just be very likely that two girls with similar interests and experiences would fall for the same man? But did Zoe fall for him, or did she settle for him? And how can I ever separate my love for Alex from the life he has lived?

With all of those unanswered questions buzzing around in my head, I take a cleansing breath, get to my feet, and proceed through the north gate. Within seconds, I arrive at La Colombe d'Or, a golden stone building with a Spanish tile roof, located on the threshold of St. Paul de Vence. I've passed it at least a hundred times, but today will be my first time dining in this famous inn and restaurant that is decorated with works of art by Picasso, Miró, and Chagall amongst others, all of them having been ardent frequenters of this unique establishment.

The maître d' informs me that our table is ready, and I should have a seat and enjoy the art while I'm waiting for my friend. He ushers me into the airy dining room with dark wood wainscotting, exposed beams, and great masterpieces hung on every section of wall between the many windows and doors. It's hard to decide if this place is a restaurant or a living museum.

I've just been seated next to a line drawing of a woman's face by Matisse when Zoe bursts in and zips over to the table. She hasn't even sat down yet and exclaims, "Okay, Jade! Spill it! I need to hear everything about your life as an escort!"

"I..I ...," I stutter.

Zoe slips into her seat and leans forward, like she's not quite sure who I am. Her eyes are puffy again today, despite the concealer that is evident at this distance. "Miriam told us. I laughed so hard! Alex looked like he'd swallowed a sock!"

She registers the alarm on my face. "Don't worry, I told him to lighten up. I was raised in a family that was uptight about sex. Well, weren't we all? But that's not the way the world is anymore. And, as you and I know, it never was like that over here." She gestures to the view out of the open window beside her. Fig trees on the terrace give way to verdant valleys scattered with picturesque houses that anyone would be thrilled to call home.

Zoe flops back in her chair, lets her eyes flutter closed, and shakes her head side to side. "I always knew you were a dark horse." Then she signals the waiter. "Sauvignon blanc, s'il vous plait! Une bouteille."

He nods and turns away.

"I can't tell you how much that news cheered me up!" continues Zoe. "Oh my god, I missed you! We are kindred spirits. All those years ago, we were the only two girls in that group who actually came here to immerse ourselves in this culture and let it permeate our flesh, because we knew that the French experience life through their whole bodies. I'm so glad you came back to Saint Paul. And you're an escort! Holy shit, Jade!"

I take a moment to laugh with her and continue my inner struggle with what to say. The waiter affords me more time by showing up with our wine. He presents the bottle to her, splashes a mouthful into Zoe's glass, and she pronounces it, "Superbe!"

"So, please," she urges me after he has filled our glasses, "I need to get my mind off my troubles. Do tell!"

I wonder how long she could continue her monologue if I didn't answer, but I decide to put her out of her misery.

I start with a smile, like I would for a job interview. I roll my

CHAPTER THIRTY-FOUR

mind back to the time before I met Alex and channel the woman who still possessed rational thought, unclouded by the fog of love. "I am currently no longer an escort, but I did work as an escort for ten years. It allowed me to buy a home and to give Belle, for the most part, what she wanted, not just what she needed. It was a steady job and I worked hard to build my brand. I was lucky to have a lot of regular clients. In my opinion, they were basically decent men who just wanted more sex than they were getting in their marriage."

"That's interesting. I'm sure there's a lot of people who would disagree with that, but I've never been interested in other people's ideas about morality. You were brave to make such a bold career choice. I'm amazed that you told your daughter."

"It wasn't easy keeping it a secret. I'm not ashamed of it, but I waited until I thought she was old enough to understand. This has shown me that I need to continue the conversation with her. I'm glad that she's talking about it, but now I know that she's ready to be told more. That it's not everyone's business and, although it was legal for me, it was still illegal for my clients to purchase my services."

"Right. I get it. But Jade, this is me, Zoe." She touches her chest with both hands. Nails the colour of ripe strawberries pressed against white silk. I wonder if Alex has ever sucked on her fingers? She checks that the waiter is out of earshot and continues, "On our hike, I told you that I had sex with two guys at the same time. Steamy bisexual sex." She lets the last three words drip out of her mouth like moans in the darkness. "You know I want more details about this. What was it like screwing a bunch of different men?"

The waiter deposits a basket of warm rolls on the table, and I make Zoe wait while I tear and butter one, then take a big chewy bite.

"Well, I do have this weird obsession for keeping statistics. So, I know that, over the decade, I had six hundred and fifty-three clients. There were some who paid for my company for other reasons; however, most of them simply wanted a blow job and some vaginal sex. It became a science to me and a challenge of sorts, first, to make them smile, to make them laugh. Then, to make them come. Then, if they booked another session, to make them come harder. We always used condoms. I got tested every month for STI's and I've never had any."

"You make it sound so . . . business-like," says Zoe. I wonder if she realizes that she has a long strand of hair twirled into a knot on her right forefinger?

"In many ways, it was. Escorting is a business, first and foremost. For the last ten years, I've never had unprotected sex. I've never said I love you unless we were playacting. I've never woken up with a man in my bed whose face I was genuinely happy to see, and I haven't heard anyone utter my real name in a moment of passion."

"Ooh, so you had a fake name? What was it?"

I can't answer that. "It's all very private, you know, like with the clients."

Somehow, my wineglass has been refilled. I can tell Zoe's not going to let me leave it at that, and I realize that Julia's story deserves to be told, even if it's only here, this one time, at this beautiful restaurant. I suck back some more liquid courage and go where my heart is taking me. "But, yes, it was hot! Lots of crazy fantasies were played out in my guest bedroom. So much cum on the sheets, the floor, the wall, on me. But, for many of them, what they wanted most was just to feel like they were good in bed and able to please their lover. So, I taught them how to go down on me, how to talk dirty, and how to go slower than slow, keeping eye contact, until the whole world becomes one big burst of good feelings."

"Did you ever fake it? Like, orgasms I mean," she asks.

"I like sex, and often I would come, but if a guy really wanted that experience and it wasn't happening for me, yes, I would. They're buying a fantasy. And I was paid by the hour. I'm good, but I'm not a miracle worker," I answer.

CHAPTER THIRTY-FOUR

"I get it. But whoa! Six hundred and fifty-three guys! I think you won the kissing contest!" Zoe mimes fanning herself with her hand.

"That is wild! Okay, but be honest. Were some of them repulsive? Like, I don't want to say losers, but . . ." she wrinkles her nose and I stop her right away. Compassion was never Zoe's strong suit.

"I honestly never felt that way. If I had, I couldn't have done it at all. I think every person is pretty cool if you take the time to get to know them, and Kate screened out the bad eggs. Most of the time, I felt like a sex therapist. That's what the experience was like for me anyway. Half therapy, half acting, and all work."

"Who's Kate?"

"My agent, my mentor. She's awesome. I would have been a lot more worried about my safety if it wasn't for her."

"So, you said you did it in your own house?"

"Hotels are expensive, too public, and I could control the ambience in my own space. It was a lot of work, but I was meticulously careful and I did pretty well with it."

"I suppose I never really gave escorting much thought. Like, I guess it happens right under our noses, but it's not really legal, is it? Is that why you decided to stop?"

"To be honest, there's nothing that says I can't start again. But if I did go back to it, I'd have to be open with Belle. I'd also change my persona and start seeing clients who would take me out for actual dates, concerts, nice dinners, and we'd have sex in hotels. But it's not a job I want to do anymore. This fall, I'm going to start teaching full-time."

Zoe hasn't taken a bite of bread yet. I have her complete and undivided attention.

"Belle is growing up so fast. I'll be on my own in a few years when she goes to university, and I like sharing my days with someone. I decided to try dating in real life and I don't want to do that and escort at the same time. Lots of escorts do, but I'm ready for a new adventure. I'm ready to find a man to date, for fun, for company, for conversation. A man who will add energy and a new perspective to my life."

I said all that because it's true. It's exactly how I felt before Alex swept through my door. I did not imagine finding a man to whom I would feel like presenting my whole heart. Showing it all off, the scars, the flaws, and especially the loneliness. I expected I might find a lover. I didn't expect to find love.

"Let me think," says Zoe, tapping her chin. "Who do I know that you might like to go on a date with?"

I choke on my wine and scramble for the linen serviette to hold against my mouth. I have to change this topic.

"What's good to eat here?" I ask.

Sensing that we are ready to talk to him, the hovering waiter hands us our menus, which look like works of art themselves. There is a list of items in a formal calligraphy font, each in a bright colour and set haphazardly on the page as if the writer was eyeballing it and couldn't stay on a straight line.

We decide on crudités, grilled sole, and crème caramel for dessert. Zoe says the pretty menu rarely changes. It's part of the charm and history of La Colombe d'Or.

The longer I sit here, in this one-hundred-year-old country inn and restaurant, the more I'm transported back in time. This is my first visit, but I've read the stories. The Fitzgeralds often dined here with the Hemingways, Picasso kept a bar tab that he paid for in paintings, such as the abstract Flower Vase which is currently hanging over the fireplace. Jean-Paul Sartre and Simone de Beauvoir were frequent visitors, escaping the winter chill of Paris for the hedonistic lifestyle of Provence. And now Zoe and I are making fresh memories here among the ghosts of some of the greatest figures of modern art and literature.

Age doesn't change people as much as we anticipate it will, and so I'm not surprised that Zoe is kind and funny and that we're having

CHAPTER THIRTY-FOUR

a good time. And yet, she hasn't opened up about her troubles. I wonder if I've given too much information and I'm afraid of sounding insincere if I inquire about her family, so I decide to ask about someone who has been on my mind.

The waiter steps up and places our starter on the table. "This is so cool!" I say and take my phone out to snap a picture. It looks like someone has just gone out to the garden and gathered and washed a bunch of radishes, a zucchini, a bulb of fennel, some spring onions and a clump of celery. Then they washed it, chucked it all in a basket and threw in a couple of hard-boiled eggs and some sharp knives for us to chop everything up ourselves. There is also a pretty silver bowl of dip.

I select some radishes and Zoe gets to work on the fennel. "Please, tell me about Bruno," I say.

"Yeah. Okay. Well, you left in October and in January, my menage à trois with Marcel and Bruno ended when they went to Paris to study at the Cordon Bleu school. I visited them there once." She sighs and looks up from her task. "It was fun, but they were busy. It wasn't the same. And the whole au pair thing ended in February, so I went back to Canada."

I realize that Zoe perceives a question as an open invitation to talk about whatever she wants. I imagine this must be a source of frustration for Alex. "What happened to Bruno?" I repeat.

"Right," she pauses to dip and munch on her fennel, then she tosses a few slices onto my plate. "He graduated and started to work in a restaurant in a fancy hotel in Paris. He was so happy. Then he got brain cancer and died six months later." She forces her eyes shut and takes a deep breath. "Marcel was devastated."

A rush of pain seizes my heart and tears pop out of my eyes. "I'm so so sorry! How do you know all this?"

"Marcel and I have kept in touch."

"You've kept in touch for twenty-five years?"

She shakes her head. "Not exactly. When I got back to Canada after the au pair job, my mom informed me that my travelling days were over. I tried to do the right thing. I went to university for journalism, then I got married as soon as I graduated. My mom and her best friend pretty much arranged the whole affair," and she gives a snide snort. "We came here for our fifth wedding anniversary."

Is Zoe aware of how callous she sounds? I don't think so. Looking at her face, I realize we're both more than a little inebriated and the wine is helping the truth to seep out of cracks in our hearts.

"Remember when we sat on Francine's grave and promised we would return to St. Paul?" I ask.

"I never forgot. We pinky swore," she laughs. "I always knew that I had left a little piece of myself here and I'd have to come back some day to pick it up. That's when I reconnected with Marcel, and he told me what happened to Bruno."

We continue to chop and eat for a couple of minutes, talking about the food and our cutting techniques. Zoe has created a long zucchini curl, a radish that looks like a mouse and another that looks like a rosebud, while I attempted to slice the onions lengthwise and ended up with a plateful of unmanageable fibres.

Should I just come right out with it and ask her if she's having an affair with Marcel? Part of me thinks that's exactly what she wants me to do.

My phone vibrates. I check in case it's Belle.

Hey

"You're smiley all of a sudden. Who's that? Your artist friend?" asks Zoe pointing to my phone.

"Ha!" I feign surprised shock at her reference to Omar. "Belle obviously tells Miriam every little thing there is to know."

I shouldn't text Alex back, right here at the table, but I can't resist.

CHAPTER THIRTY-FOUR

>*Hey*
>*Why can't I stop thinking about you?*
>>*I feel the same way.*
>*Guess what I'm doing right now?*

My heart is pounding and my head is spinning.

I stand up and announce, "I'm just going to go use the washroom before the food arrives." Then I try not to stumble as I make my way into the ladies' room.

I enter a stall and sit down on the toilet, well aware that texting from the washroom is a distasteful habit.

>>*Are you dressed?*
>*Not completely.*
>>*Are you alone?*
>*I hope so. I left Noah to pick up lunch. Then I went to the Place Neuve.*
>>*Please tell me you're not half naked in the Place Neuve right now.*
>*Ha! I was driven out of there by a raging hard on and I found a café with a private restroom outside the walls.*
>>*Holy shit. You are so close to me right now. But we're just starting to eat.*
>*Can you help me?*
>>*How's this?*

I open the top two buttons on my blouse and take a quick selfie looking longingly into the camera with my nipples barely showing through my white lacy bra.

>*Beautiful. It's working. More?*

It's really cramped in here, and I don't want to get the toilet in the picture. Should I just go right for a clit shot, or stay with the sweet and sexy vibe? I decide on a little of both.

> *Wait for it. I'm putting on a private show here, just for you.*

I open the remaining buttons and push down my skirt. I have to try a few times to get it right, but I send a short video of my hand sliding over my breasts and down my stomach, stopping just as it enters my panties.

> *Oh baby you are so sexy. I wanna see your ass.*

That sounds like a reasonable request, so I stand up and try reaching around behind myself as I bend forwards.

I hear the door open and Zoe says, "Jade? Are you in here? Oh my god, I have to pee so bad. Remember that time we peed on someone's lawn in Nice? We were so drunk we didn't even bother to go behind their bushes!"

I jerk to stand up and my phone crashes to the floor. Then it skids into the next stall.

I hear Zoe laughing and I feel sick.

"This is nasty," she says. "You're gonna have to give that thing a bath now." Her white sandaled foot nudges my phone back to me.

It landed face down.

"Too right. Thanks. I'll be out in a sec. I just gotta pee," I say. And as I do that, I take deep breaths to calm my racing heart.

> *Damn. I gotta go. This'll have to do.*

CHAPTER THIRTY-FOUR

I snap a quick picture of myself smiling and giving him the middle finger. I hope he's not too disappointed. Then I delete the videos and our conversation.

* * *

"How was your lunch?" asks Belle as she bursts into the room. She walked back into town with Daria and her mother, which I really appreciate because I needed a nap to sober up from my boozy lunch with Zoe.

I stretch my arms overhead and wiggle my toes, "Lunch was delicious and amazing. I promise we'll go there before we leave. La Colombe d'Or is literally a museum and the food was excellent."

Somehow Zoe and I polished off two bottles of wine and shots of some kind of licorice liqueur. We were all giggles as we stumbled out of the restaurant, holding onto each other for balance. Zoe started laughing during dessert when I told her about the client that asked me to dress up in a fish costume and she pretty much didn't stop until she hugged me goodbye in front of her hotel.

Belle pounces on top of me on the bed. "It's only two more sleeps 'til my party! We're going to a real French farm! With goats! And your other lady friend. You have so many friends now! Zoe, Pascale, Omar . . ." She flops beside me and flutters her eyelashes in my direction.

"Belle. About that . . . can you please not tell everyone you meet that I was an escort? It's not socially accepted everywhere. I hope it will be one day, but it isn't now."

"Sorry."

"Don't be sorry. It's okay. I love you."

"I love you, too. What did you get me for my birthday?"

"Hmm. Let me think. A trip to France, a farm party with three friends and, oh, I know." I reach into my purse on the night table, pull out the cicada keyring that I paid a ridiculous amount of money for and hand it to Belle.

Her face lights up. "I love it!" she says. And I laugh because I know she really is thrilled with her wooden insect. But, if things work out, I'll have something else to give her for her birthday that will be a much bigger surprise.

CHAPTER THIRTY-FIVE

I LOVE THE way my breasts look in the bath. Squeaky clean, erect nipples crowning bubble laden orbs like dark cherries on an angel food cake.

Alex should see this. But I've never had bath with Alex. I've also never walked in a park with him, I've never gone shopping for groceries with him, and I've never even watched the news with him. But that doesn't make me sad, it makes me excited for what the future holds. I may be a hopeless optimist, but we've gotten over the hurdle of being in a client/provider relationship. Yesterday, he texted me for sex. Not paid sex, just sleazy, it looks like we're having an affair now, sex. It's not my goal, but it's progress.

And today, I feel like I was able to catch my breath.

This morning, Belle and I assembled the party bags, which look awesome. Each one has a different painting by Picasso and Belle matched them to the personalities of her guests. She chose Harlequin for Rico, Child with a Dove for Daria, and Les Demoiselles d'Avignon for Miriam. Belle said the Demoiselles looked like they were dancing, as she loves to do with Miriam. I didn't tell her that I chose the bag with that particular painting because, not only were they prostitutes, but the women, with their masks and bold stares, look powerful and captivating. We doled out the art supplies, then finished the bags off with an abundance of poufy tissue paper and curly ribbons.

Next, not feeling at all like the tourists we are, Belle and I strolled around the now familiar cobblestone laneways of St. Paul and bought pistachio macarons for Kate, a box of assorted macarons to give to Pascale, and some gummy dinosaurs for Georges. I hope he remembers me and the elaborate dinosaur world we built in the room he shared with his sister Émilie. I know that the DuBois family had many au pairs over the years, and I was only there for one quarter of the length of time of the others, but the twins stole my heart on the first day with their big smiles and even bigger hugs, and leaving them was the most difficult thing I had to do in those six weeks.

Belle and I had a leisurely lunch of salade Niçoise and crêpes Suzette on the patio at the B&B and then Rico's family picked her up. They are going to watch the new Lion King movie in a French cinema and have dinner at a fondue restaurant in Cannes.

I spent the afternoon working on my plan for Belle's birthday surprise. I don't know why the thought of making these phone calls made me so anxious before. Having Alex in my life is changing me for the better. I'm more trusting, more confident, less afraid of adventures. It's scary, but enthralling as well, to open up the tiny world of Belle and me to new people. Love is making me want to see the unknown as an opportunity for even greater happiness.

I sink a little deeper, my body now obscured by bubbles from the neck down, and listen to the happy murmur of conversations on the street. I'm planning the next four days so that one day soon, I can live my truth. Am I satisfied with what I've accomplished so far? Alex sexting me yesterday was a victory. He still wants me. Well, he still wants to have sex with me. The world is filled with sexy women. It's not enough that he misses sex, however, we also had a great day at the beach, and we still have a date planned for Thursday.

Zoe is a mess. A beautiful, hot mess, and I'm more certain than ever that she is having an affair. I can't sense a romantic spark

CHAPTER THIRTY-FIVE

between her and Alex and, obviously, it's me he wants in bed. But that doesn't mean that their marriage is over. Not by a long shot. I feel like their marriage is a story with a life of its own and it's going to fight back against anyone trying to tamper with it. Alex is the pen, Zoe is the paper, but together they have crafted an intricate tale of family and tradition which is intent on maintaining its own trajectory towards a satisfying, if not happy, ending.

I add a few drops of lavender oil to the bath and watch it spread out over the surface of the water causing the bubbles to scurry to the sides of the tub.

Zoe texted me that she and Miriam are shopping in St. Tropez, and they bought Belle an amber necklace with a real dead spider in it for her birthday gift. She also mentioned that Alex and Noah drove to Monaco this morning to go on a helicopter flight. He must really be trying hard to get Noah back on board with their family. That seems pretty extreme, but what would I do if Belle was pulling away from me? How much would I spend and what would I sacrifice to keep her love? I'd like to say it would never come to that, but I know better. Life is full of shitty choices you never intend to have to make.

I pick up my phone to investigate where I might like to have a solo dinner this evening and a text pops up right away.

I can't believe it.

Hey

Stop, I tell myself. Don't answer yet. Don't always be there. You have to make him think it's possible that you might not respond. Perhaps he'll get a nervous flutter in his stomach and contemplate the empty sadness of a life without you. For a long minute, he needs to feel the burn behind his eyes, waiting for your text to appear.

My fingers extend toward the message.

Don't even open it. Wait.

Two minutes is all I can manage. What if he gives up?

> *Hey*
> *Where r u?*
> *I'm in the bath. And I'll prove it.*

I push my chest out of the water and send Alex a picture of my now oily, but still perky breasts.

> *Wow. Just wow. Belle?*
>> *She's out with friends. I hope you were able to finish without me yesterday.*
> *All good. And yet, today I find myself in a similar predicament.*
>> *Where's Noah?*
> *Playing boules. I'm alone. Wish I wasn't.*
>> *Hmm. We could FaceTime?*
> *Not the best. Noah said he'd call when he's on his way back, but it could be soon. Can you text me? I enjoy it so much when you describe what you want to do to me . . .*

I could tell him that he's not paying me for this anymore. I could ask him what the fuck we're doing. But I will do neither of those things.

>> *I step out of the tub, dry off, and join you in the next room. I get wet the second I see you lying naked on the bed, ready for me. But . . .*
> *But what?*
>> *I make you wait. I approach the bed, then turn around and bend forward. Exposing the holes you crave. I reach through my legs, then slide my finger down from my asshole and into . . . ooh . . . I'm so ready for your cock . . . but*

CHAPTER THIRTY-FIVE

I can't decide which one I should choose.
    Just let me text. I enjoy putting on this show for you.

I know how long this should take him. He's contemplating each image I elicit, abandoning himself to my story, becoming more and more aroused. Every time, I count five full seconds before I press send.

K

    I'm rubbing my clit with two fingers, everything is so wet because I know you are staring at me and stroking your cock.
    My clit is hard and I make quick circles. I am close . . . but I want your cock deep inside me when I come . . . so I climb onto the bed. Straddle your long hard body, and my butt is in your face. Please kiss me . . . there

Oh

    Let me text.
    Now I squat and slide my body onto your cock and you moan, as it plunges
    deeper and deeper
    and I squeeze tighter and tighter then
    fuck you faster
    you watch my ass move up and down
    fucking your cock
    you feel that now, don't you?
    the squeezing, the stroking

OMG! . . .

    Close your eyes, feel everything

I'm lying on the bed, damp and frustrated. I dare not take a moment for myself right now. I've got him where I want him. Focused on pleasure. Focused on me.

I watch the clock. Half a minute later, he texts:

> *Thank you. That was amazing. I kept imagining your perfect ass.*
> *So happy I could complete the job today.*
> *It's not a job anymore though, is it?*
> *No. It's not.*

I snap and send a selfie of me lying sideways, head on my pillow with a ridiculous smile.

> *We're so far apart, but so close. Do you feel it?*
> *Yes. You're curled up beside me. Our legs entwined.*

I feel his warm breath on my face.

> *I love you.*

Nothing.

Two minutes. Nothing.

Shit! How could I be so stupid?!

I throw my phone to the foot of the bed, roll on my side, and bury my face in my hands. There is a scream inside me. There is an enormous, frustrated scream eating away at my heart and I need to release it, but I'm far from home, in a fucking tiny town with hundreds of people walking around outside my open window, and with walls as thin as paper.

I wail mutely, pushing my face into the soggy pillow to catch my sobs, then turning my head sideways, like when I was swimming, but this time, I'm gasping for air and struggling to stay afloat.

CHAPTER THIRTY-FIVE

I just offered my heart to the sweetest man on Earth, and he cannot think of a single response.

Not a word.

Nothing.

Feeling like a pathetic desperate loser, I reach again for my phone. Of course, there is no reply. It wasn't on silent. My stupid text was sent fourteen minutes ago and it's still screaming at me from the screen. Delivered and read, but unanswered. Like an unsolicited invitation to a lame party you'd never be caught dead at. No thank you, you think, and just pretend you never saw it.

With three words, I fucked up months of cautious steps, of trying to coax Alex to see me as his shining future. Is this my punishment for daring to rob a troubled friend of her beautiful family?

I may never hear from him again.

I cry out my tears and eventually start to feel sick and like I have to go pee. I stumble into the bathroom and laugh at my hideous reflection. My face is blotchy and my eyes are so swollen, it looks like someone beat me up. There is a clock in here. An ornate wrought iron clock that tells me it's almost eight. No wonder I'm hungry.

Belle will be back soon.

I wash my face and use the toilet. Then I wash my face again and start applying make-up. I'm playing Zoe's game now. Conceal the truth.

I put on a clean bra and panties, then walk to the closet and pick out a blue cotton sundress. Camille washed and ironed it for me this morning and its wrinkle-free fabric and fresh smell offer a glimmer of comfort. I raise my arms, slip the disguise on over my head, and examine my reflection in the mirror with a critical eye. I decide that I will pass for "okay" to my unsuspecting daughter, even though a self-inflicted wound is raging underneath my left breast.

The knock at the door makes me jump. Belle would just come in.

I try to move with a purposeful step to compensate for the sluggishness in my brain, and then swing open the door.

It's Alex.

"The lady at the front said I could come right up. She knew I was Miriam's dad."

His forehead is creased, and his lips are pale. He keeps blinking like his eyes are sore.

I'm so empty right now, all I can come up with is, "Why are you here?"

He extends his arms like he might hug me, but pulls them back. "I'm sorry."

"Oh. I'm sorry, too," I answer, stunned that actual words have come out of my mouth instead of nonsensical blubbering.

Alex shakes his head. "You took me by surprise, that's all. I really care about you, Julia."

"Ha! Thanks for that. I guess I deserve it," I laugh, step back, and let Alex enter the room.

He grits his teeth. "Jade. I know it's Jade. I just . . ."

I raise my hand to cut him off. "I know. I shouldn't have said that over text. Or maybe I shouldn't have said it at all. I don't know what the fuck I'm doing." Standing up has exhausted my energy. I almost sit down on the bed but decide that a chair would be a better choice. Alex doesn't follow my lead and remains standing.

He starts to pace from the door to the window. "I don't want to upset you. And I can't believe I'm doing this to you right now, but I need your help. I also wanted to know that you're okay and I didn't want to text anymore."

"What's the matter?"

"Noah left at four to play boules with some friends. Or that's what he said. He should have been back hours ago. We had plans for dinner. He's not answering my calls or texts." Still pacing, he runs his hands through his hair. "I've been combing the streets for the

CHAPTER THIRTY-FIVE

last hour. Zoe and Miriam will be back soon. I was supposed to be taking care of Noah and making lasting memories. Making him feel like he wants to be part of our family. We had a really good time on the helicopter ride and when we got back, Noah asked to go see his friends for a bit. I thought it would be okay."

Alex's eyes are full of tears and they are starting to run down his cheeks. I stand up, but resist hugging him.

"Do you think he'd take a bus somewhere? Nice, maybe?"

"I doubt it. At home, when he's upset, he just takes off and walks to the park, or the mall. I thought maybe, with both of us looking, we could cover more territory."

"How is his ankle?"

"Pretty good. I think it's still swollen, but if he's determined to go somewhere, he's not going to let it stop him."

He motions out the window, blissfully unaware of the futility of trying to find someone who is determined to be lost.

"Let's get going then. Are you sure you don't want to text Zoe and ask if she's heard from him?"

"I texted her earlier. She and Miriam are on a bus from Saint Tropez that won't arrive in town until ten tonight. She'll just panic. The police aren't about to start looking for him this soon, but I'll call them if he's not back by nine."

Downstairs, I ask Camille and Solange if they can keep an eye on Belle if she returns before I do. Solange looks at Alex, then back at me, nods, and pushes on my shoulder, directing me towards the door. "Go. Don't worry about your little one. She can help us with the baking."

Alex and I step outside. The street is in shadows, but we still have almost an hour until it gets dark. Most of the shops are closed now, and only a few tourists are about. If Noah was walking around, we'd see him, but a fifteen-year-old boy is going to be looking for something fun to do—and somewhere private to do it.

"Do you think he'd buy drugs?"

"Possibly. It's so dangerous to do that here, though. He's not a dumb kid."

"Maybe one of his local friends took him for a ride on their moped? How about you go outside of town and ask people if they've seen him around the boules court or the museum. Find a good photo of him on your phone and send it to me, please. I'll search on the ramparts."

Alex looks like someone punched him in the gut.

"Just go!" I urge him. "I'm sure we can find Noah." I put my hands on his shoulders and look straight into his eyes. "We'll find him."

Then I stride away with exaggerated determination and don't look back.

At the south gate, I take a second to text Rico's dad that Belle may need to stay with Camille and Solange for a bit. Then Alex sends me a text with a picture of Noah, so handsome, with his wavy blonde hair grazing his shoulders as he is about to climb into a helicopter.

I begin my search with a quick visit to the cemetery. It's nearly deserted. I approach the two people I see, a little Italian lady who doesn't speak French or English, and a young man, smoking a cigarette, who says he just arrived, and hasn't seen anyone who looks like Noah. So, I go back through the gate and begin making my way along the eastern rampart.

This is the hour when St. Paul's magic is the strongest. Night is coming on and the ghosts in the walls; the soldiers, the lovers, the artists, who lived and died in this place over the last five hundred years, emerge for a breath of cool night air and gather in the long shadows that fill the narrow streets. I wonder if the ghosts ever sneak into bedrooms and studios to inhabit the bodies of the living, so they can once again feel the tickle of soft lips on skin or the joy of stroking paint onto canvas?

CHAPTER THIRTY-FIVE

Halfway along the eastern rampart, I slow my steps, then sit down on the section of the wall that juts out. This ledge was designed to be used by guards as a perch from which they could get a strategic view across the valley towards the invading Italians. I have no wish to admire the darkening view now, so I turn my back to it. I am hungry and heartsick and glad no one is around to see me falling apart.

"Argh!" I say aloud, scolding myself. I'm supposed to be searching for Noah, yet I continue to ruminate on my actions, my future, my love. The love that came to me like a burning hot star flung out of the night sky and somehow, I caught it. But I couldn't keep hold. Of course, I couldn't hold onto Alex.

What was I thinking on that sunny day in April when my old friend's husband strode through my front door? It was my last day of escorting. Was I simply too afraid to step out from behind the persona of *Just Julia* and tackle the world as myself? Do I really love Alex, or did I just decide to love him, because he seemed to fit the bill for the job of keeping Jade Matthews company in her old age? Or worse, did I instantly seize on the opportunity to best my former rival, Zoe? The girl who lured away my crush when I was eighteen years old. How ridiculous was that? How ridiculous am I being right now?

I don't trust myself to think rational thoughts about love at this moment. I shake my head and return to the urgent matter at hand. Analysis is a comfortable activity for my brain. I will use logic to solve the mystery of Noah's disappearance.

Noah is a Canadian teenager in southern France, in July. An obvious tourist.

Noah is tall for a fifteen-year-old, and he converses with the confidence of someone older.

Alex thinks that Noah would be wary of buying drugs in France. The legal drinking age here was raised from sixteen to eighteen over a decade ago. So, he's not likely to be in a bar. However, he could be hanging out just about anywhere with friends, they could be drinking or . . .

I jump up. I've got it! I'm sure I've got it, but I don't want to get Alex's hopes up just yet. I send him a quick text.

All quiet on the eastern rampart. You having any luck?
He did play boules until about 6. But he left by himself.
Just keep looking. I know we'll find him.

CHAPTER THIRTY-SIX

Conversations with Clients: 7 Reasons Why He Won't Leave His Marriage: Reason #7: The Children

Percy #124

P124: My son is being scouted for the NHL.
JJ: How wonderful for him! You must be really proud.
P124: It's literally all I've ever wanted. I never miss a practice or a game. He's such a great kid.
JJ: Do you play hockey as well?
P124: I made it to Junior A, but then I tore my rotator cuff, and I could never shoot the puck as hard after that.
JJ: Any fun weekend plans?

Percy #375

P375: My daughter and I are going geocaching.
JJ: What is that?
P375: Thousands of people do it. You hide containers filled with objects for other people to find using an app and GPS trackers.
JJ: Very cool.
P375: Yeah. My daughter was so excited last weekend when we found a cache with wildflower seeds in it.

JJ: Will you plant them?
P375:   For sure. We have a five-acre property and we're making it into a self-sufficient homestead. I've always felt that it isn't my job to prepare my child for the world, it's my job to prepare the world for my child.

"Just Julia" was marketed towards married men and so, it follows, that I've met a lot of dads. In my experience, the majority of dads had children because their wives wanted them. The minority are the dads who spearheaded the project. Hopefully, both parties discussed the topic before they got married, but these are the dads I'm referring to, the ones that actually got married because they wanted to start a family.

Deeply devoted fathers crave dynastic continuation and the sense of purpose that comes with being a father. They prioritize family time to play catch, read stories, or build a snowman. They inhabit a familiar, youthful mindset by being with their children and they feel that they are the best versions of themselves in their role as a parent. Often a quarter of their time with me is spent bragging—showing pictures, celebrating successes, and telling stories about their children.

What's different between dads and moms, though, is that when a family splits up, it's usually the dads who lose out on spending time with their children. Even if that ever stops being true, shared custody is still just half of what you had before. These dads will stay in a less than happy marriage in order to spend every day with their children.

Children grow up and move away from home. But, even as empty nesters, these dads can be so devoted to the idea of family that makes it impossible for them to leave their wife. They struggle with monogamy while wholly embracing the concept of family, and they hope that their children will escape inheriting the demons that compelled their father to stray into the arms of an escort.

CHAPTER THIRTY-SIX

When I saw those tears in Alex's eyes because he couldn't find Noah, I had my answer. It would be so much simpler if he wanted me to convert to Judaism, if he was afraid that I would take his money, or even if he still fervently loved Zoe.

I don't see how I can compete with Noah and Miriam, and I wouldn't like myself very much if I even considered trying.

CHAPTER THIRTY-SEVEN

OFFICIALLY, THE CEMETERY closes at 7:30 p.m. That's when the flimsy front gate is locked by whichever townsperson is currently employed as the caretaker. However, the gate is really just symbolic of the respectful night's sleep that should be accorded to the dead who endure throngs of tourists disturbing their eternal rest all day long, every day of the year. After hours, the sides and back of the cemetery can still be accessed through the woods that skirt the town, either by hopping a short stone wall, or by going far enough down the hill and entering through the trees. This is where Zoe and Marcel disappeared to last week. They took one of the paths that knot their way through the woods on the steep sides of the hill upon which St. Paul is perched.

I'm heading back to the cemetery, but this time, I'm not going to walk right into it and announce my presence to the young man who I assume will still be lurking there, keeping a watchful eye out for local authorities. Instead, I walk the length of the ramparts, exit the town through the north gate, and use the footpath that borders the base of the wall to make my way towards the woods beyond the gravestones.

I leave the gravel footpath and take a side trail that looks like it gets some regular, if not frequent use. The scrubby grass is tramped down just enough to guide me through the maze of pine and deciduous trees. The sun has made its quick Mediterranean exit, dropping out

CHAPTER THIRTY-SEVEN

of sight over the horizon and leaving me with only a faint afterglow with which to help me pick my way forward.

I'd like to turn on the flashlight on my phone, but I need to rely on my eyes adjusting to the dimness. It makes me move slowly, and that's a good thing, because, that way, I won't be heard.

I have a good idea where I'm headed. There were a few decent sized, relatively level, clearings in the area when I was here twenty-five years ago. I spent many afternoons in one with Zoe, Marcel, and Bruno.

I pause a moment and close my eyes. My phone vibrates, but I ignore it. I've heard something ahead. I dare not even remove my phone from my pocket for fear of the light being seen. I place one foot in front of the other, careful of thick roots and the odd rock. At a break in the trees, I look up to the right and I can make out the top of the walls, about fifty feet higher than I am at the moment. The three-quarter moon is now visible over the trees to my left.

A deep male voice yells, "Putain! Attend là-bas! Lucie n'est pas prête."

Why did that man ask them to wait for Lucie to be ready? Everyone is laughing now. I would guess that I hear between five and ten voices.

I take a few more steps and push aside boughs as I pass through some fragrant cedar trees. Like a switch has been turned on, I see a bunch of lights up ahead. Maybe fifty feet away? It looks like cellphones and one light that is brighter than the rest. This must be some kind of sex party and I'm pretty sure they are all filming it.

My phone vibrates again. It's got to be Alex, but I dare not check. How much closer can I get? How much closer do I want to get?

But what if it's Belle texting?

Shit. It must be nearly nine o'clock. I have to take a chance and move forward to check if Noah is in the group. It's getting louder, lots of swearing and rude jokes, and the grunting and rhythmic smacking of flesh on flesh. I shouldn't be here, but Noah shouldn't be here either. He's much too young for this.

About twenty feet away, I crouch down on the damp ground and conceal my body in the rough boughs of a pine tree. I feel like I'm in a darkened theatre and the one bright light is illuminating a lewd scene that I am glad is obscured by a dozen or so trees. Without trying to analyze who is doing what, I focus on trying to identify anything I can about the individuals. Some are in bright light, some in shadows, and others I can only locate by their muffled conversation. My French is good, but I'm not fluent in the jargon of the streets and I have no desire to follow any of their chatter. I am close enough though to discern two mature female voices, giving directions in an authoritative tone. This is a job for them. I pray that they will get paid what they deserve.

A group in the shadows moves forward, like a line up at the grocery store, and Noah steps into the light. I stifle a sob.

I'm crouching now, and I dare not leap up. So, I tip forward and crawl away in the grass on my hands and knees until I am concealed about one hundred feet away. I pull out my phone and check the messages from Alex.

Anything?
It's nearly nine. This is useless, isn't it?
Please text me back and then I'll call the police.

I'm glad he's waiting for my response before getting anyone else involved. At least I can save Zoe the knowledge of her son's transgressions.

I can see Noah. He's okay.
Where r u?

CHAPTER THIRTY-SEVEN

> *Too hard to explain. Please do as I say. Send Noah a text. Tell him you know exactly where he is and you want him to leave right now.*

I rack my brains for the perfect thing for him to say.

> *Tell him that you won't ever mention what he's doing with a girl named Lucie, but he must leave immediately.*

Where r u?

> *Just do it!*

A very long minute passes before Alex texts me back.

Thank God. Noah finally answered. I can't thank you enough. He said he'll be back in ten minutes. What's going on?

> *I can't text now. Just give Noah a big hug and ask him to never do that again. I gotta go.*

CHAPTER THIRTY-EIGHT

"PLEASE CAN I keep him?" asks Belle, cuddling a fuzzy brown and white baby goat that has its head nestled in the crook of her neck. When she found out that the two-day old kid's mother was unable to care for it, Belle took it upon herself to fill the role and it promptly fell asleep in her arms.

"It's not really me you need to ask, is it?" I look at Georges, whose smile is as warm as the Mediterranean sun. The wide grin from his little boy face is now on the face of a handsome man who, I found out today, is the father of two five-year-old twin boys. Their mom, Daniella, is inside the barn, feeding the animals with all the other children in tow, but Belle is walking around, showing off her baby goat and she won't put him down.

"I'll teach you how to give him a bottle now," says Georges, and he steers Belle and her bundle back into the barn.

"We're going to have to pry that thing out of her arms you know," I say to Pascale, who is standing beside me, looking right at home in rubber boots and cutoff overalls with her dark hair, now peppered with grey, pulled back into a braid that almost reaches her waist.

"I know how she feels," says Pascale. "After Alain left us, I had to drive around the countryside to pick up stock for the shop and I too, fell in love with the goats. After the divorce, I used my half of the money from selling the store to buy La Chévre Brune."

CHAPTER THIRTY-EIGHT

She waves her arms, encompassing all her land, ten rambling acres in the shadow of the Alps. There is a stone farmhouse with a terracotta tile roof and bright blue shutters, a modern grey steel barn, an outbuilding where the goat's milk soap is manufactured, and several fenced pastures. Georges explained to us that he and his mom started with twelve goats, and they are now up to one hundred and eighty. They sell goat's milk to a local cheesemaker, and they sell their soap to local shops as well as online. Daniella also planted a market garden where they grow root crops and lettuce for local restaurants. Pascale is the picture of happiness, and today, she has given me a powerful glimpse of what living your best life looks like.

I've been waiting all day for a quiet moment with her. "Can we speak in private?"

She nods and we walk to some bales of hay in the shade of an olive tree in front of the house. Pascale probably has her morning coffee out here, contemplating the ever-changing mountain landscape in the Alpes-Maritimes.

"It's been a fabulous day," I say and give her a hug. She smells like roses. She always smelled like roses.

"I'm so glad you came back to Provence," she says, smiling so hard that I see the lines of wisdom appear at the corners of her eyes. "You didn't get to stay long enough the first time."

I nod in agreement. "I definitely left with some unfinished business. How is Émilie?"

"She is selling real estate in the Loire Valley. I think she's happy. She likes a busy life."

I decide to go for it. "What happened to Alain?"

"He left us for a truffle seller in Marseilles."

My lips feel tight. I may not be ready to exorcise this demon, but I've started, so I can't stop now. "I'm not sure I should be saying this to you. It's not about something you did. But it feels like a secret that I need to tell someone," I say.

"Whatever it is, you obviously need to get it out. A secret can be an overwhelming burden to carry around. You can tell me," says Pascale, placing a hand on my arm.

"Hey," Zoe interrupts, walking out of the house with a glass of wine. Then she sits down on her own bale of hay, looking like an outcast from the eighties. After lunch, when all the gifts were opened and exclaimed over, she agreed to get her blonde hair chalked in rainbow-coloured stripes, and both she and I are sporting fluorescent pink nails. "Sorry if I'm intruding. But I overheard you and now I'm curious. What's up?"

"You're good. Stay. I need to tell Pascale what happened on the day I got the call about my dad's heart attack."

"Go on," says Pascale.

"When Alain told me about my dad's heart attack, we were alone in the kitchen. I was upset about dad and about having to leave so soon, and Alain hugged me because I was crying."

A shiver passes through me. Pascale must feel it and her hand tenses on my arm. Out of the corner of my eye, I can see that she has closed her eyes.

"He stuck his hand in my shorts."

At the same moment that Pascale says, "Oh, Jade," Zoe leaps over beside me and wraps her arms around me.

"It's not your fault, babe. Not your fault at all," says Zoe.

"She's right," says Pascale. "It makes me so sad that happened to you in my home."

"That was the end of it, though. I yelled at him, and he stopped," I say.

"It wasn't the end for you though, was it?" asks Zoe.

"I suppose not," I say. "But I'd like it to end now."

"Maybe you might like to contact Alain? You deserve an apology," suggests Pascale. "I can give you his information. Or I can tell him this myself if you'd prefer."

CHAPTER THIRTY-EIGHT

Pascale has always been so easy to talk to. "Thank you. I will write to him and let him know that touching me in that way was assault. But I want you to know that what he did is the reason why I didn't stay in touch. Even so, I never forgot about you and Georges and Émilie. I lost my mother a long time ago, and you were the perfect mom for me to model myself after."

"Merci," says Pascale and she kisses my head.

I turn to Zoe, wishing she would say something funny to lighten the moment, but her face is running with tears.

"I just can't fucking take this anymore!" she says, downs the last of her wine, and walks back into the house.

CHAPTER THIRTY-NINE

"GEORGES LET ME name the baby goat. I called him Bonbon because he was so sweet," says Belle when we slip under the covers, in our pajamas, way past Belle's bedtime.

I love that name! Your party was so great! And now you're twelve years old! I can hardly believe it," I say. It's been a long day, but I've got one more revelation to make.

I reach over to the bedside table and pick up my phone. "I've got another surprise for your birthday," I tell her. "I've been thinking a lot about the fact that you would like to meet your father. I reached out to the five other ladies who were on the bridal shower trip to Mexico with me. I asked them to send me every picture they had of the trip. In one of the photos of all of us in the restaurant, I was able to identify Carlos, your father, in the background. He's standing sideways, serving someone a drink."

Her face is a silent scream, wide mouth and eyes. She lunges for my phone. "Oh my god! Really?! That's him?"

"Yeah, it's him. The girl who sent me the picture remembered him as well."

"So, does he want to meet me?" She pops out of bed like she's ready to get dressed and leave for the airport at once.

"Not so fast. I told you he was from El Salvador, and he was only working temporarily in Mexico. I hired a private detective who is going to try to track him down. I don't know how long it will take,

CHAPTER THIRTY-NINE

or if it will even work. But I promise to tell you everything I find out. You're a big girl, now. And, whatever happens, we'll always have each other."

"So they haven't found him yet?"

"Not yet, but they're looking."

She gets back into bed and hugs me. "Send me that picture, okay?"

"It's on its way now," I say, and hit send.

When I was raising Belle by myself for all those years, the thought of anyone else having a claim to her terrified me. But I'm now convinced that she will never stop probing me, and that trying to find out whatever I can about Carlos and his family is the right thing to do. I need to help Belle find the answers to the questions she has, as well as to the ones she hasn't even thought of yet.

Ten minutes later, Belle is asleep beside me, iPad clutched to her chest. I reach over, ease it out of her grasp, and give her a kiss on her temple.

I know there are many aspects to her personality that have nothing to do with the half of her DNA that she got from me. I had only known Carlos for a few days and all our exchanges were pleasantries until, feeling drunk and lonely on my last night in Mexico, I decided to proposition him. I only remember that he was friendly, kind, and gentle. But Belle has the right to know everything she can about her father, and he has the right to know that he has a daughter.

I hesitate to turn my phone off for the night. Alex sent me two texts today, but I ignored them both. I wanted to focus on Belle's birthday and I'm trying to quell the sadness that rises up inside me like bile whenever I think about his rejection of my love. Even if I did make the horrific choice to tell him that I love him over text, the result would have been even more painful if I had to witness his dismayed reaction in person.

Alex wants an explanation of what Noah was doing with Lucie, and I will tell him. But, for Noah's sake, I wanted Alex to have some time to get over his initial panic so he can proceed cautiously with his son. The obvious parallel between the actions of father and son is disturbing, but there is a world of difference between their methods. It just proves that almost everyone craves physical attention and that men are very resourceful in their ability to find it. I'd like to think that Noah's choice to participate in the lurid sex party was a spontaneous decision, not a calculated act. But either way, he did agree to leave the woods immediately when he was found out.

Sleep still feels far away. I'll see if Alex is awake now.

What's up?

His reply is immediate.

Thank you for answering. It sounds like the birthday party was a big success.

It was great. How was kayaking?

Beautiful. But Noah was quiet. I was glad we went with a group. I don't know how to talk to my boy anymore. Will you tell me what he was doing? Please?

I will, but I don't want to text.

We could meet at the hotel tomorrow?

I don't think that's a good idea. I have another one. You're supposed to be golfing on Thursdays, so let's go golfing. We can tell people what we're doing that way. No more sneaking around.

I didn't know you golfed.

There's a lot of things you don't know about me. Can you get a tee time? I drop Belle off for her day at the museum at 9.

I'm sure that can be arranged. Thank you. See you in the morning. Goodnight.

CHAPTER THIRTY-NINE

I put my phone on silent, curl up onto my side facing away from my sleeping daughter, and try to cry myself to sleep with as little noise as possible.

CHAPTER FORTY

ZOE AND HER kids are getting in a taxi for Nice as Alex and I set off to golf in Grasse. She still has rainbow hair, now pulled into a ponytail that is secured with a pearl encrusted scrunchie. I suspect that she is suffering from a wicked hangover, yet she somehow always looks pretty and put together.

"Since when do you play golf, Jade?" she asks.

"Since I had a job as a cart tart during the summers in university. I got lots of tips and a few free lessons," I laugh.

"Well, you're a better sport than I am," says Zoe. "Alex has tried to get everyone in this family to golf with him, but none of us would bite."

She approaches me with her arms open for a hug, then whispers in my ear, "I hope he doesn't bore you to death talking about the physics of his golf swing."

She has no idea. No idea what a wonderful companion her husband is, how much I desire him, or how happy he makes me by being exactly himself. And that sucks, but so would spending the rest of my life feeling like a total shit for breaking up my friend's family by informing her of this when Alex doesn't love me back.

Zoe moves on from me, puts her arms around Alex, gives him a peck on the cheek, and says, "Don't forget you're taking Miriam and Belle to the concert tonight."

CHAPTER FORTY

"Right, Ed Sheeran live under the stars in Cannes. Wouldn't miss it for the world!" he says pointing his finger at his daughter who is beaming at him with her chin thrust forward and a satisfied grin spreading across her face.

The concert was another birthday present to Belle from Miriam. She is as generous as her mother, although, if I may be cynical, it's not her own money that is funding Miriam's benevolence. Thanks to Alex's job, along with a hearty dose of hereditary affluence, the Greens are a wealthy family, and, on the surface, they seem to inhabit a world filled with sunny days. Just like magic, money infiltrates its way into their everyday life and affords them the time and space to explore their interests. Miriam talks about how her schedule is packed full of fun activities like shopping sprees at secondhand stores, volunteering to walk the dogs at the Humane Society, and cooking up four course meals with her friends. She is determined that she will expand her schedule to include regular sleepovers with Belle once we're back in Canada and that she will introduce Belle to her large posse of teenage friends. I imagine the Green's sphere of influence as a spiralling world with Alex at the centre, quietly doling out money, along with his love and protection. It's got to feel good to be able to orchestrate that kind of quality of life for the people you love.

Miriam and Belle informed me that the drive from our house to Miriam's in Toronto is only twenty-seven minutes, and the assumption seems to be that I'll be the chauffeur. Am I destined to be a permanent odd man out—that single friend that gets invited with her daughter, and who then tags along on outings like a loose thread? Will I be helplessly stuck inside the fantasies in my own head, imagining Alex naked when he greets Belle and I at the front door, hoping to touch his hand as we pass the potatoes across the dinner table, or closing my eyes and basking in his voice as he holds forth about his lab's latest scientific discovery from a lawn chair in the backyard on a sunny summer day? Can I really become a neutral spectator to the life of the man I love?

"Hey, Jade!" Zoe motions towards me and calls, "Don't let him try to tell you that it's not really golf unless you play two rounds in a row. I swear that man can think of nothing else!"

I force a smile and wave back at her. Then we all climb into our respective taxis and Alex laughs at Miriam who is making faces in the back window as they pull out in front of us. I can barely see Noah because he is slumped low with his hoodie pulled down over his baseball cap. But he's there, with his mother and his sister, not hanging around with whichever lowlifes it was that enticed him into the woods two nights ago.

In the back seat, Alex and I are separated by a chasm of about eight inches. This hurts, but I'd still rather be here than anywhere else. I love looking at Alex's strong profile and smelling his woody cologne. His presence is scintillating, as usual, and I can't help but feel the happy flutter in my heart and the sweet ache in my loins.

But I can try to ignore it.

I decide I'd be better off chatting than letting my imagination run wild when there's no scenario in which I can end up feeling anything other than frustrated, so I lean right up against the car door and start talking. I begin our conversation by explaining my plan to use a private investigator to find Belle's biological father, Carlos.

"I'm really impressed and, to be honest, shocked, by your decision to try to find Belle's father. You must be terrified. The guy could be a serial killer for all you know."

"I'm fairly certain he is not a serial killer. He was a sweet guy. He even brought a bunch of towels from the pool cupboard so we wouldn't get all sandy while having sex on the beach," I laugh at how lame that must sound. "Anyway, I have to make an effort. If we don't find him, Belle will eventually be angry at me for not trying sooner. It's something that could come between us."

CHAPTER FORTY

He nods again. "Being a parent is tough."

"And wonderful. This trip has been a great experience for Belle, and I want you to know how grateful I'll always be to you for bringing us here. But now she just wants to go home and meet her dad. I spent all breakfast explaining to her that it may never happen."

The taxi driver, ignoring us, is chatting with someone through his phone, but Alex lowers his voice, "What was Noah doing the other night?"

He's waited long enough to hear this. I explain the scene in the woods in as few words as possible. "A long line of men and, it would appear, boys, were having sex with two women in a wooded area on the hillside. Someone was filming it, probably just for their own amusement, but who knows?"

"Oh. I see," Alex says, and he looks away and shakes his head.

"Try not to be angry with Noah."

"He took a lot of money out of my wallet that day."

"Good," I reply.

He looks back at me, confused.

"I hope some of that money made it into the hands of those women."

"You would say that," Alex says. Then he sees my perturbed reaction and puts his hand on my arm as if in apology. "And I understand completely."

"You'd better understand," I say. "Sex work is work. People need to acknowledge that. But what happened there was not okay. Whoever it was that enticed Noah to go into the woods that night was exploiting him for money."

I take a deep breath, grateful that Alex hasn't removed his hand from my arm and say, "Sorry. I know I'm preaching to the choir. It just startled me when I saw that Noah was actually intending to participate."

A new thought occurs to me. "Those women are at fault for not checking the age of their clients. But, they could also be survival sex

217

workers trying to make a rent payment." I throw up my hands. "It's a fucking mess."

"You're right. But thank god you were there! I'm amazed that you figured out where Noah was. And crawling around on the hillside in the dark! You could have been hurt."

"I'm okay," I say quietly, and turn my head to look out the window in case a rogue tear manages to erupt from my eyes.

His concern for my physical well-being should be touching, but it underscores his avoidance of the damage he has done to my heart. He's acting like I never said I love you. Do people declare their love for him so often that it isn't worth comment? Did he think I was joking?

Or is he overwhelmed? I had months to mull over this quagmire called love. He has barely had any time to wonder about our divergence from a transaction-based relationship. Up until a week ago, I was still his dirty little secret.

I take a few deep breaths and realize that, as much as I want to be angry with him, Alex's physical presence in this small space, and his hand that is still on my arm, are instilling a welcome state of calm in my soul. He may not have fallen madly in love with me on this trip, but something curious did happen. We became friends. And, by putting ourselves and our families in close proximity, our daughters created a connection that could alter the path of their lives.

We pass the last few minutes of the ride through the French countryside in contented silence, like we used to do when we watched the baby robins from my upstairs landing.

"Ah!" says Alex when the undulating fairways and manicured greens of the Saint Luc Golf Course come into view. "I'm so glad you suggested this!" And he lifts his hand and taps it on mine in a brief gesture of thanks.

Inside the clubhouse, I use the washroom while Alex pays for us, then we head back out to pick up our rented clubs and pull carts.

CHAPTER FORTY

"I usually bring my clubs with me. It's not quite the same this way," he explains as we make our way to the first tee along a path lined on both sides with lush palm trees.

And in that moment, I realize how much of a sacrifice Alex made to arrange our Monday and Thursday meetings to coincide with his golf dates. I've spent enough time on golf courses to recognize the difference between the guy who does it to get away from his nagging wife, the guy who does it to impress his boss, and the guy who feels that, given the right alignment of the stars, he could have become a professional golfer. Alex is definitely the latter and this is his happy place.

The marshal directs us to play in a foursome with two energetic brothers from Marseilles who begin the round by arguing about which of them will get to drive their golfcart. They seem intent on outperforming each other with the enthusiasm of pro wrestlers.

Alex and I are walking, and, from our comfortable distance, the brothers' antics provide an amusing distraction. On the second hole, the taller one attempts to hit his ball through a lilac bush, and it gets stuck inside. On the sixth hole, the balding one removes his shoes and socks to retrieve his ball from a water hazard and then sinks in the mud up to his knees.

"It's a funny game, isn't it?" Alex says as we approach the seventh tee. "Makes people do crazy things."

I laugh, "To me, a round of golf is four hours of being in one's own little world. Plus, there's always beautiful scenery, old and new friends, and lots of laughs. It's enough time to feel like you've stepped away from your life, but not so much that you forget about it entirely."

"Well said," says Alex. But he looks confused, like he wants to say something else and changes his mind.

Then he steps up and hits a perfect drive over the water hazard and we watch it bounce out of sight down the fairway.

I know that Alex's mind is preoccupied by his family, but I am sensing the tension fizzle out of his frame with each stroke. There is a familiar rhythm to this game that is perhaps making his world seem less off kilter. He takes easy strides, the corners of his lips resting in a half smile, his shoulders slack—and, just like I used to do in bed, I find it easy to follow his rhythm as we make our way around the course.

On the twelfth tee, I catch him looking up and down at my bare legs and I decide that we don't need to say it out loud. I don't need to hear him tell me it's over. If we do this right, maybe we can slip into a new routine. I'll just have to learn to live with it. I haven't lost anything I truly possessed. I came to France and watched a silly dream float away like a red balloon whose string was too insubstantial to hold on to. For now, I'm happy to be playing this game with him. And I have learned an important lesson. Love does not conquer all. It barely scrapes the surface of a well-crafted marriage.

"Great shot!" Alex says to me as I tee off on the long par three from the ladies' tee. The brothers race off in their cart to search for their balls in the cedar hedge and the two of us fall into step.

"Thanks, this is really fun," I say, and I decide that this collegial atmosphere would be a favourable one in which to open up about the past. "I told you before that I'd tell you how I came to have the sketch of Zoe that is in my house. I could do that now if you'd like to hear it?"

"I would. Yes."

"I spent six weeks in St. Paul with Zoe in 1999 because we were both au pairs. In our time off, we hung out with a lot of local boys and one of them was an aspiring artist named Raphael. He drew that sketch."

"Zoe mentioned him a couple of times over the years. She has a similar sketch to yours, smaller and not framed, that she keeps with some other souvenirs of France in her bottom drawer. I can't

CHAPTER FORTY

believe now that it took me so long to put them together," he says. Alex looks happy to have solved the mystery. "But why did you hang Zoe's picture in your bedroom?"

"Well, what happened was that Raphael asked us both to model for him, but he also asked us both to keep it a secret. I didn't discover what was going on until the day I learned about my father's heart attack."

We have arrived at my ball. Alex waits for me to take my chip shot, then asks, "And what was going on?"

"Zoe wasn't just posing for him; she was having sex with Raphael."

"Huh," Alex shakes his head, then bites his lower lip. I can see he's trying to put two and two together. I wonder how much of her past Zoe confided to him before they got married. She must have had at least ten sexual partners by the time she left St. Paul. But what does that matter? It was her business to tell him or not.

I continue, "Well, I had a huge crush on Raphael. By accident, I walked in on him and Zoe in a very compromising situation. I was jealous and I overreacted. The next day, before I left for the airport, I snuck into the studio and stole her sketch. I had fully intended to take one of the ones he had done of me, but when I saw the sketches of Zoe, I just grabbed one and ran," I raise my hands in resignation. "The sketches he did of Zoe were far better than the ones he had done of me. I suppose I hung it there because it's beautiful. And it's sexy. And if I'm being totally honest, maybe I wanted her to have to watch me getting some for a change."

Alex chuckles and says, "Well, now I know."

"Now you know," I repeat. Now that he knows, it still doesn't change a thing.

On the green, the taller brother, whose name is Claude, asks Alex for advice about lining up his putt.

Claude makes his par and decides that he needs Alex's help with every aspect of his game. Alex is eager to impart his wisdom and I'm happy to take a back seat for the rest of the round and observe him doing something he loves.

It's nearly two p.m. when we head to the clubhouse for some much-needed air conditioning, baguette sandwiches, and beer. The conversation flows, because we have eighteen holes of good and bad golf shots to discuss, as well as the putting successes or failures of the golfers we are watching through the floor to ceiling window as they finish up on the last green.

When we're almost done our food, I say, "In the interest of complete disclosure, there is something else I would like you to know."

Alex looks apprehensive, but says, "Go ahead."

I swallow hard. "I wasn't sure, but I was fairly certain, when you arrived at my house the first time, that you were Zoe's husband."

"How did you know? Kate said she never tells last names."

"It was your voice. I've listened to the Zoe's Green Family podcast since she started doing it two years ago. I always felt a little sad about how everything had ended between us. Zoe and I were pretty good friends during the short time I was here."

Alex nods. "So, what did you think afterwards, when, I suppose, you googled pictures of Zoe Green's husband and it confirmed your suspicion?"

I will not lie to Alex. I look down at my plate at the half-eaten tomato and cheese sandwich and scrumpled serviette. "I thought you were the most amazing lover I had ever known. And I have known a lot of lovers. And not one of them made me feel anything close to what I felt with you."

Alex puts down his beer. It makes a louder noise than he must have intended, and I'm taken aback. "What is happening here, Jade?"

I think of Miriam, a teenage girl who idolizes her father. And of Noah, a boy who needs the guidance of someone he can look up to. I look at the tight lines around Alex's eyes and answer, "Nothing.

CHAPTER FORTY

Nothing is happening here. We're two acquaintances who had a nice day playing golf. That's it."

* * *

I always give Alex a lot of credit for being super intelligent, but the penny doesn't appear to drop until we're in the taxi, halfway back to St. Paul, after ten awkward minutes of silence.

"So, if you knew who I was, you also knew that it would be likely that you would run into Zoe in this postage stamp sized town," he says.

"I tried very hard not to be recognized. My suitcase is full of unflattering dresses and big hats. But yes, I took that risk and I apologize for it."

Alex leans back and sighs, "If I'm honest, I took the biggest risk by inviting you here in the first place."

I would like to ask him, *So then why did you bring me here?*, but I've been in the business for ten years. I know why. When you mix sex and danger, it makes a very potent drink.

The air conditioning doesn't seem to be working in this taxi. I feel itchy with sweat and my hair is clinging to the bare skin on my back.

"You did take a huge risk," I say after a pause. "You offered me and my daughter a free trip to France. It was impossible for me to turn down an opportunity like that. I can afford to give Belle a decent life, but not one that includes European luxury vacations."

My phone vibrates. I check the message from Zoe, then inform Alex, "They've just picked up Belle, and the girls are getting ready, whatever that means, at your hotel. It was really kind of you to volunteer to take them to the concert tonight. I'm going to have a nap."

He doesn't respond. He looks sad.

Why am I feeling sorry for him? He's the one who ignored my love text.

I'm so frustrated with myself. I know very well that this is how men work. Why did I think he would toss away his life for me when all he was interested in was hot sex with no commitment?

I need to be a lot stronger than this. I need to believe in my core that self-love is enough. And, on top of that, I should prioritize the love I have for my child which is a precious gift. That's enough. It's been enough for twelve years. It can keep being enough for as many more years as I have left.

"I wonder what Zoe will be doing tonight?" Alex ventures.

I stare at him blank faced. Why do I keep getting the feeling that he is asking me to spy on her? "Maybe you should ask her yourself," I suggest.

"You're right," he says and wipes his hand through his sweaty curls. I remember washing his hair for him in the shower. Massaging his scalp with my fingers while he knelt down in front of my slightly parted legs and flicked my clit with his tongue. How did we get from there to here? Oh yeah. Feelings. I caught a bad case of feelings that I'm striving to purge from my heart.

"Oh, for fuck's sake!" I say, throwing up my hands in frustration. I can't watch this train wreck of a marriage anymore. Zoe is too distraught and emotional to be able to keep this festering secret under wraps much longer and I'd rather be the bearer of bad news than have one of his children find out by accident. "I will tell you everything I know."

Alex looks like a starving man who's just been handed a loaf of bread. "Thank you so much, Jade." And he gets that wide eyed and super focused look.

That's something I love about Alex. He's a fabulous listener, very attentive and he never interrupts me. No. That's just a good quality I will appreciate about him from now on.

"Here goes," I say. "Not only did she have sex with Raphael, but Zoe was also having sex with Marcel when we were au pairs. I think

CHAPTER FORTY

that Raphael was just a fling. Zoe was seriously into Marcel and when we were on the hike last weekend, she couldn't wait to tell me about their crazy hot sex that continued for her whole au pair stint."

Alex's face is giving nothing away. He's waiting till he has all the information. I take a deep breath and get ready to deliver the final blow. "One week ago, before she knew I was in St. Paul, I saw Zoe and Marcel in the cemetery. She was crying and he held her for a second. But they looked guilty about it, and they left the cemetery together and went into the woods."

He's still not saying anything.

"So, there's your answer," I say like I've spent too much time explaining a simple math problem. "I think they're having an affair. It's probably been going on for years."

Alex scrunches his mouth up to one side. "That can't be right. Marcel and his husband Bjorn are close family friends. We were all at their wedding . . . uh . . . nine years ago, I think?"

"I don't know what you want me to say now," I answer. "I'm not a detective. I'm a teacher who used to be an escort. That's all I've got."

He scrolls through his phone and shows me a picture of a bunch of beautiful, smiling people standing on a pier with blue waves rolling behind them. Marcel, with a lot more hair and a neat beard, is standing beside a hunk of a man whose bulging muscles refuse be contained by the open necked dress shirt he is wearing. To the left of Marcel stands Alex, looking like a million bucks in a black tux, and Zoe, ridiculously photogenic, in a shimmering pink cocktail dress. To the right of the grooms are much smaller versions of Noah, in a navy suit, and Miriam, in a turquoise pouf dress with a garland of daisies in her hair. Everyone is fluid and smiling like somebody just told them a great joke.

"Your kids are so little there!"

"Gay marriage was legalized in France in 2013, and the wedding was two years later, in Nice. There were only twenty guests, and we had a fabulous time. The kids call Marcel and Bjorn uncle. Both men were kayaking with Noah and I yesterday." Alex shrugs his shoulders, opens his hands, and shakes his head in disbelief. "Marcel and Bjorn have even stayed in our home in Toronto several times over the years and used it as a base to travel around North America."

"Did you know about Zoe and Marcel's relationship?"

"When Zoe and I first visited St. Paul in 2004, she introduced him as a former boyfriend, but he and Bjorn have been together since, well, around that time. I have to say that I think you're wrong. I don't know what you saw exactly, but I really don't think Marcel is interested in Zoe in a sexual way. He's devoted to his husband."

I peer at the picture one last time. "Hmm. It's easy to see why. That man is stunning." Then I add, "You all jumped in the water after that picture was taken, didn't you?"

CHAPTER FORTY-ONE

A COOL BREEZE from the open window wakes me up on my bed at a quarter past five. After golf, I came back to the B&B for a soothing shower, then I fell into a restful sleep. I got a lot of things off my chest today and I'm basking in an eerie state of detached calm. I can finally stop trying to win this game of love that I was obviously not equipped to play in the first place.

I gave it my best shot, and I lost. I was not able to pry Alex out of his marriage. And even if my suspicions are correct, and the heart of his family is a being eroded by festering secrets and the infidelity of one, if not both, parents, I accept my defeat and I'll leave them to their fate.

I'll probably hear any sad news second hand from Belle through Miriam.

I must admit that, to my knowledge, neither Zoe nor Alex has ever expressed the desire to get divorced. Alex can find himself a new escort now, and life can return to normal for the Green family. Noah will also likely see sense and mature from his experiences this summer.

I concede. It was a great dream while it lasted, but I bit off way more than I could chew.

I do have one tidbit of ammunition left in my pocket. "Hey, Zoe. Funny thing. Your husband used to be one of my clients." But, no. I'll keep that to myself, along with the identities of all the other Percys

I've known over the years. I'm bound to run into one or two more of them at some point in my life. I won't compromise Kate's work or *Just Julia*'s stellar reputation by breaking client confidentiality. I'm not spiteful, just sad.

Alex and the girls will be on their way to the concert soon. Miriam has a cellphone, so I text her an overly smiley selfie with a thumbs up and write, *Have the best time ever!*

Miriam texts me back a picture of her and Belle in matching plaid shirts, ripped jeans, and high-top sneakers.

While I'm staring at their lovely, exuberant faces, my phone vibrates and I smile at what pops up, feeling an instant connection to home.

> *Hey girl! I hope you've got those macarons. FYI, I've had four of your regulars call me literally sobbing because they miss you so much. Okay, I'm exaggerating, but if you ever change your mind, I'd be thrilled to work with you again.*
>
> *I'm sure I can guess who's asking for me, but Julia is well and truly gone and I no longer have any desire to lock lips with the flounder guy. Thanks so much for having my back for the last ten years. I know I got lucky with you. I'll see you at the gym next week, with the cookies.*

There are only two more sleeps until Belle and I return to Toronto. She is beyond excited to find her father. I am eager to redecorate my guest room and invite friends and family to our home. I am also ready to abandon my monotonous routine of changing the sheets and attending self-care appointments that are aimed at making me look ten years younger to charm men that are ten years older than me. I will replace those chores with the pleasant tedium of high school marking and the intellectual stimulation of learning Spanish with Belle.

CHAPTER FORTY-ONE

I look out the window at the rows of solemn pale stone sarcophagi adorned here and there with garish red flowers. I wonder why the bodies of the dead are put to rest above ground here, instead of being buried?

Francine's grave always looks the most poised to me, the most graceful. I hope she knows that, even in death, her presence has made a difference in the world. It reminds me of the transience of human existence and the necessity to savour every moment. I let my gaze rest on her eternal stone bed, wondering if Francine ever had to relinquish the greatest love of her life.

This may be the last time I'll return to St. Paul. There are so many other places to see. It still baffles me that Zoe keeps bringing her family to this tourist mecca every couple of years. It would make sense if she and Marcel were having an affair, but, if Alex is correct and they are just friends, I can't imagine why she is so attracted to this particular location.

Since I probably won't be back, I think I'll act like a total tourist this evening and have dinner at Le Café de la Place, the iconic restaurant that faces the outside of the walls of St. Paul. They have a curated selection of good food and plenty of room to dine al fresco and people watch. I'll sit at a table with a red umbrella under the tall plane trees and be entertained by the locals playing boules and by the departing tourists as they juggle small bags filled with trinkets, medium sized bags filled with home décor, and large wrapped paintings destined to impress in every corner of the globe.

I'm also curious to see if Lucie and her associates might be hanging around, plying their trade. My close encounter with that bunch left a sick feeling ruminating in my gut. I may have been mistaken that Alex is my future, but one path forward that I feel compelled to explore is taking shape in my mind. I will use whatever influence I have to expose the unjust aspects of sex work. I'm in a good place to help others who are still in it. I've got a few thousand followers on my blog and, instead of ending it, I'm going to out myself and invite them all to come with me on a new adventure as sex work moves towards legalization in many places around the globe.

Instead of *Conversations with Clients*, I'm going to have conversations about the business side and the legalization of sex work. I may only have the time and energy to put out one or two podcasts a month, but once I do, the words and opinions of the people who are most affected will be there as a record at this pivotal moment in history. Maybe, just maybe, sex workers will start to get the respect they have always deserved. I want to be a part of that change.

When we're back home, and Alex and I have managed to put some time and distance between us, I'll ask Zoe to teach me everything she knows about podcasting.

* * *

I'm sipping a glass of Chateau Miraval rosé, watching two young moms play boules while their red cheeked children cheer them on from their perch on the curb at the edge of the pitch. A couple dozen tourists are gobbling down their daily specials and whipped cream covered waffles, so they won't miss the bus back to Nice. There is no sign of either sex workers or pimps, although I'm not convinced that I'd recognize either.

"You are without your daughter this evening?" comes a smooth male voice.

I look up and see Omar, in ripped jeans and a neat black t-shirt. I surmise, from his dustless appearance, that he hasn't held any chalk since he last cleaned himself up, and that, from his soapy smell, this was likely a recent occurrence. His thick, black curls shine in the slanting sunlight as I motion to an empty seat at my small square table.

CHAPTER FORTY-ONE

"Yep," I answer him. "Belle chose Ed Sheeran over yet another salade Niçoise with her mother," I laugh. "Would you like to join me?"

"Thank you, I will," he says and sits down.

"You saved me from drinking alone," I say.

Omar signals to the waiter who nods and goes inside without asking for his order.

"How was Monaco?" I ask.

"Different. Something new for me. I drew a two hundred square foot mural for a store in a mall." He leans in, pulls out his phone and shows me a picture of a three-dimensional beach scene in the triangular space below an escalator. It looks like I could walk right into it. There are people playing beach volleyball, sunbathers, rogue sharks, scuttling crabs and funny pranksters. Every person's outfit has the logo of the Italian fashion brand Uccello, a blue U with wings.

"That's fabulous!"

"Thank you, I think the mural turned out well, and it won't disappear with the next rain," he laughs.

"So, you don't always draw on the ground?" I ask.

He shakes his head. "I have contracts to design weekly chalkboards in many restaurants. Sometimes I work on commissioned pieces for clients' homes, and I even do illustrations for children's books. The tourists love the street art, though, and I admit, I do like to work with a crowd. I love hearing the oohs and aahs." I love the way he says the last bit, closing his eyes, puckering his lips, and drawing out the syllables.

My salad arrives along with a glass of pastis and a croque monsieur for Omar. Our conversation flows from music, Omar likes British pop, to travel, he has a trip planned to Australia in the fall, then to pigeons, which Omar is convinced have all made a pact to shit as much as possible on his art no matter where he goes in the world. He asks me about the seasons in Canada, about being a single

231

mom, and about what I think he should draw for the St. Paul crowd tomorrow. "A dragon you can ride, a balloon that carries you away, or a giant-sized Venus flytrap about to snap you into its stomach?"

"Do they even have a stomach?" I laugh.

I watch him swallow a bite of the grilled ham and cheese sandwich with béchamel sauce oozing out over his chin, then wipe away the liquid with his cloth serviette. He tilts his head, squints at me, and does a little bounce in his seat. "I've got it! It's been puzzling me since the first time I saw you. I kept asking myself who you look like."

I haven't heard this in so long, but I'm happy to hear it again. "I think I know, but you can go ahead and tell me."

"Odette! You could be her twin sister!"

I'm blushing, and a sweet rush passes through my body. No one has ever said that to me in Canada. Not one of my clients felt that I was hot because I look like a famous French musician with long brown hair, fabulous cheekbones, and sensuous eyes. It's amusing to inspire that silly happiness in someone else when they know very well that you're not that famous person, but part of their brain can trick themselves into thinking that they are in the presence of a celebrity.

I want to reach out and touch Omar's hair. I imagine placing my lips on that tender spot on his neck just beneath his ear.

"Can I interest you in a game of boules?" asks Omar, bringing me back to reality.

"Oh, yes please! I've watched it so many times, but never actually played. This is turning out to be the sporty day of my holiday in Provence!"

We finish our dinners and each pay the waiter for our own meals, which is great, because I don't want to be beholden to anyone. However, I have an awkward moment as I am about to stand up and I wonder how much time is left for us to fuck? It freezes me to my seat. It will obviously take some time for me to get escorting out of my system.

CHAPTER FORTY-ONE

My next thought is, how long has it been since I thought about Alex?

While Omar disappears inside the restaurant, I close my eyes, purse my lips, push out warm breaths from deep in my lungs, and repeat inside my head, "Let this go. You can let go of anything," until I feel light enough to rise.

Omar emerges with a mesh bag with six silver boules and one smaller white ball, and we walk together to an open space in front of the restaurant. He draws a circle about fifty centimeters in diameter. "This is called the cochonnet," he says, then he stands in the circle and tosses the smaller white ball, which stops rolling about thirty feet away.

"That means piglet, doesn't it?" I ask.

"It does." He smiles at me and continues, "Each of us has three boules. Mine are smooth and yours are striped. You can go first and try to toss a boule as close as possible to the cochonnet."

My throw lands about two feet away.

"Not bad for a beginner," he says. "But watch me. Use an overhand throw, so you can get some spin on it. Then it will land and stay put where you want it."

He leans forward and releases the boule. It lands with a thud within a few inches of the small white ball.

"Now, you try to knock my boule away," he instructs.

"Sure," I say and, to the surprise of both of us, I proceed to do exactly that.

"Woohoo!" I yell and raise my arms.

In the next instant, we are hugging. I've always been fascinated by the moment when the wall of personal space that two people keep between themselves is broken. The French usually get it over with as soon as possible by hugging and kissing strangers on the cheek. It is not so in North America, and I've trained myself to follow the lead of my clients. If I make the first move too soon, they may get a wary look in their eyes.

But my hug with Omar is a spontaneous and welcome dive into the wealth of each other's physical energy. This feels wonderful, I think, and then he releases me and starts to plan his next shot.

Omar wins the game thirteen to four and I'm proud to have made any points at all. We are putting the balls back into the mesh bag and he says, "It's been a lovely evening. Thank you for dinner and a challenging game of boules."

Did he just wink at me?

Is he waiting for me to make the first move? To give a sign? I have almost no experience with this type of thing. I'm not even sure what I want. Is it enough that I don't want to be alone this evening? I could invite him back to the B&B. We could lie down on the bed and run our hands along each other's bodies. We could have a hook up, a one-time only encounter with an almost total stranger, simply because we are curious, and we want to fulfill our physical urges. We'd use protection. It would be safe. No judgement. Just fun.

I close the gap between myself and Omar, then I reach out to stroke his hair. It feels like curly strands of fine silk. I inhale his intoxicating just washed, but now a little sweaty, scent. Then I weave my fingers into his hair and ask for permission with my eyes. He gives a brief nod. I lick my lips, then press them against his. No tongue, we just let our lips explore the full surface area and yielding flesh of each other's lips. It's fabulous.

A group of teenagers at a nearby table whistles and comments on our bold public display of affection and it prompts us to extend the kiss even longer.

When we ease apart, I say to Omar, "Thank you for a lovely evening. This was perfect. Go with the dragon tomorrow. Everybody loves dragons."

And I skip through the gate into town without looking back.

On the Rue Grande, I hesitate in front of La Cave. It might be nice to go in there for one last drink. The night is still young. I could sit

CHAPTER FORTY-ONE

on a barstool and reminisce about the time I kissed two French boys at a party there, even though it was Raphael, who was watching us, that I was hoping would find me irresistible.

My phone rings.

It's Zoe. I anticipate that she will be crying, but when I hold the phone up to my ear, there is no sound at all.

"Zoe? It's Jade. Did you call me?" I ask.

"Oh, Jade," her voice is barely a whisper. "I'm at Francine's. Please come now." And she hangs up.

CHAPTER FORTY-TWO

FRANCINE'S GRAVE IS halfway along the leftmost row. Perched on it, looking small and forlorn like a lost kitten, is Zoe.

"I wonder if Francine enjoys these pajama parties?" I ask as I approach and take a moment to read the inscription one more time. *Ici repose Francine Malamaire Née Giuji décédée le 16 décembre 1913 à l'âge de 27 ans.*

Zoe hangs her head and concentrates on kicking the heels of her white sneakers against the pale grey sarcophagus. "Do you believe in ghosts?" she asks, and I can tell that she's doing her typical thing of beating around the bush. I will be patient while she edges ever closer to divulging her truth.

"Why else would we keep returning here if there were no ghosts? We'd meet in a bar, and then we could get a drink," I joke, half serious. But I don't mind. I enjoy the solid feel of the flat stone supporting my weight as I ease onto it beside Zoe.

I take a deep breath and contemplate the distant Alps, the lush surroundings, and the serene air of early evening that all somehow combine to make me feel closer to understanding the state of my heart.

I lick my lips and savour the last traces of Omar's kiss.

Zoe turns her head so I can see one bright blue eye. "Do you believe in reincarnation?"

"I never really thought about it."

CHAPTER FORTY-TWO

"Well, Francine died in 1913. That's over a hundred years ago. It's possible that she has been reborn a couple of times since then."

I can see where this is going. "So, maybe one of us is Francine?"

"Which one?" she asks.

"All we know is that she was born Francine Guiji. At some age, who knows? It could have been as young as fourteen, she married Monsieur Malamaire. Then she died at the age of twenty-seven. It could have been from an accident or an infection. But it was most likely in childbirth—but, if so, was it her first child or her fifth?" I'm surprising myself with all the hypotheses we can make from such a short epitaph. "I've never been married, so you're probably the reincarnation of Francine," I point at Zoe.

Zoe nods. "Makes sense, I suppose. But we know more than that. She must have been Catholic, and she died in mid-December. Maybe that Christmas, there were presents under a tree that she had placed there, and her family had to open them without her. We can also assume that Francine Guiji must have come from money to be eligible to marry Monsieur Malamaire, who prized his dead wife so much that he buried her in this fancy cemetery. I doubt this was a love story. Francine was probably forced into marriage by her parents," Zoe pauses, "also like me."

"Really?" I'm taken aback. Where is Zoe going with this?

"Well, yeah, really. My parents were very persuasive. When I turned twenty-four, they made it clear that it was time for me to grow up, get out of their house, and marry a respectable boy. They even threw in a lot of cash to sweeten the deal. They bought Alex and I our first home."

"Wow. I knew your family had a lot of money, but . . ."

"Alex's mother and my mother were close friends," she says by way of explanation. "I'm pretty sure it was all decided before I turned one year old. And they orchestrated the rest of our formative years as a means to an end. They even let me have a bit of a going off the rails phase, so I would realize that I needed a dependable man like Alex who would be able to keep me in the lifestyle to which I had become accustomed."

This is sad. So pitiful to look back on two decades of marriage as if they were a farce orchestrated by a couple of crones. But who am I to throw stones? Haven't I been trying to manipulate Alex since I first set eyes on him? What can I say to Zoe?

"I'm sorry," I say, and it feels like the most truthful words I have uttered, and the only words I have said to Zoe that weren't part of my calculated plan. That felt really good. So I say it again, "I am so very, very sorry."

Tears have started rolling down her cheeks. "Oh, don't get me wrong. I love Alex. I love his patience, his intelligence, his determination. I love that he always takes care of us and that he is tidy around the house. I love that he's good with money and he knows how to fix things. I could have done a lot worse. If I had chosen for myself, I'm sure I would have picked a real winner," she laughs, and, looking back into the past, says, "Raphael." Then she shrugs her shoulders and flips her hands open, meaning, need I say more?

"I would have chosen Raphael, too," I say.

Zoe heaves a big sigh. "In retrospect, I would have preferred to stay free and single my whole life. But it never once occurred to me that I had that choice."

This is all very interesting, but not actually enlightening because I am already privy to much more of her life than she is aware.

Zoe never gets to the point. I clear my throat and ask, "You told me to come here right away because...?"

"Yes. That. I need to tell someone something, and I want to practice it on someone first." She smiles at me. "I choose you."

"Okay." I nod, knowing full well that she has no one else to tell anyway. I'm sure she's got lots of friends back in Canada who would immediately phone three other friends to fill them in on the big

CHAPTER FORTY-TWO

revelation the instant Zoe was finished. Zoe believes I'm trustworthy and she called me to this special place because we know that we can open up here, in the cemetery, and that the dead will hold onto our secrets for us.

"You don't have to tell me," I say. Then I place my hand on her arm and she leans closer. The concealer over dark eye circles isn't working at all today. I smile to keep my tears at bay. "Because I think I already know."

"But?" She winces like she's in pain.

I raise my hand. "It's gonna be okay," I say. She drops her shoulders and waits. I continue, "I saw a picture this afternoon. Alex showed it to me on his phone. It was a group shot at Marcel and Bjorn's wedding. I thought there was something odd about it and I just figured it out."

I can't read Zoe's face. What if I'm wrong?

But I'm not wrong. Zoe's words have absolutely confirmed my suspicions. "Marcel is Noah's father," I say aloud, to Zoe, and to our dead friend, Francine.

Zoe bursts into sobs and buries her face in her hands. She's nodding and gasping for air. I put an arm around her narrow back. It feels like Francine has sat up, disturbed from her eternal rest, and her arm is reaching around Zoe from the other side. I look over at Francine and smile. She has an unlined face, long auburn hair, and heavy eyebrows, and her eyes are sparkling brown. She looks like a young woman who knows how to take charge.

My eye is caught by a large man in black, standing at the gate.

"Off the graves! The cemetery is closed now. There is no sitting permitted!" he growls at us.

"Fuck that guy!" snaps Zoe.

"Come on. We'll go to my room, and you can talk to me there," I say, standing up. Then I stop and ask, "Where's Noah?"

"At the concert," says Zoe, wiping snot onto the back of her hand.

"Ugh! You are gross. Don't you put that on Francine!"

Zoe tries to swipe me with her gooey hand, but I jump away in time.

The gatekeeper is in our face now and doesn't seem to care at all that one of us is an emotional wreck. He waves his arms and yells, "Allez!"

Then he follows two steps behind as we make our way out through the wrought iron gate into the south end of town and head to my room.

* * *

I pour two glasses of rosé and try to hand one to Zoe, but she doesn't react, so I place it on the table beside her. "You didn't just buy those tickets a few days ago, did you? It was going to be a family thing and you gave up your ticket for Belle, right?"

She looks up at the ceiling and starts pulling on her hair. "Family things are too hard. The three of them keep looking at me like I have two heads and they can't decide which one to chop off."

"I get it, I really do. It's hard being a mom and a fallible human being at the same time. I estimate that we still have a couple of hours to figure out what to do for the best. So, go on and tell me how it happened," I say. "You had sex with Marcel sixteen years ago. You would have been twenty-eight years old."

I prop myself with a pillow, lean back against the headboard, and congratulate myself on doing a great impersonation of a psychiatrist, but really, I'm just relieved that she has stopped crying.

"Okay, here goes." Her hand jerks and she looks surprised that several loose strands of yellow hair are now wrapped around her fingers. I wait while she pulls them off and watches them fall to the floor, then begins anew, "For the first four years of my marriage, I couldn't admit that my exploring days were at an end, and my mind

CHAPTER FORTY-TWO

was still fixated on Marcel. I kept reliving the crazy times I had with him and Bruno over and over in my head. Whenever I had sex with Alex, I imagined it was Marcel."

"And, I assume, twenty years later, that you are still doing precisely the same thing."

"How the fuck did that happen?!" she slaps the arms of the chair and bounces up to start pacing the room.

Does she want me to sympathize with her, or to give her advice? Is she even listening to me? Maybe what I say now doesn't matter at all, so I'll go with my instincts and try to push her into finding her own truth. "You know, this would all be no big deal. I know lots of men who keep playing out the same fantasy over and over again. It's what gets them off. It's that magical image moment that brings them to orgasm. I get it. And like I said, it would be no big deal what goes through your head in bed, except that you tried to make it real again and, in doing so, you had someone else's baby." I realize that anyone in the hall could hear me, so I lower my voice, "And then you kept that fact a secret from your husband."

"It's lucky my kids look like me," she says.

I cock my head in disbelief. "Miriam isn't his too, is she?"

"No. She's daddy's little girl, no doubt about that. I've been a model wife for the last fifteen years."

I wonder when Alex first started seeing escorts, but then I tell myself it's none of my business.

Zoe has discovered her wine. She takes a long drink, then sits back down and says, "Marcel said that if I don't tell Alex by the end of the day tomorrow, he will."

"Marcel knows?"

"Yes."

"Since when?"

"Last fall. They stayed with us for a week in November. He guessed. Well, he can do math as well as anyone else. I think he

241

always suspected and now he wants to try being a dad. Or maybe Bjorn wants to try being a stepdad. Or maybe they just both think I'm doing a shitty job of being a mother." Her tone of voice is sarcastic, but I don't think she means it.

"So, you married Alex in 2004 and in 2008, you came to Saint Paul and had sex with Marcel?" I summarize.

"We came here over the Christmas holidays. There are hardly any tourists in the winter, but the town is all decorated. It's really pretty," Zoe has pulled her legs up into the chair and she's scratching her left arm so hard I can see white lines on her tanned skin from across the room.

"Stop doing that," I say. "You'll make yourself bleed." But she doesn't look up. I continue, "So, Marcel decided to give you a baby for Christmas? What the fuck?"

"I knew I shouldn't have done it. Alex and I were trying for a baby. Marcel and I had sex twice, once at the restaurant and once in my hotel. We couldn't keep our hands off each other. It was . . . incredible. The way he kissed me was like . . ."

"Stop!" I yell at her, "I get that you want to talk about your hot sex, Zoe, but this is so much bigger than a random affair." I wait till her hands stop moving, and remind her, yet again, "This is about Noah."

"How did you guess? What gave it away?" she asks.

"There's something about his jawline, and wide cheekbones, that take after Marcel. And when I saw Marcel's wedding picture where he's got more hair, his resemblance to Noah was even stronger."

"You're good," says Zoe. "If Noah ever starts to lose that mass of curls, it will be much more obvious."

She contemplates her unscratched right arm but pulls her hovering hand back and reaches for her drink instead. She takes such a big mouthful that she can't swallow it all and spits some of it out onto her white shorts.

CHAPTER FORTY-TWO

"Oh my god!" she laughs. "I'm such a bloody mess! But I have to tell you how good this feels to finally say all this out loud. I know that my whole fucking world is gonna come crashing down in the next twenty-four hours, but bursting that bubble makes me feel like I've escaped some kind of prison. Whatever happens next can't be any worse than the hell I've been living in all these years."

I cannot follow her logic, or lack of logic. "Didn't you bring this on yourself? You could have cut all ties with Marcel after Noah's birth and no one would have been the wiser."

She's managed to empty the remaining half of her rosé in the last ten seconds. I walk over to our little fridge and take out a bottle of water.

Zoe shakes her finger at me. "Uh-uh . . . that's not true. I would know. Even if it took till I was a senile old lady, I would eventually let it slip to Noah, or Marcel, and they would be angry that they never got to know each other. This way, they usually got to see each other once a year."

"But it wasn't okay when Marcel figured it out, was it?"

"Nope," Zoe shakes her head and purses her lips. "He was really upset. I begged him not to tell and he gave me until the summer to 'make it right' as he said."

I remove the cap from the water, pour some into Zoe's glass and take the rest with me back to my perch on the bed.

I think about what it will mean when Zoe "makes it right." It's going to crush Alex. I try to imagine how I would feel if someone told me that Belle was not my biological child, but I just can't contort my mind to go into that place at all. Then I think of Carlos, who doesn't even know he's a dad. I've got no right to be frustrated with Zoe. There's a striking similarity between our stories that I'm not eager to point out right now, but it gives me even more reason to treat her with compassion.

I think I hear Solange's voice downstairs. When Zoe and I came in, Solange and Camille were moving around the furniture in the two ground floor rooms. She told me they have a family of ten from Greece arriving on Saturday. I'm sad to think of leaving the happy little refuge Belle and I have called home for the past three weeks.

I turn my attention back to Zoe and force a smile. "Well, now you can make it right. You can tell Alex, Noah, and Miriam," I say, certain that this is the correct advice, but not sure in which order they should be told.

Zoe takes a drink of her water. "That's not wine." She scowls at the offending liquid but takes another sip. "Don't forget the grandmas and the grandpas. I'm more afraid of them than anyone else."

I move to the edge of the bed to be closer to Zoe. "Like I said. It will be okay. At the end of the day, love will win out. We just have to plan the best way for you to do this." I'm imagining a giant group hug scenario where everyone is okay with everything. "A way that puts Noah's feelings first. People's initial reactions to the news are really going to stay with him. He needs to know that you all . . ."

There is a knock. I hear Alex say, "Jade! I'm here with Belle," and the door opens into the room.

Alex and Belle enter side by side. He's got his arm around her shoulder and she is leaning her head against him. Her face looks flushed and her eyes are dull.

"What?" I say.

Zoe drops her glass of water.

I jump off the bed and hurry to my daughter "Are you okay?" I ask, knowing full well that something is not right.

"I'm really sorry," says Alex. "We came back as soon as I realized what happened."

"What's wrong, baby?" I wrap my arms around her, and she starts shaking and crying.

"I didn't do it on purpose. It's not my fault," she mumbles into my chest.

CHAPTER FORTY-TWO

Alex puts his hand on my shoulder and starts talking to me in a forced calm voice, "Belle ate two gummy bears with cannabis. Miriam found them in her brother's suitcase and shared them with Belle when they were in the van on the way to the concert. About an hour later, the girls started to show symptoms and we figured out what they had done.

"What the hell?!" says Zoe and she darts to the door to look in the hall. "Where are the kids?"

Alex reaches his other hand out to calm his wife.

"At our hotel. Miriam didn't know they were drugs. She just thought they were candies, but she only ate one. She'll be fine. They'll both be fine. I called a friend who's a doctor and she talked me through it." Alex continues in his professional voice, looking straight in my eyes, "I'll take you and Belle to the hospital if you'd like, but her heart rate and breathing seem to be normal. She really just wanted her mom. My doctor friend suggested we should get her to drink some water and get a good nights' sleep. It should wear off in about six hours and she should be okay in the morning."

My heart is beating so hard it hurts and anger is flooding through my chest. Two nights ago, Alex told me that he was sure Noah wouldn't buy drugs in a foreign country.

"We're having the special dinner tomorrow," sobs Belle. "It's our last day. What if I can't see my friends again?"

I squeeze her tight and run my hand along her long dark hair. Her hands on my shoulders are cold. I need to get her into bed. "Is there anything else you want to tell me before you leave?" I say to Alex.

Alex looks beaten. "Again, I'm so sorry. Please call if you need anything," he says and follows Zoe, who has already left.

CHAPTER FORTY-THREE

SURROUNDED BY THE happy chatter of shopkeepers and locals, Belle and I wait for our taxi at the north gate at eight fifteen in the morning. I close my eyes and focus on the hum of the rising heat as it burns off the residual morning dampness while the scents of exotic flowers and trees tickle my senses awake. It's going to be another fabulous day in Provence, but we won't be here to enjoy it.

"Are you still mad at me?" asks Belle.

I hug my daughter again, for what must be the thousandth time in the last thirty-six hours. "I was never upset with you. You didn't do anything wrong."

"Why do you look so angry then?" she asks as we break apart.

"I'm not angry. I suppose I'm disappointed." Belle's face crumples and her chin starts to quiver, so I give her another squeeze. "But not with you. Not for a second. I just wish things had turned out differently."

My mind is taken back to the last time I said good-bye to St. Paul, twenty-five years ago. I was standing in this same spot under the plane trees, in a pair of ripped jean shorts and a white elastic tube top, waiting for the taxi with Pascale. I had a stolen sketch in my backpack, and I felt utterly jaded at eighteen years of age. I was certain that I had learned everything there was to know about hurt and betrayal. I believed that I had been wronged by Zoe, Raphael, and Alain.

CHAPTER FORTY-THREE

Belle is correct. I'm not okay, but, this time, who do I blame? Noah, perhaps, and myself. Actually, just myself. I had such high hopes for this trip. In my far-flung fantasy, I would figure out what was keeping Alex tied to his marriage and then convince him that he should choose me, his hired escort, as his new life partner. And I would claim my prize in the space of three weeks.

I didn't expect to get thrust right into the heart of Alex's family, or to rekindle and strengthen my friendship with Zoe. I also hadn't anticipated that our daughters would bond on a dusty trail in the Alps over their shared love of ABBA. But one thing led to another, and, in the end, I found the answer to my question which also turned out to be the roadblock to my happiness. Alex Green is the fucking father of the year. His heart turns to mush when it comes to his progeny, and he wouldn't be that exact person I love if he put anyone else but Noah and Miriam first.

What will Alex do when he finds out that Noah is not his biological son? I know that he'll never stop loving him. Alex might even double down on his attempts to save his marriage because his children give so much meaning and direction to his life.

I believe that I've figured out one common thread among married men who hire escorts. They are able to experience different aspects of their life separately. In the same way that some people don't exercise unless they go to a gym, these men only fulfill certain sexual desires when they're with their escort. Maybe it's not the scenario they would choose, but they manage to derive a great deal of satisfaction from a brief sexual encounter, enough so that they can wait for a period of time, then come back for more. Alex didn't want to muddy the waters of his marriage by opening his heart to two women, each with her own set of emotional needs. Hedonistic sex is a commodity he could purchase and with Julia, he got excellent value for his money. Zoe is his wife. He made a commitment to take care of her and integrity matters to Alex. It's that simple. I see that now. He doesn't hate me. He doesn't love me. He doesn't need me. Perhaps he wants me, but I am not special. I am not Zoe, his life partner. I am not and never will be, his wife. Zoe made one mistake fifteen years ago. She's not a terrible person. I believe that Alex will fight to keep his family together.

"That man is waving at us, mom," says Belle, pulling me out of my head.

It's our taxi driver, and, in no time, our three suitcases and two carry-ons are loaded into the little van. I'm going to have to pay extra for the third suitcase. It's full of the pieces of art Belle created during her various lessons, as well as a lot of shoes.

As soon as we pull away, the taxi slows down to let a busload of tourists cross the road. Belle waves at the Colombe D'Or, a landmark at the entrance to town. "Bye restaurant with famous paintings!" she calls. Then she looks at me, beaming. "Rico and Daria said it was the best dinner they ever had. Thank you for taking us there yesterday. I know it cost a lot of money."

I'm glad that Belle is leaving here with mostly happy memories. "I can't believe you ate the escargots. I'm glad you were feeling okay, and we got to see your friends one last time. When Daria comes to visit us at Christmas, we can take her to the CN Tower, go see a play downtown, and go to the art gallery. It'll be wonderful."

"Can we put the pictures of me with all of Omar's drawings up in my room? That dragon yesterday was the best!"

"We can absolutely do that."

Belle gives me a sneaky sideways look accompanied by a slow nod. "I saw the way he looked at you, mom. Omar likes you."

I laugh, "He thinks I look like a famous French singer." I flip my hair and make a silly duck face at her. "I like Omar, too. He's a nice man, that's for sure. But there are also nice men in Canada."

"And there are nice men in El Salvador," she says, drawing out the last syllable, and I wonder how I'm going to keep this nosey

CHAPTER FORTY-THREE

preteen from trying to set me up with every handsome man we meet.

"Bye palm trees! Bye smelly perfume stores! Bye art galleries!" she waves out the window, then flops back into her seat. "I'm going to miss St. Paul so much! Maybe we can bring my dad here when we find him?"

"One step at a time, please."

"When I was packing, I counted, and I only bought nine pairs of shoes. So that means I have to come back."

"Maybe you can come back when you're eighteen and be an au pair, like me."

"And Miriam can come with me? Like Zoe was here with you."

"Who knows?" I say wistfully. "I don't think it makes sense to plan so far ahead. Just enjoy today. Enjoy every little thing you can about today. And tomorrow will take care of itself. It's what I'm going to try to do from now on."

I check my phone. Zoe has only sent one text since she left the B&B two nights ago.

I'm so sorry, Jade. Miriam is asleep now. I'm sure the girls will be fine, but Alex and I feel terrible about what happened. Noah feels very badly about it, too. Thanks for your help. You're a dear friend and you've given me courage. I'll let you know how it goes.

And, then, nothing since.

Alex hasn't contacted me at all. But that is not surprising. If Zoe followed through with her plan, he would know her secret by now. He's not thinking about me. His life is breaking into tiny little pieces and I'm not there to wrap my arms around him and hold on and tell him everything is going turn out alright.

CHAPTER FORTY-FOUR

Season 1 Episode 1

WELCOME TO MY *first ever podcast, Sex Work is Everyone's Business! My name is Jade Matthews and I worked as a paid escort in Toronto for ten years. My clients were exclusively married men who were looking for a safe, fun, and discreet encounter. Interesting men. Attractive men. Decent men, who did their research, consented to identity checks, put on the condom, and paid a fair price for the service they received. And yet, every single one of them committed a crime. Bill C-36, which has been in force in Canada since December 6, 2014, is called the Protection of Communities and Exploited Persons Act. This act made purchasing sexual services an offence for the first time in Canadian criminal law and it comes with a maximum sentence of five years in prison.*

However, the law does not criminalize the sale of one's own sexual services. That is how I was able to work, claim income, and pay taxes like an average citizen, while working in the sex industry for a decade.

Sex work is a fascinating, multi-faceted field. The laws surrounding the sector of prostitution vary greatly from country to country. For example, prostitution is completely legal in Germany and Greece, so much so that workers can draw a government pension. In Saudi Arabia, it is punishable by death. Prostitution is illegal in every US state except parts of Nevada and Maine, which has recently adopted

CHAPTER FORTY-FOUR

similar laws to Canada. And so on. Prostitution is legal, limitedly legal, and illegal each in roughly one third of countries around the world. But, legal or not, it is a multi-billion-dollar global industry, and it will, without a shadow of a doubt, continue to thrive in the future. In my opinion, full and fair legalization is the only answer and it's desperately needed to help the sellers, the buyers, and the ordinary citizens of the future to achieve the safest and healthiest outcomes. Do you disagree with me? Great! Let's talk about it.

You might be tuning into this podcast for a business opportunity, a sexy tidbit, a hearty laugh, or a heated debate. We've got it all. I'm going to talk to anyone brave enough to get open and honest about the oldest profession in the world. As well as sex workers, I'd like to chat with doctors, parents, pimps, and politicians, actors, clients, critics, and connoisseurs. Let's expose it all with the aim of sifting out the truths and finding out what works.

Rather than asking all of my guests the same set of questions, I've decided to focus each podcast on one question, although I'm sure we'll get onto a lot of titillating tangents along the way.

In future episodes, I'm going to try to answer: What does a typical sexual encounter for money look like and is there even such a thing? What is a fair price for sex? and Who would suffer if prostitution was legalized?

This week, for my inaugural episode, I'm going to look for an answer to a question that has plagued me for a long time. Why are there far fewer male escorts than female? It's almost impossible to hire a male escort in many cities and the selection is not at all comparable. Is it a matter of low supply or low demand? Or is it something else entirely?

I've got two guests here today to help me answer this intriguing question. My first guest is a dear friend, my former agent, who is going to have to use an alias. I'll call her Shelly. Shelly kept me safe and busy for ten years, but remember Bill C-36? It also throws her into a murky legal scenario because she profited off my work by taking a fair portion *of my fee for the work she did screening and scheduling the clients. Currently, Shelly represents six female escorts and one male one in Toronto, Ontario, the largest city in Canada.*

My second guest is a male escort for women who works in Vancouver, British Columbia on the west coast of Canada. His name is Duke Grayson, and you won't want to miss the insightful and touching stories of his hundreds of paid dates with women.

So, lie back, open your mind, and enjoy the show!

CHAPTER FORTY-FIVE

I'M ON MY hands and knees scrubbing the kitchen tiles and watching yellow leaves flutter down off the birch tree in my yard when I hear the doorbell.

"Miriam's here!" screams Belle as she darts down the stairs and whips open the door.

"Ahhhh!" the two girls leap into each other's outstretched arms and bounce up and down like a giant basketball made of two people.

This spontaneous euphoria continues for half a minute until Belle realizes that she has something even more exciting to share, "I've got a half-brother! He's the cutest baby in the entire world! Come and look at the pictures!"

Belle takes hold of her friend's hand just as Miriam grabs her backpack from Alex's outstretched arm and the two girls race up the stairs to Belle's bedroom.

Alex is standing in the doorway. The sun is sneaking in through little spaces around his tall frame. It's like he's frozen, the way he is in my mind. Not wanting to come in. Not sure if he should leave.

I let my gaze hold him there a little longer. I can feel his heartbeat from across the room. If I thought I might need a moment to reconnect, I was wrong. There is absolutely no doubt in my mind about how much I love this man. None whatsoever.

"So, he's not a serial killer?" asks Alex, grinning.

"We got the news and skyped yesterday. Carlos and his wife

Benita own a restaurant in Santa Ana. They have a ten-month old boy named Diego and he is absolutely adorable. He has Belle's smile."

"I'm glad it's working out for you," says Alex.

I sense that he is trying to find a reason to stay. I'm grateful for that.

"Please come in." I motion to the couch in the living room where we had our first chat five months ago. I've moved the furniture around and there is a TV in here now. "Or we could sit out back?"

"I'd like that," he says.

We never went outside before because of the need to protect his privacy from nosy neighbors. Julia had a strict indoor only policy.

Alex looks down at his feet and then at the scrub brush in my hand.

"You're fine," I say. "Go through the kitchen. There's a nice place to sit at the back of the yard." I'm proud to show off my little oasis, a Japanese style garden with perennial plants, water, and rocks.

I watch through the window as Alex makes his way along the winding gravel path and sits down on the stone slab bench beside the koi pond, in the shade of the twisted willow. I pour two iced teas and fill a bowl with pretzels. The familiarity of this simple act fills me with a ridiculous amount of joy.

As I step outside and walk towards Alex with my wooden tray, I shorten my steps to allow another image of him to burn itself into my memory. He's sitting on the bench leaning forward, with his elbows on his knees and his chin resting on his hands. He needs a haircut. His curly salt and pepper hair is almost in his eyes. He is motionless, except for a slight rhythmic tapping of his left foot. Socks and sandals. Because he likes to keep his feet clean. Tears tug at my eyes, and I force them back with a smile.

I ease down next to Alex, place the snacks on the flat rock in front of us and take a slow breath. I want to initiate conversation, but I'm uncertain. I'm afraid of what he might say, and what he might not

CHAPTER FORTY-FIVE

say. And I'm scared that my heart is going to fall right out of my chest onto the squishy mounds of pale green moss at our feet.

I gave up hope in St. Paul when I saw how much Alex loved his children. But I know, from Zoe's short texts, that the two of them are now separated, headed toward a divorce that was initiated by her.

That's no surprise. After examining the seven reasons why married men don't leave their wives, I concluded that Alex was probably not staying because of religious or cultural reasons, nostalgia, a strong attachment to his home, or an unbreakable love with Zoe.

However, he is a man who values logic and reason, who seeks contentment and peace, and who is devoted to his children. If divorce ever crossed his mind, Alex would have been more than a little afraid of the inevitable emotional upheaval and also somewhat concerned for how it would affect his financial situation.

Besides, few people would leave a good thing without knowing that they had something even better to go to. What percentage of marriages break up because one of the parties has fallen in love with someone else? That's a statistic I cannot find. But it formed the basis of my strategy—the plan to make Alex become so enthralled with me that it would supersede his need to be a full-time participant in the lives of his children.

Sadly, Alex couldn't bring himself to love me. There wasn't a strong enough connection between us. I can't make something out of nothing. It hurt like hell for a long time that he didn't see in me the future that I saw with him, but I accept it now. At least I tried.

We're watching the stream of bubbles from my water feature that appear, spread out and then pop, all within seconds. It makes a soft gurgling sound that blocks out the traffic from the road and the conversations of neighbours on the other side of the fence. I'm happy to say nothing. To be present with Alex in this moment. It feels like we are marking the end of what we shared inside my house, a relationship that was wild and spontaneous, where each moment was savoured precisely because it was not meant to lead to anything else. Scenes of pure unadulterated pleasure. We created them. Now we are letting them go.

Zoe said that for her, separation was necessary and cathartic. I believe that Zoe has stopped thinking about Alex's feelings, not because she is heartless, but because she needs to do this in order to define the edges of herself as an individual who is no longer part of a couple.

Belle and Miriam orchestrated this sleepover weekend, and I knew I would see Alex. He could have waved to his daughter from the car and watched her walk into our house, then driven away. But I never thought for a second that he would.

Of course, I wanted to see him. Of course, I had a shower this morning and styled my long hair with the gentle curls that he used to like to twirl around his fingers—but I kept telling myself that it wasn't because I was getting my hopes up. Alex and I had a strong physical attraction, but he ignored my declaration of love. We continued on friendly terms for a short while in St. Paul, but he could see that I was angry when Belle was accidentally given drugs, and he has made no effort to reach out to me since that night.

If our girls are going to remain friends, it makes sense that Alex would be trying to maintain an amicable relationship and that he would agree to chat with me in my garden. I grip the corner of the hard granite bench to stop my hands from shaking.

"I listened to your podcast. It was fabulous," Alex offers.

"Thanks," I say. "Who did you like best? Kate or Duke?"

"To be honest, I was just excited to hear your voice."

What does that mean? Does he miss me?

I follow his eyes up to the highest window at the back of the house. Miriam and Belle's heads are visible, moving around. They must be dancing. I can just make out the tune of "Take a Chance on Me" by ABBA through the open window. I could make a joke about

CHAPTER FORTY-FIVE

that, but I know I talk too much when I'm nervous. And I can't forget the time I blurted out my feelings in a text.

I force myself to stay silent.

Alex continues, "Duke's story about his ninety-year-old client was eye opening. I was surprised at how much work he has to do, choosing restaurants, researching conversation topics, giving massages . . ."

"Essentially, it's caring about all the needs and desires of your client. Same as what I did, but I think Duke has a lot less sex and gives a lot more foot rubs."

"Do you miss it?" Alex asks. And I know he doesn't mean do I miss the sex.

"I miss the black and white aspect of it. I enjoy having a task to do and getting it done. Knowing that I did a good job. Seeing their gratification. It was very satisfying for me in that way."

"Yeah. Duke's job seemed more complicated than yours."

"I think women just have more trouble asking for what they need."

"I never could figure out what Zoe needed." Alex shakes his head.

"It was never your job to do that. It was hers."

Alex pushes his beautiful lips into a hard line and closes his eyes. I watch silent tears spill down his cheeks, and I fill the moment with nibbling pretzels and sipping my drink, because I'm not sure if he would welcome the hug I so badly want to give him.

He wipes the tears away, sighing deeply, before rubbing his thighs and, almost whispering, says, "It's over."

"I'm sorry," I say, and I reach over to squeeze his hand. It's warm. His skin is rough. I let my forefinger run along the length of his bumpy knuckles.

"Are you in touch with her?" he asks, and he pulls his hand away to await my answer.

"She gave me podcast advice and sent me pictures of the apartment she and Noah are renting in St. Paul. Zoe wanted to live in La

Minette since we were teenagers. Looks like she got her wish. Do you ever get the feeling that our cat Zoe always lands on her feet?"

I regret that at soon as it's out, but Alex doesn't appear to register the resentful tone in my voice. I remind myself again to listen more and say less. "How is Noah?"

"I wish I knew. No idea. But he's got Zoe, Marcel, and Bjorn. He's going to stay in France for a year to get to know Marcel and his extended family. He's registered for high school in Vence. It's going to be an adjustment—gut wrenching—but he's very capable, when he puts in an effort. At least Miriam is ecstatic to be an only child. But that could just be an act. I'm sure she'll eventually miss her brother."

"She's got you," I say.

He nods, then stands up to admire the huge stalks of bamboo that act as a screen to the neighbours behind me. He runs his hand along the jointed stems and I watch his shoulders relax. "This is beautiful. Did you know that bamboo generates thirty percent more oxygen than trees?"

I smile. "I didn't. I just think it's gorgeous. Kind of exotic."

He pivots to admire the rest of the tiny garden, my green oasis with subtle accents of stone and wood, then sits back down.

"I didn't see a robin's nest on the front light," he says.

"It's finished now, but the second clutch had four healthy babies," I assure him.

At that moment, a robin flies into the yard and lands on a submerged rock in the pond. It proceeds to dip its head repeatedly in the water and flap its wings and tail sending off spray.

"I guess this guy will be heading south soon. Will you feed the other birds that stay for the winter?" asks Alex.

"Yes. The cardinals are my favourite," I answer. "Did you know that they get the red colour in their plumage from eating things like dogwood berries and mulberries?"

"I did not know that. You really are a bird lover," says Alex.

CHAPTER FORTY-FIVE

He hasn't forgotten where we started.

"I don't know," I tease. "I would say that I love birds as much as the next person. From my experience, everyone seems to like birds."

"I suppose I'll have to take your word for that. You've definitely known a lot more people than I have."

I don't mind at all that Alex is referring to my time as an escort. It actually warms my heart to be able to share a joke about it.

Alex touches my fingers with his and says, "Miriam and I have started counselling. It's been helpful. I'm learning to express my feelings. It would appear I have a lot of baggage I didn't know about."

The girls are in the kitchen now.

I so want to hear what he's going to say next, but I see Belle standing in front of the stove with a pot in one hand and a large knife in the other.

"I'll just be a second," I say, and dash inside to head off the catastrophe.

I tell the girls that cooking is not an option at the moment. I appease them with some mandarins and an old box of Turtles which they convey up to her room.

As I'm about to step back outside, my phone vibrates in my pocket. I look through the open door at Alex, who is still sitting, leaning forward, looking conspiratorial. He points to his phone, then at me.

I pull out my phone and read his message.

Sorry, this is late.

He lowers his head to compose another text and I hold my breath. My phone vibrates again.

I love you too.

I stare at the words while my heart explodes inside my chest. My hands are shaking, but I manage to reply:

> *Meet me at the side of the house, under the trellis.*

We come together in the dappled shade of the tangled wisteria vine. Alex pulls me into his chest and my arms find their place around his neck. Our first kiss as boyfriend and girlfriend feels like magic.

"I loved you from the moment we met," I confess.

"I knew you were special," he says, "but it took me awhile to get to know the real Jade."

He slides his hands on my cheeks and caresses my face. "Such a beautiful name. Such stunning green eyes," he says. "It's all I want to see forever, now. *Just Jade.*"

ACKNOWLEDGEMENTS

Thank you Rebecca Eckler, for offering short chats with writers about anything. You were honest and supportive, and you made me believe in myself.

Thank you, James Dewar. For working with me through the first draft, for making me take more time to explore each moment, and for suggesting an important character.

Thank you, Jan Field, for the editing support, and for so many lunches that keep me on track and having fun.

Thank you to the Writers' Community of Durham Region for being a wonderful resource and a welcoming group of friendly faces.